To Survive
is *Not* Enough

Ruth Lindemann

Lindemann, Ruth
To Survive is Not Enough

1st edition
Library of Congress Control Number: 2016947100

ISBN 978-0-9905827-5-5 (paperback)

Published by

AquaZebra™
Book Publishing
Cathedral City, California
www.aquazebra.com

Editor
Mike Foley

Cover/interior design
Mark E. Anderson

AquaZebra™
Web, Book & Print Design
www.aquazebra.com

Printed in the United States of America

Dedication

This book is dedicated to the memory of the two million Jewish children who were rounded up from every corner of Europe to be brutally murdered.

AND

To the Child Survivors of the Holocaust and the righteous gentiles who risked their lives to save them.

Any proceeds from the sale of this book will be donated towards projects dedicated to teaching tolerance among people.

Chapter 1

Hedy tucked the little ones into their beds. There were two beds and two blankets for eight children. She gave each one a small piece of bread and a pat on the head.

"Go to sleep!" she admonished. "We are leaving early tomorrow."

"I want my mama." one of the little girls whined while several of the others began to whimper. The damp, cement walls sent back faint echoes of their high voices. There were no bars on the doors of the old prison cells, but there was no escape.

Hedy and her charges had been lodged in this ancient fortress for almost a year waiting for space on a train. In order to placate the children, who ranged in age from 5 to 8, and still believed everything she said, she now told them another of many lies.

"If you go to sleep right now, tomorrow I will take you to your mama." she whispered to the small girl who clung to her hand. Eight pairs of eyes looked at her with such hope and expectation that she could hardly breathe from the shame that clutched her heart.

Yet she knew she dared not become fond of these children.

That night, like she had done almost every night since the catastrophe, Hedy lay awake for several hours going over every detail of the life she had before that fateful day when her world disappeared and felt as if she lived on another planet.

Hedy at fourteen longed for her mama with as much fervor as the youngsters in her care. Every night she tried to relive the warm, safe feeling of contentment at just being in the same room with her lively mother. After three years she had trouble remembering exactly how her mother looked, but the memories of the good times were vivid.

From the time Hedy was three years old her parents took her by train from the small Polish town, where her father worked for the textile mill, to Vienna, Austria to visit her mother's large family. There they spent their time visiting the many cousins and Hedy's grandparents, who lived in a spacious apartment near the Schotenring. (An area of upscale specialty shops and elegant coffee houses.) She was taken to the children's theater in the Volksteater, the exhibits at the various museums, performances of ballet and age appropriate concerts at the Musikverein (the famous Vienna Concert Hall).

These twice a year excursions were the highlight of her young life. She lived from one trip to the next and endlessly told their housekeeper, Konstanza, about every detail.

Hedy's father, Paul Mandel, was a sales representative for a well known Polish textile mill near the German border. He traveled regularly to the largest cities in Europe, taking orders from wholesale fabric houses. It was on one of these trips that he had met Hedy's mother, Mathilde. She was working as a secretary and head bookkeeper in the office of the largest fabric wholesaler in Vienna.

While waiting in the reception area for his meeting with the buyer, Paul began some informal banter with the pretty woman behind the desk. Thinking her to be the receptionist, he thought a slight flirtation might get him to the buyer sooner on his next visit. It was a pleasant pastime and the young woman seemed to enjoy the repartee.

During his meeting with the buyer, he found out that the woman at the reception desk was filling in for the receptionist and was actually the head bookkeeper and private secretary of the owner of the company. After the meeting Paul went to find Mathilde. He found her in her office. When he started to apologize for what might have been considered rude behavior, she stopped him in mid sentence.

"I know how traveling salesmen act. Receptionists have my sympathies." She laughed. And added "So, you think I am too beautiful to sit behind a desk and should be in films?"

He smiled his most beguiling smile and said in a convincing tone, "I must admit that I tend to say that to all the female receptionists I encounter. However, in your case it is the absolute truth. And what's more you know it."

She did not know what to say to such a firm statement but Paul continued talking.

He told her he was a well brought up person from a very respectable family and he would prove it to her if she would have dinner with him that evening. As it turned out she invited him to dinner at her home and within a year they were married.

Paul and Mathilde moved into the home that Paul's uncle had provided for him since his parents had died when he was in his teens. They also inherited a Greek housekeeper named Konstanza, whom the uncle had brought along to Poland after a business trip to Berlin.

Konstanza was the child of a high ranking German diplomat and his Greek housekeeper, who had come to Germany with the family after the German embassy was closed in Athens. The paternal relationship was never articulated and her father never acknowledged her but he sent her to the best schools in Germany, where she also learned French and English. Her name was a combination of Konrad and Estanza.)

After her employer, Konrad, died, Estanza decided to return to Greece. By then Konstanza was sixteen and working for a German family. The father of this family had met Paul's uncle Marcus during their school years in Stuttgart and since they were in a similar business had remained friends.

Marcus Mandel was in need of a housekeeper for his recently married nephew, Paul. Konstanza was serving dinner the evening Marcus was dining with his school friend and it was evident that she was competent and intelligent.

Before she would accept the position in the Mandel household she made Marcus promise to never reveal her background. The Poles had a strong animosity (well deserved) for Germans. "Being Greek is much better! "She had declared at the time.

Paul had worked at the textile mill since graduating from Gymnasium (high school) and learned about business from his competent uncle. A few months before he died his uncle had sold the business to a competitor, who had kept Paul on staff and six years later he was in charge of sales for most of Europe.

A year after the wedding Paul and Mathilde Mandel became the parents of a blond haired, blue eyed daughter that gave them joy and many sleepless nights. In other words, she was a normal baby. They named her Hedwig and called her Hedy.

Mathilde had traveled to Vienna for the birth of her daughter to be near her mother and the doctors that she trusted, so Hedy was by birth Viennese. Paul came to this beautiful city on business at least twice a year so it was convenient to bring his wife and daughter to visit with the extensive family while he conducted business. Konstanza remained in Poland where she kept the house ready for the Mandels. She communicated with Poles only in very broken Polish and much hand signaling. She didn't want anything to do with Austrians either.

For the first eleven years of Hedy's life she spent her summer vacations in Austria, visiting the lakes, mountains, forests and cultural offerings of Vienna. The family returned again in December for the lively Christmas celebrations. Although the Mandels were Jewish, they enjoyed the colorful Christmas market, the toy store window displays with moving trains and other animated scenes. There were festivities and plays with Catholic friends, special baked goods only served during this season, and presents. (The grandparents called them Chanukah presents while friends referred to them as Christmas presents.)

For Hedy's fifth birthday a special celebration had been planned by the family in Vienna.

It was the summer of 1933 and Paul stopped traveling to Germany, taking orders by mail or telegram. (It was inadvisable to use the telephone and soon all the mail was censored as well.) Hedy heard talk about finding a bypass around Germany in order to get to Vienna, but in the end there was no alternative. Even five year old Hedy felt the tension as they neared the German border, but the train passed through Berlin and on to Munich and they had not been treated differently from other passengers. They had arrived in Vienna without incident.

It had been her first children's birthday party and had turned out to be her last. The apartment of her grandparents was decorated with streamers and balloons. Grandfather, had performed a professional puppet show for which he had practiced for several weeks. The six children and ten adults had laughed with delight and then devoured the chocolate cake (a Sacher Torte, 6 thin layers of chocolate cake with raspberry jam between each layer and a chocolate glaze over all,) made with painstaking care by her grandmother, then washed down with hot chocolate topped with whipped cream.

That summer had been the last carefree time of Hedy's life. Reliving those happy hours during the cold nights distracted her from the constant hunger pangs that clawed at her belly.

∼

Five years had passed with little change in the routine of their lives. The trips to Vienna were shorter and then stopped altogether. There was talk of the grandparents moving to Poland because of the hostile atmosphere in Austria. There was an undercurrent of tension and Hedy heard fear in the voices of her parents as they began to argue about what to do next.

After many whispered arguments Mathilde left for Vienna. Her father had died and she had to help her mother with the burial plans and possibly arrange for her to come to Poland to live.

After four months of weekly letters and urgent phone calls all communication had ceased. Paul had made several trips to Warsaw to the German Consul (Germany had annexed Austria and it was now the German state of Ostmark) to make inquiries with no results. He wrote letters to the cousins and received no answers. His wife and her mother had vanished in the aftermath of Kristal Nacht. (The murderous, well organized riot that took place in all German cities, towns and even the smallest villages. Jewish stores were looted, their owners beaten and arrested, almost all the synagogues were looted and burned.)

By the morning of the 10th, of November 1938 thousands of Jewish men were transported to Dachau concentration camp. Overnight the Jewish communities in all of Germany were destroyed. The most productive, patriotic, philanthropic decent segment of German society was imprisoned or forced to flee. The master criminals and their thugs took over and became absolute rulers of Europe, driving the best minds into permanent exile.

Even during 1938 Hedy's life had continued in the well established routine her mother had prepared for her. Piano lessons, with hours of practice, French lessons, without much practice since her mother was not there. The French teacher, an elderly Pole, who had spent his youth in Paris, had stayed an extra hour to converse with Hedy and Paul in French.

Konstanza and Hedy became used to Paul's pacing during the day but soon his footsteps echoed throughout the apartment into the late hours of the night.

The German invasion of Poland was almost an anticlimax for the Mandel family. They had been expecting this day and Paul had loudly proclaimed, almost on a daily basis. "I must do something."

It wasn't until his employer had told him not to come back to work and the friends and co-workers he had known all his life turned their backs on him when he walked by, that he made the decision to travel to Nazi Vienna to find his wife.

The last Hedy had seen of her father was at the train station where she and Konstanza had come to see him off. The three of them had stood silently in a small circle. Each of them in turn looked over their shoulder to see if they were being watched. Swastika flags hung from the high ceiling and huge portraits of the German leaders hung on the sooty walls.

There were no tears, no promises, no declaration of love. Only a very tight embrace from an ashen faced Paul who swung up to the west bound train with a clenched jaw and empty eyes. He had a plan to pass as an Aryan since his blond hair and deep blue eyes were more like the ideal German the Nazis envisioned than most of their leaders. He had thought to take Hedy with him, as she had his coloring and spoke German with a Viennese accent so that no one would take her to be Polish. But in the end he thought she would be safer with Konstanza. He decided to travel alone and stop off in Berlin to contact old friends who he fervently hoped could be trusted.

A few days after Paul's departure the men came in the middle of the night. Konstanza had opened the door that was vibrating from the pounding fists. There were two men wearing shiny, black boots, black uniforms and carrying heavy guns, which they pointed at the frightened woman. Behind the men, had stood a Polish neighbor, wearing a swastika armband and a wide grin.

"They won't hurt you." He had said to Konstanza. "Just tell the dirty Jew girl to get dressed, pack an overnight bag and to hurry up."

Konstanza had helped Hedy pack some underwear, a sweater, pairs of extra socks and then she insisted that Hedy wear her warmest winter coat over her best dress. She had stuffed the pockets of the coat with bread and cheese.

The men wandered around the apartment taking inventory and slipping small items of interest into their pockets.

Hedy and Konstanza pretended not to notice. As Hedy had started towards the door, to her complete surprise, Konstanza whispered to her in perfect French. "Do whatever you need to do to stay alive."

Hedy had joined a group of Jews being marched towards the train station. Along the way there had been armed Germans holding dogs on leashes and some of their Polish neighbors wielding clubs and pitchforks.

That train ride in the cattle car had been the first of many such trips in the next two years. Compared to subsequent trips this one had been almost comfortable. Mothers and children clustered together and the few men offered coats and suitcases for the women to use as seats and pillows. Hedy had found a place near the door where she could lean against the wall. David, the boy who lived across the hall, sat down next to her.

He was two years ahead of her in school and they had sometimes walked home together. During the last few months he had taught her how to play chess.

After the doors were rolled shut it was dark inside the cattle car. Children began to cry, one woman had started to sing a lullaby. David took Hedy's hand in his and stroked her arm with the other. Then he had put his arm around her shoulders.

"You are the prettiest girl in Poland." he whispered in her ear. Strangely these words gave her a little jolt of pleasure. In the next few hours she shared her bread and cheese with David and he gave her bites of the apple he had brought along. The train had rumbled on into the night and as the daylight began to seep into the cracks near the roof, Hedy went to find the hole in the floor to relieve herself. When she had come back to David after waiting what had seemed like an hour, David went to find the hole. Then they had sat in their prime spot and David put his arm around Hedy's shoulder as before. Soon his other hand had moved to cup her small, developing breast. At first she thought to remove his hand but as he gently squeezed the soft flesh she felt her nipple harden. As he continued to alternately squeeze and massage her right breast she became acutely aware of the warm twinges of pleasure between her legs. As his hand moved to her left breast she turned her face to look at him, but it was too dark to see his eyes. Suddenly their lips met. A flash like fireworks blazed before her closed eyes. "He is kissing me." were the words that formed in her mind. "My first, real kiss.", Her whole body was immersed in pleasure. At first Hedy had been totally ignorant of the implications of those feelings. Only after it was all over, after the train had arrived and she had been pushed into a long line of females and had lost sight of David, had she understood what she had experienced with him.

∼

Now she would be escorting her young charges on what she surmised might be their last journey. These children couldn't live much longer. Their emaciated little bodies could barely hold up their heads. Yesterday they had stood in a long line for many hours until they arrived at a table where women were writing names and dates into a thick ledger. The Germans kept meticulous records so as to account for how many Jews had been murdered to date. (These records were sent to Berlin daily.) No one was to be overlooked. Each child of this orphan transport was given a card with a number that was duly recorded in the book and the card hung around the child's neck. Then they were sent back to their cots to await the train in the morning.

The night finally passed and Hedy had not slept. As daylight came creeping along the cement walls of the onetime school room and the children began to stir, she pushed her memories into the background. She herded her charges to the latrine, although it was too late for the two younger ones. They filed by the trickling faucet without being allowed a drink as the guards came to march them to the waiting train.

This morning there was no bread or warm water, the

children were too tired to complain. They filed dutifully into the cattle car and pressed against the walls as more and more children were loaded into the car. They were ordered to raise their hands over their heads as this made more space available Eventually the doors were rolled shut and bolted. As the train began to move Hedy closed her eyes and tried to close her ears as well to the muffled crying, praying and pleading for air, water and bread. She fought down the panic rising in her throat and tried to keep her mind blank.

"Do not think!" She told herself. She counted backwards from 100 over and over in all the languages she knew. She even knew how to count in Hebrew as she had briefly attended Hebrew school when she had been nine years old. She tried to keep herself as numb as possible. Thinking could lead to hysteria and certain death. Kostanza's last words echoed in her brain. She had promised to stay alive as long as possible.

That day and night passed and they arrived at another place with long tables, where those that had survived the train ride (many had suffocated during the trip) lined up to be counted and recorded. They were told to take off their clothes but keep the cards around their necks. There was to be a medical examination.

The children were herded into a tent like structure and Hedy was still outside, shivering as the cold morning air hit her body. She tried not to think about her nakedness. What did it matter who saw her? As usual there were several men standing guard. She had schooled herself to ignore them. After all they were not real humans. She kept her head down and covered her breasts with one arm and instinctively put one hand over her pubic area.

Suddenly a pair of black boots were standing close beside her. Before she could look up a blanket was thrown over her head and her arms were pinned down as the rough cloth was wrapped tightly around her. In one motion she was picked up and carried away. She could feel herself being pushed into a small space. Then she heard a car door slam, the sound of a motor and by the feel of the vibrations she was inside a car, most likely on the floor. What felt like hard shoes poked into her back. She wanted to scream, but her mouth was totally dry and no sound came out. She concentrated on breathing and managed to wiggle her head around just a little. This gave her a small pocket of air. The blanket was scratchy but this was the warmest she had been for a long time and in spite of her discomfort she fell asleep.

She woke up suddenly and felt herself being lifted out of the small space. Strong hands clutched her around the waist and carried her up some stairs. Her head bobbed with each step and she was helpless to hold it still. Then there was the sensation of being thrown down and she could feel that she was now lying on a mattress. A cold rush of air came over her body as the blanket was jerked away from her. Simultaneously two hands gripped her wrists and pinned her arms above her head. She had a glimpse of a black form as her legs were being forced apart and held firm. A woman spoke a few words.

Something was being inserted into her vagina. It was soft and cool, prodding her slowly and then quickly removed. She had felt that strange sensation with David. A sensation that also came to her when she dreamt of him.

Her legs were released and the woman spoke again in a strange language that Hedy had never heard before. She tried to move but her wrists were still being held. Then a man was standing over her. He was dark, like an Arab, but he spoke to her in German.

"Do as you are told!" He barked "and you will not be hurt. If you disobey you will be beaten. Do you understand?" When Hedy did not reply immediately he hit her on the legs with a short length of rubber hose. It smarted and she whimpered.

The man with the rubber hose kept asking if she understood but Hedy's mouth was so dry she could only moan and whimper. He kept hitting her over and over until another man somewhere in the room spoke to her in Polish.

"Do you understand that you will be beaten until you answer?"

The blows kept coming and so did the question. She urinated on the bed. The pressure on her wrists slacked a bit and she heard the woman speak again. The man replied and the beating resumed. At last Hedy had enough saliva in her mouth to speak.

"I understand!" she answered in barely audible Polish.

A man spoke in the strange language and the woman holding her wrists released them and got down from the head of the bed. Hedy didn't move. She closed her eyes and waited for whatever might come next.

Hands lifted her off the wet blanket and covered her with a soft cloth. She heard heavy footsteps receding and a door slammed. Hedy lifted her head slightly and saw a woman, wrapped in a black robe, standing beside the bed. Another woman, a younger version, also wrapped in black, stood on the other side.

Hedy desperately wanted to ask where she was and who they were, but not wanting another beating she just lay still and watched the women, watching her.

The older woman spoke to the younger one in the strange language. Then to Hedy's surprise the younger woman asked Hedy, in strangely accented French, if she spoke French.

"Yes!" Hedy whispered.

"We will not hurt you but you must obey every command." The younger woman continued in French. "You must answer all questions truthfully. If we find out you lie, you will be beaten."

They proceeded to uncover her and pulled her to her feet. The two women looked at Hedy with curious and searching eyes, but not unkindly. When Hedy began to tremble the younger woman spoke again.

"You must be bathed first and then you will eat and drink." Seeing Hedy draw back she added. "You must obey or the men will come back and beat you. We don't want that?"

She asked conspiratorially.

Hedy shook her head slowly and they led her to the bathroom. Her head felt light from hunger and as her stomach growled loudly. She took a quick look around her and saw they were in a large room that looked like the bedrooms that she had seen in American movies. A narrow bed with an ornately carved headboard, a framed picture of a man wearing an enormous white Turkish hat, dark, heavy furniture, oriental rugs over shiny wood floors. Two windows along one wall with heavy, black drapes almost closed, but she could see leafy branches moving in the wind outside.

The bathroom was larger than her bedroom at home and tiled from floor to ceiling in dazzling white tiles with a blue trim around the ceiling. The toilet was walled off on one side of the room the women motioned for her to use it while they filled the tub with water and placed a heavy towel over a heating rack against one wall.

Hearing the running water, Hedy was overcome by thirst and she thrust her head into the sink, turned on the faucet hand, letting the water run into her mouth. The women came up beside her, taking her arms they guided her into the bathtub. The warm water was the first she had felt in over two years. Tears of gratitude came into her eyes, even as the water began to sting very painfully on her bruised legs.

The women washed her body with a soapy sponge and then undid the long, golden braid and proceeded to wash her hair with a sweet smelling shampoo. After they were done with rinsing the soap from her hair they dried her with the warm towel. As Hedy sat on the edge of the bed wrapped in the towel, the older woman began to comb out her hair, which fell like a cascade of raw honey to the middle of her back.

A tray of food had appeared while they had been in the bathroom. Hedy was told to first drink the hot, milky, sweet tea. There were no utensils. The women showed Hedy how to wrap the flat bread around the chunks in the bowl and then put the whole piece directly into her mouth.

A few years ago Hedy would have been shocked at this procedure. In Europe it is considered very bad manners to touch food with anything but a knife and fork. (Soup was always eaten with a proper sized spoon. Drinking soup from a bowl Oriental style was considered totally uncivilized). But by now it had been several years since Hedy had seen a fork or even a spoon. In the camps bread was stuffed directly into the mouth as fast as possible and soup was slurped up right out of a bowl.

After a few bites of the spicy morsels Hedy became a little dizzy. The women allowed only one more bite, urged her to drink a little more tea and took away the tray. The younger one brought a white garment from the closet and laid it on the bed. It was a one piece with a round necked, short sleeved top joined at the waist by a pair of pantaloons. There was a slit from the middle of the waistband that went between the legs to the middle of the back of the waist. The split fabric overlapped at the waist.

The older woman showed Hedy how to get into the strange garment through the slit and demonstrated how to part the fabric for relieving herself.

"Get into bed!" ordered the younger woman.

Hedy noticed the light fading from the window as the women guided her under the feathery covers. Her head sank into the pillow and in a few seconds she was in a deep sleep.

Chapter 2

The stately villa, one hour's drive from the center of Berlin, was surrounded by a ten foot high wall that hid the beautifully landscaped garden from the road below. A half a mile of tree lined gravel road led up to the iron gates and continued another half a mile to the portico of the main entrance. The castle like structure had been built for a member of the Rothschild family, nearly a century ago. No expense had been spared to make the home as comfortable and modern as those times would allow.

When the Nazis came to power, they immediately confiscated the property. The Jewish owners had fled to Switzerland and had taken the blueprints of the structure with them. The subsequent modernization of the building was made more complicated by the lack of those blueprints but soon it was suitable for hosting foreign dignitaries and diplomats. The fund for the rewiring, depluming and redecorating had been stolen from Jewish bank accounts and supplemented by Middle Eastern potentates who had sent laborers, little more than slaves, to do much of the work.

The former Rothschild Villa had become the summer home of important families from countries that supplied the Third Reich with cotton, sugar and crude oil.

When WWII had disrupted the French and British hold on the Middle East, the Arab leaders joined the Axis Powers. So it was that the most powerful personality of the region, The Grand Mufti of Jerusalem and Palestine became a personal friend of all the members of the German High Command. He and his numerous household took up residence in the plush villa outside Berlin as the guests of the Third Reich. In his retinue were four young men he had brought to Berlin as his personal secretaries.

On more than one occasion the Grand Mufti joined the tours of inspection to the various concentration camps and at least once he visited Auschwitz-Birkenau where the Feuhrer himself had proudly shown off the efficiency of his extermination plan for Jews and other undesirables. The Mufti was impressed and planned to implement a similar "final solution" in the Middle East as soon as the war against the despicable allies was won. He was confident in the German victory. They were invincible.

He thought, as so many other supporters of the Nazi fiends, that when they had killed all the Jews in the world they would stop killing. He was ignorant of their plans for eventual enslavement or extermination of all other races, leaving only Aryans in charge of the whole world.

The Grand Mufti hated Jews. He saw how they had arrived in large numbers from western Europe and Russia. They cultivated the land that had been bought from Arabs by the Rothschild's and modernized the towns with electricity and sanitary facilities. They brought running water to places that had depended on brackish wells, medical clinics to rural villages, and paved roads to the cities. In the cities there were streetcars, buses and modern hospitals and even schools that educated girls beyond puberty. They were improving the lives of all the people in Palestine, clearly undermining his power and authority.

When North Africa became a battlefield and he was no longer safe in Bagdad or Damascus he had fled to the protection of the Third Reich. He planned to return to Jerusalem and eliminate the Jews as soon as his Nazi friends were in command of the region.

The Grand Mufti, like all Madras educated men, had been taught from childhood that women were the property of the men in the family and legally the spoils of war with other tribes. In his broadcasts from Berlin he openly urged all Muslim men to kill Jewish males and impregnate their women, making them Muslim property. It was during one of the inspection tours of a death camp that he decided to lead by example. And simultaneously squelch the rumors about his private life.

Upon his instructions his body guard and one of his trusted secretaries had brought him girls of a certain description; Blue eyes, blond hair, slim body, pre-teen or early teen, who would most likely be a virgin.

So far two girls had been brought to the villa in Berlin. They had proved to be unsuitable and needed to be "sent away" Their graves remained unmarked in the beautiful gardens.

The two women he had ordered to "care" for the girls had failed. The older one, the mother of the younger, had been in his household since he was a youngster in his mother's house. The daughter was educated in a school for serving girls. She was probably his cousin or niece. She could read Arabic and spoke French and a few words of English.

He hoped she would be able to communicate his needs to the new girl, His secretary, Omar had informed the Mufti that she was being groomed. The bodyguards had disciplined her and seemed to understand what was expected at the moment.

"She speaks some French." Omar told the Mufti "That should be helpful in explaining her duties."

"Where is she now?" The Mufti asked.

Omar seemed to hesitate before answering. "She is sleeping. Jasmin gave her food and a sedative in her tea. She needed to rest."

"I want to see her!" The Mufti demanded. "Take me to the room!"

Omar led the Mufti down a long corridor and around a corner to another long hallway, to the spacious bedroom. As the men entered the older woman jumped up from the floor and bowed very low. The younger woman remained sitting on the floor at the foot of the bed. The room was dark, except for a small kerosene lamp on a table by the bed. The heavy, blackout curtains were tightly drawn over the windows.

The Mufti looked down at the sleeping girl with squinting eyes then turned to the woman standing behind him. "Is she a virgin?" he asked quietly. The woman nodded. He pushed her aside and went out the door followed closely by Omar, who closed and locked the door, putting the key in his trouser pocket.

"She is the one I saw at the camp. Slim, (actually they all looked like skeletons) blond, presumably she has blue eyes?"

"Yes." was Omar's muted reply.

"You say she speaks French?' The Mufti went on in a hopeful tone.

"I was told that she has an education." Omar's voice was flat as he asked. "When would you like her to come to you?"

"Perhaps tonight, so that Jasmin has all day to train her on the proper behavior in my presence."

Omar looked steadily at the floor, pretending to examine his highly polished shoes in order to hide his pained expression. He fought to keep his features expressionless before looking up again and bowing slightly as the Mufti strode off towards his quarters.

As the Grand Mufti's personal secretary and interpreter Omar had rooms nearby. They were not as spacious or as elaborately furnished as those of the Mufti, but certainly better than the room where the women were quartered.

As Omar came into his living room he noticed that his servant, Yusef, had laid out a tea service beside his wing chair. He sat down and bending double at the waist, covered his face with trembling hands while his whole body shook with stifled sobs.

He had volunteered for this job, for which he was uniquely qualified. He was providing a valuable service, was saving the lives of many people and helping defeat the evil that was threatening to engulf the whole world. The evil that had already trampled large areas and millions of people under its heavy, black boots.

If he were to continue to be successful he had to sacrifice his personal feelings, stifle his natural inclinations and somehow bury all sense of decency and morality deep inside himself. He was a very good actor and played the role to perfection. There was no sign that he was boiling like an underground geyser. Most days it took all his inner strength to keep it in check.

Chapter 3

Omar had been recruited by the Zionists when he was in his teens The local leader of the underground section of the Haganah in Cairo had been scouting for likely candidates and when he saw the file of Oskar Menkes he set out to make his acquaintance.

The files showed that Oskar's father, Rudolf, had married Rosa Kalisher, the only daughter of a Jewish cotton merchant. They had two daughters who were just starting school when Rosa had died giving birth to Oskar. Two years later Rudolf Menkes, a cotton exporter with family roots in Vienna had left the youngsters in Cairo in the care of their faithful Egyptian housekeeper named Amah, while he traveled to Vienna to find a wife and new mother for his children.

A distant cousin had an eighteen year old daughter who had corresponded with his late wife and Rudolf intended to court this girl, marry her in Vienna and bring her back to Cairo as his wife. In the correspondence there had been mention of weak lungs and a doctor's advice for Amalia, (the young cousin) to live in a warmer, dryer climate. Egypt certainly had all of that.

The trip to Vienna was successful. The cousin, whose maiden name was the same as his, was very reluctant, at first, to allow her older daughter to go so far from Vienna. But Oskar's father was very persuasive and the fact that he was handsome, courtly and rich helped persuade Amalia's family to agree to the marriage. They were married within the month and departed for Egypt. Amalia's young sister,

Mathilde was devastated.

When long letters arrived from Cairo, describing the life and culture, the endless desert, archeological sites and warm, dry weather, eight year old Mathilde consoled herself with the thought of how the warm, dry climate would be so good for her sister's health.

Eventually the letters became shorter and disillusioned with her life, Amalia complained of the constant heat, the relentless blue sky. She preferred to live in the dark and kept the drapes drawn to shut out the relentless sun. One sad day a telegram arrived in Vienna. Amalia had died of her lung infection.

Since Oskar's father traveled most of the time he left the children in the care of Amah. They were sent to a Jewish school, but at home Amah observed all the rituals of her Muslim faith and took the children to her Mosque every Friday.

Oskar's father developed cancer and died in the home of his in-laws. He had traveled to Vienna to seek medical care for his condition. Subsequently he had lost a leg, was nursed by a very reluctant Mathilde and after a few months died in Amalia's old bed. His lengthy illness had drained his assets and all that was left was the house at the outskirts of Cairo. The three children were near penniless orphans with no immediate family for support.

The house was sold and the proceeds divided among the children with a small stipend for Amah. She offered to care for the twelve year old Oskar while he finished his Bar Mitzvah preparations, then send him on to Vienna to join his sisters. They were all to stay with a distant cousin of their mother's while learning skills for employment.

After the Bar Mitzvah ceremony and graduation from public school there were no funds left for a passage to Vienna. In order to continue his education, Amah enrolled Oskar into a Madras where Muslim boys were educated and trained to become religious leaders. It was the best Arab school in Cairo and there was no tuition

During a street soccer game when Oskar was fifteen,

he was approached by a member of the Zionist Youth Organization. It was 1933 and getting Jews out of Germany and into Palestine was their main mission. When the other boys asked about the man who had taken him aside, he told them he was a soccer scout for a professional team.

On Amah's advice Oskar had kept his Jewish origins a secret and she had enrolled him in the Madras as Omar and using her family name. Oskar's family had not been religiously observant, yet his father had strong moral beliefs that he had instilled in Oskar at an early age. Oskar knew many passages of the Torah and learned even more passages of the Koran. He found there was wisdom in some of these words but neither Rabbi nor Imam aroused spirituality in Oskar's soul.

He had been following the news from Europe and knew about Fascism and Zionism. At the Madras the boys were told of the evil, Jewish conspiracy to take over the world. Oskar listened and kept his thoughts to himself. He spoke only Arabic while at the lower school. However, when two years later he was enrolled at El Ulum university in Cairo he excelled in French, English and German (which he spoke with a Viennese accent).

The Zionist contact explained what they wanted him to do, and why it needed to be done. Oscar understood completely. By the time he was twenty he was a trusted aid to the Grand Mufti of Jerusalem as well as a competent agent for the Zionist cause. He was to gather information and pass it on to his contacts. His skill with languages was valuable and he was not to risk his life as he would be difficult to replace.

In the Madras the students were taught that females were indispensable as they were needed to produce sons and do the manual labor that was needed to raise them properly but that they were totally interchangeable especially if they didn't live up to expectations.

Most of the boys had very little contact with females. They had been enrolled in the boarding school almost as soon as they could walk and talk and seldom returned to their homes except for important holidays or funerals for the male members of their families. Although they saw westernized women, (mostly French, English or German) on the streets of Cairo, they did not identify these strange beings with the women in their households. The real women in their lives were little more than shadows who served them food and drink and then disappeared into their own quarters.

They were taught that Allah had created females to do any kind of work that needed to be done by hand, that men found distasteful or boring. A man's hands needed to be free to wield a sword and protect his family not carry parcels, or pull a cart.

Of course a man needed to earn a living and in many cases he did that by selling products in the Bazar that had been handmade by his wife.

Almost from the start of his religious education, Oskar saw through the hypocrisy of the Imams that ran the Madras. Although it was one of the many acts forbidden in the Koran, they frequented prostitutes, (male and female) had sexual relations with each other and with their pupils. Alcohol was also forbidden, but there were other, actually more potent methods to add pleasure to living. In fact Oskar lost all respect for organized religion very early in his life. Even while attending Cheder, (the Jewish day school) he realized that the Rabbis didn't always adhere to the rules laid out so clearly in the Torah. However they didn't seem to be as blatant about it as the Imams. He felt that their attitude towards women was only slightly more enlightened than the Muslims, however the Jewish men seemed to treat their wives and daughters with more respect and at times almost like equals.

～

Oskar never knew his mother who, he was told, had died shortly after he was born. The few years that he had a stepmother were the happiest of his life. She was kind and thoughtful and his father always treated her with deference.

She urged the family to take outings to the historic sites around Cairo, to visit the world class museums, attend concerts and lectures by famous archeologists both Egyptian and European.

The Jewish families with roots in western Europe, like their counterparts in Austria and Germany, celebrated both Jewish and Christian holidays. There were family gatherings where men and women mingled and even danced together. Oskar, who spoke fluent Arabic, since that was the language Amah spoken to the children when their parents were not around, overheard the servants discuss these shocking events that meant these infidels would surely go to hell. They did not envy their lifestyle but felt sorry for them.

After his sisters left for Vienna and the house was sold Oskar and Amah moved to a two room apartment in the Arab part of Cairo within walking distance of the Madras.

Oskar, or Omar as he now thought of himself, was one of the few boys who lived at home. He came back to the small, but very clean, apartment every night, shared a meager but healthy meal with Amah, did his homework and most evenings went out again to meet friends. By the time he was fourteen there were girls in his life. He couldn't afford prostitutes, but there were always young, experienced females who would provide sexual favors for a small gift or just for an insincere declaration of love. His encounters were always consensual and there was no feeling of guilt on his part and the women seemed to enjoy his company.

One night, a few days after his sixteenth birthday, he came home nearly an hour before his usual time. He let himself into the apartment and saw, what he thought, was a strange woman sitting at the kitchen table. She sat with her elbows on the table, her head in her hands and a cascade of black ringlets fell down her back. Her shoulders were shaking as if she were crying.

Instinctively Omar called out. "Amah!" As he always did whenever he walked into the apartment even well after midnight, for he knew she didn't sleep until he was home. The head with the black ringlets turned toward him. It took a few moments before he recognized Amah. She put out her hand towards him, touched his arm gently and motioned him to sit down. During those few seconds Omar had a flashback to when and where he had seen those black (now streaked with a bit of gray) curls before. They had glistened, reflecting the lights of the chandelier in the dining room of the big house in which they used to live. Amah and his father were sitting at the table holding hands, speaking in earnest whispers, oblivious to the eight year old boy watching them.

He had come down to get a drink of water for himself, after calling for Amah and getting no response. He had not continued into the kitchen, but stood listening. They were speaking in Arabic and he only heard disconnected phrases.

"Nothing we can do" was uttered several times. "We must wait and see" Paul said at last. Then the two of them had stood up. For the first time in his life Omar saw two adults kiss in a passionate embrace. The scene had left an impression, but as he had made his way back up the stairs, forgetting all about being thirsty, he had ascribed it to the enigma that was "grownups" and had forgotten it until this moment. Now, Amah took his hand in hers, very much like in the scene he had just remembered.

"There is something I must tell you." She said in a low voice, almost a whisper.

Omar kept staring at her hair. He was thinking how beautiful and what a shame to keep it hidden.

"Before I say anything more, "she pleaded, "I must ask you to forgive me and your father for deceiving you." Her wet eyes met his puzzled look. When he didn't respond she continued. "Omar, I am weeping because today is the anniversary of your father's death. He was the love of my life. The last four years I have mourned him every minute of every day. My consolation has been that he left me his son and that is all I live for."

Omar reluctantly turned his eyes away from the shining curls of her hair and focused on her sorrowful eyes. "Amah," he said softly and there was love in his voice. "You have been like a mother to me and I feel like I were your son."

"Omar," She breathed his name. "In my mind you have always been Omar. It is what I named you the day you were born." Her hands tightened around his and she took a deep breath. "Omar, you really are my son." As she spoke these words she lowered he eyes. She was terrified of what she might see in his face.

Suddenly for the first time, he realized that this woman whom he had seen every day of his life was beautiful. Her dark almond eyes, wide, expressive mouth and smooth olive skin, her oval face framed by her magnificent hair were reminiscent of a painting by Vermeer. He could well believe that she was his mother. He kept looking at her with this new found wonder until she finally raised her eyes to his.

"I have never lied to you." she said "Only left out some details of your life you should know."

"Mother," the word felt strange in his mouth. "Tell me the details, please." The love was still in his voice and Amah sat back in her chair, relief showed in her lovely face. Still holding Omar's hands, but not quite so tightly, she took a deep breath and started to tell him about his origins.

"Your father's parents came to Egypt as a young couple, financed by a family connected to a banking house. They were instructed to invest in the fast growing cotton industry. Your grandfather was an astute businessman. He bought land, started a cotton mill, and soon was exporting to textile mills all over the vast Austrian/Hungarian Empire. At first your grandparents rented the big house, where you grew up, from a Turkish Pasha and eventually bought it when he returned to Turkey. My parents were part of the sale. Originally they had been sold to the Pasha when they were children, grew up in the household and married each other. Your grandfather kept them on the staff.

By the time your father was born my mother was the housekeeper and my father worked as the groundskeeper. I was born two years later. Your father and I had no siblings and so we spent our early childhood playing among the many rooms of the mansion and in the extensive gardens.

When I was twelve I was sent away to a girls' school in Alexandria. My parents were Ahmadi and believed in educating women, as well as men."

Hearing the word "Ahmadi" Omar's eyes widened. Amah saw his expression and hesitated a moment while he interrupted her.

"The Imams spoke of this sect along with several other. They said that these people were infidels and traitors."

Although he had long ago stopped believing anything the Imams said, he remembered their words. Seeing his puzzled expression Amah interrupted her narrative of Omar's origins to give a brief explanation of the Ahmadi beliefs. She lowered her voice slightly and began to explain why mainstream Islam ostracized the followers of this sect.

"The Ahmadis are Muslims, we worship Allah, memorize the Koran, and follow the admonitions and teachings of Mohamed. Unlike Shia and Sunni we do not proselyte and interpret the teachings of Mohamed to mean that we should live in peace with all other humans as we are all created by Allah. Ahmadis have two beliefs that conflict with mainstream Muslim teachings and their politics: Even females should have a secular education and very importantly in these time, that the Messiah will come when the Jewish people are safe in their own nation. Unlike most Arab Muslims we support the Zionists. The British pretend to support the creation of a Jewish State, but incite the Arabs in Palestine to protests and even riots. We need their help, but they can't be trusted."

The sixteen year old Oskar (now known to all as Omar) gazed in astonishment at this woman who had raised him, but had never really known.

"Enough politics!" she said. "I will continue with your origins. Her voice resumed a more normal tone as she had inadvertently lowered it when speaking of her beliefs.

"As I said, I was sent away to boarding school and getting mail from anyone except ones parents was not allowed. Rudy was sent to Vienna to continue his education. Four years went by. When I was sixteen I graduated and on my way back to Cairo I saw Rudy. He had just arrived in Alexandria on a ship from Germany, and we met at the train station.

We had grown up like brother and sister, but that day we realized we had very different feelings for each other. We knew that our love was forbidden, but it existed anyway.

At first we tried to deny our feelings, but we saw each other every day. I was helping my mother run the house and keep the accounts, Rudy was being groomed to run the cotton mill. Sometimes we managed to be alone for an hour during the night, sometimes it was only for a few minutes. It was heaven and it was torture. Then in the spring of 1910 a marriage was arranged for Rudy with a woman from Vienna. Rosa Kalisher was kind, thoughtful, and a good wife to Rudy. She was from a wealthy family with an uncle who was a financial adviser to the Kaiser. She never mentioned her important connections or put on airs like so many European women did who lived in Egypt. She was older than Rudy but seemed younger and more naïve.

Rudy and I accepted our fate. In those days married couples of the wealthier class had separate bedrooms and we could have arranged to be together, but even if that had occurred to us we would not have done so.

In 1912 your sister Ilona was born and in 1914 Ida came along. Soon the war was raging in Europe and your grandparents decided they needed to return to Vienna to give support to the Kaiser. They were lost at sea after the ship was torpedoed. Rosa's parents died in an epidemic and the young couple was alone.

My mother also got sick and then died during the war and I took over the household, minded the girls, and did the accounts. Rudy and Rosa were very busy with the cotton mill. Business was booming. All the combatants needed cotton for uniforms.

Towards the end of the war Rosa became very sick. She was nauseated all the time and the doctors in Cairo were at a loss about what could be wrong. They tried different diets, baths, bed rest. Then she seemed to be getting better. I suspected that she was pregnant.

～

One day in November 1918 the war was over. A feeling of elation filled the very air around us. That night Rudy served champagne after dinner and invited my father and me to toast the "peace". My father declined as he said he was in mourning and didn't drink alcohol in any case. He urged me to go and represent the family. I only had one glass of champagne and got very dizzy. Rudy told me to wait for him, while he took his daughters upstairs and quickly checked on Rosa, who was still suffering from daily nausea, then he would escort me back to the small house I shared with my father.

I fell asleep on the sofa and as Rudy woke me up, I thought I was in one of the frequent dreams I had about the two of us. I put my arms around his neck and kissed him with all the pent up passion of many years. There was no going back. He carried me upstairs and I suppose you were conceived that night. But after that night we didn't have the strength to stay apart.

Rosa was indeed pregnant but she was also diagnosed with terminal cancer. After the diagnosis had been confirmed, Rudy wanted to take Rosa to Vienna but by then she was too ill to travel and besides the British Hospital in Cairo had a good reputation with many European doctors on call. Rosa was admitted about a month before the baby was due and kept as comfortable as possible. The girls were sent to friends who spent the summers in Alexandria. We had decided I should stay with Rosa to help nurse her. My Hijab hid my own pregnancy.

Rosa's baby was stillborn and she died a few days later. Rudy had her buried within 24 hours, as is the Jewish (as well as the Moslem) tradition. We did not tell the girls yet that their mother had died. I had been staying in a hotel near the hospital and as luck would have it my baby was born a day later with the help of a hotel maid and Rudy. He then called his daughters and told them that their mother had died and that they had a new brother.

Rudy and I talked about getting married but there were

insurmountable social and religious obstacles. There was also a strictly enforced law against such a union in Egypt. Finally, we decided that the girls needed a European woman to teach them the proper manners and customs they would need to know for the time when they would be sent to school in Vienna.

After about a year Rudy came back from Vienna with your stepmother. Amalia was barely eighteen years old but very sophisticated and knowledgeable about Viennese society. Her mother was a distant cousin on Rudy's father side of the family and a well known dress designer and seamstress for upper class ladies.

Not only did Amalia have impeccable manners, she knew how to run a family. You children took to her and I was delighted in how she treated you and your sisters with warmth, but also loving discipline.

Amalia had weak lungs and was not very strong. There was an understanding right from the start that she should not have children because of her health. I don't think Rudy ever slept with her, but they were good friends and she always treated me with respect. If she knew, or guessed about my relationship with her husband she never gave an inkling of it. I was very sad when she died."

"So was I." Omar had interjected.

They sat in silence for a few minutes then Amah released Omar's hands and stood up. "Good night, my son" Amah said. There was a quality in her voice Omar had not heard before. He kept sitting in his chair, staring into space, his mind working hard to digest and absorb the things he had just been told. Finding out that the woman who had been at the center of his life was his mother was a welcome surprise and so was the feeling of warmth and well being that he recognized as joy. It would be many years before he felt so totally elated again.

Chapter 4

After Oskar Menkes became Omar Samir he hardly remembered being anyone else. After his graduation from al Azhar University in Cairo he was soon recommend to the Grand Mufti of Jerusalem, the religious guardian of every Muslim Holy site in the Middle East. The Mufti needed an interpreter, translator, and corresponding secretary. Because he spoke German, albeit with a Viennese accent, Omar was chosen to accompany the Mufti when he fled to Berlin to avoid arrest by the British for instigating violence in their Mandate Palestine. The Mufti was welcomed warmly by the leaders of the rapidly expanding Third Reich and paid handsomely for his service in organizing an Arab Brigade to help the Germans occupy North Africa.

The villa where the Grand Mufti and his entourage were ensconced was several miles from the center of the city, which made access to the brothers and cabarets, which were located in basements and air raid shelters throughout the city, difficult and dangerous.

Berlin was in war time mode. At night the city was totally blacked out and only air raid wardens were allowed on the streets, along with Gestapo patrols who arrested anyone on the street without proper permits. Despite these restrictions and the nightly bombings, night life flourished. Soldiers and civilians found ways to maneuver the dark streets, often waiting until daylight to find their way home.

Since the Mufti and his aides were outwardly devout Muslims, who did not drink alcohol, or eat pork, the beer gardens, famous for their drunken orgies and pickled pigs feet were off limits and were to be publicly ensued. Numerous servants had come with the Mufti from Jerusalem but only the four personal secretaries saw him daily. Each of these men had an area of responsibility and conveyed the Mufti's wishes to the staff members under their charge. Amir, slim, tall like the Mufti himself at six feet, with a bushy, black mustache on an otherwise clean shaven face, directed the decorators who saw to the buying and placing of art work, furniture and accessories that would add to the comfort and pleasure of the Mufti and also made profitable investments. Amir also was the valet and poison taster for the Mufti. He had a master's degree in chemistry from al Azhar University and was seldom further than an arm's length away from the Mufti.

The other secretary was really a body guard and looked it. His name was Jamal and was usually on the other side of the Mufti from Amir. Besides being the bodyguard, his duties were to oversee the cooks, the cleaning crew, the gardeners and to discipline all the staff at his discretion. Jamal was built like a wrestler with muscular arms, broad shoulders, held up by a square body that exuded power. His handlebar mustache drooped below his chin. With his gleaming bald head and fierce black eyes, he looked like the Mongol raider, which he was. A short piece of rubber hose was always visible hanging from his belt.

Abdul, who was secretary of finance was a short, quiet man who had been with the Mufti all his life. They had grown up together in the same tribe and their fathers had been friends. Abdul covered his balding head with the exact type of fez that the Mufti wore over his thick rust colored hair. Abdul's mustache was thin and graying and he shaved about once a week. He dressed in robes that emulated the Mufti's garb and moved and talked like a shorter version of the Mufti.

Omar had grown into a well built man. At twenty-four, he had broad shoulders, narrow hips, and moved with the graceful motions of a jungle cat. He had wavy, jet black hair, bushy black eyebrows over warm black eyes that were shadowed by long lashes which had been the envy of his sisters. Like most of the men in his generation, he grew a mustache. His was a thin line across his upper lip and came to a point on each side. He seldom wore a hat.

In public the four men of this inner circle were usually in attendance on the Mufti, with Amir standing close by his side while the other three kept a few feet away. They usually spoke to each other in polite phrases about the weather, the war news, or commented on the food they were being served. There was no hint of hostility in there cordial remarks, but it was obvious that they were not close friends.

The Mufti admired the achievements of Alexander the Great, the Greek general who had conquered almost the whole Middle East and had started on India before he died. To insure the loyalty of the rulers of the various countries he had conquered, he married their daughters. (He rarely consummated the marriages as he preferred males in his bed.) Since the Mufti had the same inclinations, he chose his retinue carefully. They came from competing tribes in the Arab world. This made an alliance between his aides unlikely as they tended to mistrust each other.

The Mufti assured the loyalty of his "secretaries/body guards "by promising them that they would be at his side when he would rule the whole Middle East. But for extra insurance he provided "protection" for Abdul's wife and sons in Jerusalem. If Abdul were to be implicated in any harm to the Mufti, his family would pay a heavy price. In the case of Jamal, the Mufti had irrefutable evidence that Jamal had murdered an important official of the British High Command in Palestine. If any harm came to the Mufti, Jamal would be hanged or spend the rest of his life in an English prison. Amir was not likely to do harm to the man he loved, but if there were ever any suspicion of betrayal the Mufti had no compunction about turning him over to the Nazis to be imprisoned as a sexual deviant.

The two women the Mufti had brought into exile with him, Jasmin and her daughter Leia, were there to allay rumors about his sexual orientation. His mother and sister remained in Jerusalem. His hatred for the Jews was so powerful that on several occasions he had urged his Nazi friends to bomb the holy city in order to kill as many Jews as possible, regardless of the danger to his family or to the lover who had helped him gain his powerful position.

Oskar, who was now Omar, had the Mufti's complete trust because the imam from the madras vouched for him without reservation. Omar had entered the madras as an orphan without links to any family or tribe. Amah had advised Omar to immerse himself in the teachings of the Koran. For the duration he was to put aside all the Jewish lore he had learned and concentrate on learning about Islam. "Half the people in the world are Moslem." Amah had told him, "There must be something worth learning in their teachings."

Omar found out that Islam and Fascism had some beliefs in common. They taught that it was best that absolute power over life and death should be centered on one man. This man can enforce the law (Sharia in the case of Islam) as he sees fit. The slightest misstep and the culprit can be killed and all his possessions confiscated. (This was similar to the days of the Catholic Inquisition, when an accusation of heresy could mean the end of a family while all their assets went to the Church).

Despite the moral guidelines and admonitions in the Koran, corruption was (and still is) rampant and each tribal family must look out for itself if it is to survive. Tribal loyalty was always the first concern. Nationhood was a European concept that did not easily fit into the Middle East Culture.

Omar was aware of that mentality and thus could not, in his heart, pledge allegiance to anyone or any cause. In the present circumstances, he was very careful to say only what the people in power wanted to hear. If he ever even hinted at his true thoughts and feelings, he would be dead or worse.

Some nights he threw himself onto his bed, fists clenched, grinding his teeth, his shirt damp with sweat. There were many mornings when it took every ounce of his will power to get ready for another day of attending the Mufti instead of killing him.

Two days after Omar and Jamal had snatched Hedy from the line going into the gas chamber, The Mufti had not yet sent for her. There had been a reception at the Japanese Embassy one night and on this night the treasury secretary of the Third Reich was coming to the Villa to deliver the monthly stipend for the Mufti ($10,000 American in small bills). It was a bribe for organizing the Muslim troops to fight the British in North Africa.

An intimate supper was planned for the treasury secretary, the Mufti, Amir and Omar, who would act as German interpreter. The fact that he spoke German with an Austrian accent was an advantage because from Hitler on down, many of the members of the German High Command were Austrian. Jamal and Abdul would have a free evening, but were to remain in the villa in case they were needed.

Jamal spent the afternoon in anticipation that evening's entertainment. He paced the plush carpet of his room, fingering the length of rubber hose in his belt. His hands were itching and he could feel the excitement tightening in his groin.

In the fall of 1943 there were many air raids over Germany and as the time came to draw the blackout curtains the roar of heavy aircraft filled the Villa. Jamal pulled the drapes closed in his room and walked out the door, locking it behind him. Abdul was coming out of his room across the hall.

"Do you have the key?" Abdul asked and received a curt nod in reply.

Looking around to make sure the hallway was empty the two men sauntered casually to the room where the women were kept.

Earlier that evening Abdul had brought Jasmin a tray of

food, a bar of soap, a stack of toilet paper tissue and some lotion that Jasmin had asked for. Abdul and Jasmin ignored the admonition that women were not allowed to converse with unrelated men. They had known each other as children, had played with the Mufti and his sister in their family courtyard. That afternoon they spoke about the weather, (it was getting colder and they hated the German winters) and how it would be many months before they would walk in the garden again. Their only outings would be to prayers on Friday and to the basement to do laundry each Monday.

During that visit Abdul and Jasmin had discussed the training of the new girl and how it would go better this time since she spoke French and Leia could translate the Koran as well as the house rules to her in that language. Abdul had advised patience so as to avoid the digging of more graves.

Jasmin and Abdul had agreed they wanted to avoid the unpleasant experiences with the last two girls, who's deaths had been unfortunate. The first girl had been the feisty, sixteen, year old daughter of a former Jewish officer in the Kaiser's army. Like her father, she could not accept the position of being subhuman. When she refused to obey orders, even after repeated beatings, Jamal in frustration had punched her in the face with his ham like fist. The blow had broken her neck. She had been buried by the Arab gardeners who asked no question. The second girl, a twelve year old from an Orthodox family, spoke only Yiddish (a distorted German mixed with Polish and Hebrew). She did not understand German commands and being whipped into unconsciousness did not improve her cognition. She had also refused to eat or drink and after about a week her already emaciated body gave out.

"Digging graves is hard work." The gardeners had grumbled while preparing yet another grave. Jamal had taken out his sidearm and asked the men in an even voice. "Do you want to join the Jewish sow?" Thus the gardeners realized without being told that digging graves was considered part of their job.

Abdul and Jasmin glanced at the sleeping girl on the bed and with a quick nod to Leia Abdul left the women to eat their food, saying nothing about returning later with Jamal.

Chapter 5

The three women in the Mufti's Villa sat in their accustomed places as they ate the food Abdul had brought to them earlier in the evening. The dish made with rice was especially delicious. For a brief and painful moment Hedy was transported to the fragrant kitchen where Konstanza sometimes prepared Greek dishes. The scent of caraway, anise, roasted sesame seeds and other mysterious ingredients had filled the air while Hedy had watched the various forms take shape in preparation to be cooked.

Leia sat on her low stool while her mother Jasmin sat cross legged on the pillow by the bathroom door. Hedy sat on the bed, also cross legged, and looked around her. Leia had been reading to her from the Koran in Arabic and now she was translating some of the text that she felt were important for Hedy to know. Her voice had droned on in an expressionless monotone while she read in Arabic but in her accented French the words had more meaning. Hedy looked around the small room. She saw a bed and a nightstand beside it, a table between the two windows. A Kerosene lamp was lit on the table and threw an eerie light around the room. There were several large cushions on the floor and the other two women slept on those while Hedy slept in the bed. All three of them slept with their clothes on and their heads covered at all times. This was the most clothes Hedy had worn in two years and with winter coming she thought it might be a good thing.

That morning they had all three bathed in the bath tub, one at a time in the same water. Hedy got the warmest water as she was considered a guest as Leia had told her. Jasmin was next and then Leia got to bathe in the tepid water. Hedy noticed that there was no door to the bathroom and the water closet was behind a partition. The only place for any privacy.

With her legs still smarting from the beating two days ago Hedy tried not to think about what might happen to her in this strange place. She had learned to push fear into the background of her mind, keep her thoughts on what had to be done each moment. She found relief in remembering her childhood. Yet no matter how hard she tried to concentrate on what her life was like before she was taken away, the hate-filled faces of the people that shouted insults and accusations at her as she was marched to that first train ride, often filled her dreams. Many of those angry people were her former friends and neighbors. She had wanted desperately to stop and ask them what she had done to arouse such hatred. "Why? Why?" was still echoing in her head.

While Leia told of the many rules concerning the restrictions on women in Islam, Hedy listened with only half a mind. Leia's soft voice explained how "a woman's hair is an abomination and must never be seen in public, how a woman's voice is abomination and must never be heard in public or be raised in song. A woman must never complain about her circumstances. Whatever fate befalls her is the will of Allah and she must submit. Islam means submission and in submission lies true faith and salvation."

Hedy realized that she had heard very similar words from the Rabbi in Hebrew School. The difference in the two faiths seemed to be the consequences of disobedience. In Islam it meant being beaten or stoned to death whereas in Judaism, revised over the centuries from the harsh wording in the Torah, the consequences were not spelled out except that God would be displeased.

Leia went on about the duties of a wife. "She was to obey her husband in all things and if he was displeased with her, he was encouraged to beat her. But he must limit himself to using a switch no larger than the circumference of his thumb. "This admonition also sounded familiar to Hedy. Similar words were read to her out of the Torah.

Not for the first time Hedy began to feel that religions were cruel and a tool for the powerful to control the mass of people. She remembered that admitted Atheists like her mother's brother, several of her father's friends and even Konstanza, were the most moral and compassionate people she had known.

A key was turning in the lock, the door flew open, then Jamal strode into the room with Abdul at his heels. The two men took a quick look around the room at the startled women. Leia and Jasmin quickly looked at the floor, but Hedy instinctively glanced up at Jamal. Her blue eyes grew large with fear as he stared back at her, his black eyes blazing with rage. Abdul locked the door and stood waiting.

Jasmin cowered down on her pillow, drawing her prayer beads through trembling fingers. Leia, who throughout her sixteen years had sustained many beatings for things she had done or not done, expected the worst from the man who now stood over her. She knew he did not need an excuse, he often beat her for his pleasure. She sat very still, her head down almost touching her knees. Jamal stood over Leia and shouted "Straffe Stelle!"

Leia quickly got down on her hands and knees, grabbed the hem of her long robe, throwing it up over her head. Then reaching back with both hands she pulled the slits of her undergarment apart, exposing her white buttocks, which were mottled with bruises.

In broken German, Jamal ordered Hedy to follow Leia's example. Then yelling "Straffe Stelle!" over and over several times. Hedy sat on the bed frozen with fear. Jamal spoke to Abdul, who immediately grabbed Hedy's arms, threw her face down on the bed. He sat at the head of the bed, holding her firmly by the wrists with her head between his legs he braced his feet flat against her shoulders. Hedy felt her legs being pushed up so she was on her knees with her feet braced against the foot of the bed. Jamal jerked the black robe up over her head and pulled the slits of her undergarment apart.

For a moment he stood looking at the white, mounds of unmarred skin. Hedy couldn't even so much as squirm and when the first blow fell the pain was like fire had been set to her buttocks. Each blow hurt worse than the last. Her screams echoed through the room and became louder and louder. Suddenly the pain became mixed with a feeling of pleasure. It began in her groin and grew in intensity until it enveloped her whole body. The screams of pain mingled with screams of overwhelming pleasure. Then everything went black as Hedy fainted.

Jamal raised the rubber hose one more time, but when the blow got no response he reluctantly stuck it in his belt. He motioned Abdul to release the unconscious girl. Abdul climbed off the bed, wiping his sweaty palms on his trousers. His gold rimmed spectacles were opaque with moisture.

Jamal's moustache and bald head glistened with sweat and there were black stains on the underarms of his brown uniform shirt and on the front of his khaki pants. Hi breath came in short gasps as he backed away from the bed. Abdul unlocked the door, waving Jamal out in front of him. Without a backward glance they went out the door. Their receding footsteps were muffled by the deep carpet in the hall.

Slowly Hedy regained consciousness. The pain coursed through her whole body but centered on her buttocks. She vaguely recalled the feeling of intense pleasure then without warning she began to cry. Hedy had not cried for many years. She had shed no tears when her mother left for Vienna five years ago or when her father left for Berlin a year later. There were no tears when she said good-by to Konstanza. There had only been those fierce orders from Konstanza. "Do whatever you need to do but stay alive!" She had come near crying when she and David had been torn apart upon their arrival at, what she later learned, was a transit camp for sorting out those who would be sent on to a death camp. Now her tears mixed with the perspiration on the damp sheet. Her violent sobs shook her whole, aching body and every move was agony.

Jasmin put down her prayer beads and straitened Hedy's scrunched up form to lie flat on the bed. She pulled the black robe back to uncover her head. Then she began to rub a cooling salve into her red and quickly swelling skin.

Leia got up from the floor, adjusted her clothing, and came to sit by Hedy's head. She began to stroke the golden hair that had become uncovered during the attack, and pushed a few strands away from the face of the sobbing girl. Leia was murmuring words of comfort first in Arabic and then in French, but Hedy's aching head was still echoing with the words that Jamal had kept shouting at her.

Finally she asked Leia, "What means 'STRAF-FESTEL-LE?'"

Leia answered in French, "Punishment Position" then she began to weep softly as Jasmin led her to the bed of pillows on the floor.

Chapter 6

Hedy spent the next day lying on her stomach. She was able to stand up and eat a little of the food Jasmin pressed into her hand. She had thoughts of starving herself but the pungent odor of the spicy food aroused her appetite and she decided to eat after all. In fact, she scraped out the bowl and licked her fingers. Both of the Arab women urged her to drink water several times during the day, but she was reluctant to move because of the excruciating pain. The only relief was lying on her stomach. The swelling had gone down in her buttocks, but the flesh was still blue, green and yellow with red streaks crossing over it all.

When Abdul came to bring them food the next day, Hedy buried her face in the pillow when she heard the key in the lock fearing it might be Jamal. He did not look at the bed where Hedy was trying to keep her body from trembling. He just set down the tray, took the old tray and left.

Hedy found sitting painful so she stood up to eat. As her body regained some strength she took more interest in her surroundings as well as the landscape beyond the window. There was a park with grassy squares, rows of trees along a walkway through, what would be, flower beds in the spring. There was a bench at the end of the walkway and she saw what might be a lilac bush. Just the thought of lilacs reminded her of the bush near her home. Some of the trees were evergreens like the pines in Poland, but most of the trees were bare and the overall scene was gloomy and colorless. Late the next afternoon there was the sound of a key in the lock.

47

Jasmin made sure that Hedy was lying face down on the bed, then she and Leia sat down on the floor beside her.

Omar came into the room, locked the door and stood over the bed. He addressed Jasmin in Arabic. "The Mufti wants to see her." Then turned to Leia, who kept looking at the floor. He added in French. "She will not need a head covering he wants to see her hair. The robe she has on will do."

Jasmin lifted her head slightly, but not looking at Omar she said a few words in Arabic. Hedy understood the word "Jamal" and flinched visibly on the bed.

Then Omar continued in French. It was clear that he wanted Hedy to understand him. "Uncover her wounds!" he ordered Jasmin in a tone that expected obedience.

Carefully she folded the robe up towards Hedy's trembling shoulders and gently pulled apart the slits in her bloomer like pants. Omar's expression did not change as his stomach squeezed into a tight and burning knot, while his fists clenched until his fingernails cut painfully into his palms. One word escaped his lips. It was both a question and an exclamation. "Jamal?!" Leia raised her head a fraction to give a slight nod.

He spoke a few words to Jasmin in Arabic and left the room.

Omar had seen flesh like this before and the rage that it aroused in him was dangerous. He had to fight to control it. There was too much at stake. He could not kill Jamal outright, which is what he desperately wanted to do that very moment. He must find a more subtle way to get his revenge.

Blinded by rage and unshed tears Omar made his way to the Mufti's quarters. As he entered the ornate room, the glare from the crystal chandelier was all he could see. When his vision cleared he saw the Mufti, Amir and Abdul were playing cards. They looked up expectantly. Omar spoke in Arabic, trying to keep his voice even and unemotional.

"The new girl is very ill, just like the others." He paused to control his voice and added under his breath "Jamal has beaten her almost to death. She may still die of her wounds."

The Mufti, his reddish beard and sandy hair glowing in the bright lights, was studying his cards. It was Amir who looked at Omar with a smile and asked if he should deal him in for the next hand.

No one looked up as Omar left the room. When he got to his own quarters, Omar began to pace up and down the sitting room. Yusef, came in and with hand signals asked if he should bring food or drink. Omar dismissed him with a wave of his hand and then changed his mind and called him back. He started to tell Yusef about the girl and how he wanted to kill Jamal. Yusef seemed to read his mind. He was unable to speak, so he and Omar communicated with sign language or a word or two on a small piece of paper that was immediately destroyed.

Although it had never been mentioned they both knew that the room had listening devices hidden somewhere and that the Mufti had someone listening to everything that everybody said in the whole Villa.

Now Omar wrote the words "Jamal must die "on the tissue that they kept around for that purpose. Yusef moved his hands around his body and pretended to push back long hair to imitate feminine gestures and had a questioning look on his face. Omar smiled in spite of himself and nodded. Yusef wrote one word on a slip of paper. After Omar had glanced at it Yusef tore it up, flushing the scraps into the toilet and went to his room.

Omar kept pacing, trying to clear his mind of the rage so he could think clearly about what he must do. Try as he might he could not get the discolored skin of the Polish girl out of his mind. The excruciating pain she must have endured was beyond his imagining. He had been beaten in the Madras when he had forgotten or omitted a line in the day's readings. It had smarted, but the humiliation had been more painful.

The last time he had seen the results of a beating, one which he might have instigated, was in Cairo a few days after his sixteenth birthday. He had earned a little money running errands in the neighborhood and had just spent it in a brothel.

A girl had been sitting on the steps as he was leaving and he almost fell over her. She looked too young to be an employee of the establishment and he had asked her what she was doing there alone like that in the middle of the night. She had told him she worked there as a maid, excused herself for being in his way and started back into the house. Her manner and her speech intrigued Omar. She was slim, had light colored hair, very large black eyes in an intelligent and expressive face. He wanted to hear her voice again. What is your name?" he had asked in a friendly tone.

"Yadira," she had whispered. Then swiftly ran inside.

Several weeks later, Omar was walking by the same brothel, trying to decide if he could afford to go in when he saw Yadira sitting on the steps as before. He stopped to talk to her. Politely he asked how she was and offering her a candied almond from a bag in his pocket. He wanted an excuse to stay there with her, her voice was soft, with an accent from the south of Egypt. She accepted the almond and began to answer his questions.

She was sixteen, the 6th child of ten children. Her father was a shoemaker, The fact that he worked with his hands meant that he was a very poor man. She was to marry a neighbor last year, a man over sixty years of age, and she refused. Subsequently her father sold her to the owner of the brothel. He said he had no choice, he needed the money for food for the other children. Since she had refused to get married he had to get rid of her somehow.

Omar and Yadira had talked longer then they thought and the owner of the brothel found them there on the steps. The brothel owner asked Yadira for the money she had collected for her services. When there was no answer he kicked Omar down the stairs and dragged Yadira inside.

Two days later Omar had gone by the brothel. This time he had decided to go inside and ask for Yadira. The owner let him in after Omar said he was prepared to pay and gave him money for half an hour. A young boy showed him to a cubicle, where Yadira was lying on her stomach on a narrow cot, moaning softly into her folded arms. The brothel owner stood at the door behind Omar, who stared with revulsion at the blue, green, and yellow of the swollen flesh of her bare buttocks.

"I should give you a thrashing too!" The brothel owner barked at Omar. "She's not going to give away her time to a thieving free-loader again."

Omar felt guilty the rest of his life. He had helped bring girls to the Mufti because he knew they were safe from sexual assaults from the Mufti and it would save a Jewish life. Now that he realized what had happened to the other girls, Omar had to eliminate Jamal but without implicating himself. Yusef had spelled out the method. Omar took down his copy of Shakespeare plays and spent the night reading and re-reading "OTHELLO."

Chapter 7

Hedy spent several more days in a trance like state as Jasmin gave her sleeping powder in the spicy tea. She slept restlessly, and when she awoke, Jasmin gave her a little food and more tea. After three days went by Hedy's pain was receding, and she began to wonder where she was. Who were these strangely dressed women? What language were they speaking? Why had she been beaten so savagely?

Then she remembered that in this new world beatings were what some people did and some people endured and there did not have to be a discernible reason for the brutality. She had watched helplessly as two of her little charges, boys of about five years old, were beaten to death right in front of her and the other children. Their only crime had been that they were Jewish and had the temerity to still be alive.

As her strength returned Hedy became more restless and started pacing around the room. One morning she stopped to look out the window and discovered that the building threw an L shaped shadow over the park below. It looked like a large, two-story structure and they were in the eastern end of it.

Hedy began to question Leia. She found out she was in Berlin, (the city where her father had disappeared). Hedy had read about the Moslems and how they lived mostly in the Middle East and were Semitic, and like Jews were descendants of Abraham. What was a Muslim household doing in Nazi Germany, the capital of the racist Arians ?

Leia pointed to the picture of the man with the rust colored beard that hung above the little table and began to tell Hedy in her Arabic accented French about the "Dear Beloved Grand Mufti of Jerusalem and all Palestine."

"He is the most powerful and wisest leader in the Muslim faith. He is a learned and holy man who knows all the Islamic laws. He interprets the holy Koran. He is the judge when a dispute arises between two Muslims. He decrees who shall live and who shall die. He is the guardian of all the holy places in Jerusalem and head of the Islamic council in Palestine and all of Islam. To us he is the most important man in the world. Our Dear Beloved Mufti protects us and guides us."

Hedy then asked Leia what they were doing in Berlin. Leia told her when the British had tried to arrest the Mufti for inciting the Moslems in Palestine to fight off the British rule he had been invited to come to Berlin, where he offered to help recruit Moslems in Europe to help the Germans conquer the world and kill all the Jews.

"Why would this man want a Jewish girl in his bed if he hates Jews so much?" was Hedy's next question.

Leia replied "The Mufti has decreed that Jews are the enemy and must be killed wherever they are found. But he has also told the Muslim men that is was pleasing to Allah for them to capture Jewish women, impregnate them and convert them to Islam."

Upon hearing all of this from Leia, Hedy was speechless and momentarily stunned. In the next few moments she fought hard to control the panic that threatened to overwhelm her. Thoughts of Konstanza and her demand that she "stay alive" brought her mind into focus and she began to think about ways to escape or failing that, ways to delay her eventual death, by her own hand if need be.

It was clear that Leia and Jasmin were not going to help her escape. Leia had made it plain that both women thought that she should feel very blessed and honored to be chosen to share the Mufti's bed. They were not her enemies but they were not her friends and Hedy was certain that they had drugged her. She felt a lethargy that was unfamiliar. She would need to stay alert and watch every move these women made and make sure that they also ate and drank everything they gave to her.

She decided to engage Leia in as much conversation as possible so the detailed questioning began.

"Leia," Hedy said, "You told me who the Mufti is, now tell me who you are."

"I am Jasmin's daughter." She answered patiently.

"Oh yes,?" Hedy said in a tone that clearly indicated there was more to tell.

There was no response from Leia, who briefly raised her eyes and sighed.

"Who is Jasmin, really and why is she here in Berlin and not in Palestine ?" Hedy continued to probe. Is one or both of you a wife to the Mufti?' Hedy knew that Moslems were allowed multiple wives.

Leia took a deep breath, got up from the floor and walked to the window. She glanced down at Jasmin, who as usual was sitting on her pillow on the floor next to the little table, eyes following the prayer beads in her hands.

"We are related to the Dear Beloved Mufti" Leia said while pointing to the portrait on the wall over the table. "He is Jasmin's cousin, uncle or half brother."

Jasmin's mother was a wife to several men in the household. She died without telling Jasmin who her father really was. Perhaps she didn't know and for a girl it is not important."

"So, where is your father?" Hedy continued to probe.

"He is in Palestine, and employed in the household of the Dear Beloved Mufti's mother." Leia replied with a firmness in her voice that indicated she was not going to talk further about this subject. She did however continue to talk about the Mufti. She pointed at the pictures in the room that Hedy had not noticed previously. Now Hedy studied the pictures while she listened to Leia's gushing praise of the Mufti. According to Leia he was wise above all other men, kind, generous to his people, heroic in his fight against the British and the Zionists.

"And best of all", she added, "he was the personal friend of the great German leader. He had allied his people with the Third Reich. Thousands of Muslim troops were under his command. He was the salvation of a Greater Arabia and would soon rule the whole Middle-East."

Hedy didn't know much about the Middle East. She had read a few paragraphs in school about the turbulent history, about French and British colonialism in the arid desert areas. There had been references to the "Silk Road" from China to Europe that passed through the region, to important spices from there and more recently the discovery of oil.

Looking at the portrait above the table, Hedy saw a man about her father's age with a trim beard, wearing a large, white fez that covered most of his head. She remembered seeing pictures in an album of her aunt Amalia, her mother's older sister, sitting on a camel with the pyramids of Giza behind her. The man standing beside the camel had been wearing the same type of hat.

Leia was still talking and Hedy heard her say how she loved the German leader, calling Hedy's attention to the other pictures in the room. One was of the grim faced demon sporting his little mustache and black lock of straight hair on his forehead. The other framed photograph was of the two evil men, who had sworn to kill all the Jews in the world, shaking hands, surrounded by several handsome young officers.

The two young women were sitting on the bed when the sound of the key in the lock sent Leia scrambling to the foot of the bed where she quickly sat down on the floor, drawing the black scarf up to cover her smooth, black hair.

Abdul came in carrying a tray of food which he placed on the table under the Mufti's portrait. Hedy sat cross-legged on the bed, her hands and teeth clenched tightly, aware that her trembling body was shaking the bed. Abdul didn't even look her way. He addressed some Arabic words to Jasmin, who nodded without looking up. Then he stood in front of Leia, who lifted her head but kept her eyes down as he spoke to her. It sounded like he had asked a question and paused for a reply. Hedy saw Leia nod her head and resume her bowed position. Then Abdul went out the door, locking it behind him. The women got up to wash their hands in preparation for eating the food on the sideboard.

Jasmin brought water from the bathroom sink to make tea in the samovar that had a place of honor next to the food under the Mufti's portrait. Leia began to fill their bowls with the food from the tray. While they ate Jasmin spoke at length to Leia. Hedy tried to catch words or phrases to remember and perhaps to connect with something familiar. Occasionally a word sounded like Hebrew. Was there a similarity?

While she spoke, Jasmin kept waving her hand in Hedy's direction and it was clear that the words she used meant. "Tell her!" Hedy had learned her first Arabic words.

Abdul had told the women that the Mufti was leaving Berlin in a few days to review the Muslim Brigade in Bosnia. He would be gone for some time and they were to do the laundry the next day.

Leia told Hedy about the laundry routine: Every Wednesday Abdul and Jamal escorted Jasmin and Leia to the basement laundry room where a wagon sized cart of dirty clothing and linen awaited them that had been thrown down a huge laundry chute.

"The men will lock you into this room tomorrow while we go down to do the washing." Leia told Hedy. "We will be gone all day. On washdays we do not eat until we are done."

Leia continued, "On Thursday we go down to fold and iron the clean clothes. Then we put them back into the carts. So on Friday our Dear Beloved Mufti will have clean garments and linens for the holy day."

Hedy still ached from the beating, but was able to move around without wincing. She wanted, desperately to get out of the room. Perhaps find a way to escape. Although from what she had seen of the high wall around the property it did not seem likely. There was also her terror of Jamal. If she were alone in the room he might come back to assault her. Over the last two days she had tried to understand why he had beaten her so ferociously.

She had asked Leia if he had beaten her or Jasmin. The answer was "Yes, of course. But he no longer beats my mother, at her age she doesn't need to be punished."

"Why are you punished?" Hedy asked. Wanting to find out how to avoid future beatings.

"I don't always know exactly, there are so many rules." Leia sighed.

"What did I do to deserve the beating?" Hedy asked anxiously.

"It may have been a warning." Leia speculated.

"About what ?" Hedy was still puzzled

"Non Muslim women, even some Muslim women, do not behave properly and need to be punished so they will remember their place." Leia explained, nodding her head as if she were agreeing with herself.

"He needed to let you know what will happen if you disobey or misbehave."

Hedy listened to these words in disbelief. In order to avoid future beatings, she needed to know the rules. According to Leia there were only a few, but they could be interpreted at will by any man. An example was that a woman was forbidden to raise her eyes to a man. Hedy remembered looking into Jamal's glittering eyes and shuddered. According to what Leia was saying, if a woman did not look a man in the eyes when he thought she should, she could be punished as well.

Leia explained, "The Koran gives a man the permission, even the duty, to beat a woman who displeases him. The Koran is merciful and limits the size of the rod to be used for beating an errant woman. It is to be no thicker than the man's thumb." Then she added to emphasize the compassion of the holy words. "Beating pregnant and nursing women is not advised."

Hedy brought the discussion back to the laundry, with the hope of getting out of the room for a few hours.

"I could really be of some help with the laundry," Hedy offered.

Leia looked at her skeptically

"I have done lots of washing and know how to wring out clothes and hang them to dry." She added hopefully.

Leia and Jasmin held a short conference, then Leia told Hedy. "We need permission from the Dear Beloved Mufti. If he says you can help us you can come along."

So it was that Leia, since Jasmin could neither read or write, wrote a note on a piece of paper with a stubby pencil she found in the nightstand and pushed it under the door for the night guard to see. During the night the note came back with "yes" on the back.

Before dawn the next morning Abdul brought hot porridge, flat bread and dried fruit.

"We must hurry." Leia said. "He will be back in half an hour and we must be ready."

When Abdul and Jamal came they opened the door and stood in the hallway. Leia had warned Hedy to keep her hair well covered and reminded her about keeping he eyes directed to the floor. Hedy didn't need reminding to keep her eyes down.

The women formed a single line behind Abdul while Jamal brought up the rear, fingering the rubber hose in his belt. They walked down a long corridor then down a narrow stairway to the lowest part of the villa, that was even below the kitchen.

Three large vats had to be filled with water. Coal had to be brought from the coal bin in one area of the vast cellar area and piled under the vats to heat the water.

The two younger women carried water to the vats in two heavy buckets, which they filled from a faucet on the wall near the clothes chute. Jasmin brought coal from the dark side of the room in a coal hamper and began to start the fire with a match and a scrap of paper she took out of a pocket in her robe. She blew on the sparks with a bellows that lay beside the tubs, then started to sort the clothes into three piles.

The first vat was for soaking the white clothes in boiling water, the second for washing and scrubbing the clothes with a washboard in the strong lye soap, the third vat was for rinsing the washed items.

Then the women wrung out the laundry as well as they could by hand and carried each item to a clothesline strung along one end of the room. The dim light from the bulb that hung from the ceiling near the washtubs barely reached to the clotheslines. The rest of the cavernous room was in total darkness. A good place to hide, Hedy thought.

Jasmin began to throw the white laundry into the boiling water of the first vat, she stirred it around with a flat paddle then used the paddle to dump them into the soapy water of the second vat. Leia then pulled the pieces out of the very hot, but not boiling, water of the second vat and scrubbed them on the washboard inside the tub. She handed them to Hedy to wring out and dump into the cold, clear water of the third tub. Hedy's job was to wring out the rinsed laundry and put it into a basket. Then both girls dragged the heavy basket to the clothesline area at the other end of the room, where they hung the wet laundry over the lines. When the basket was empty they went back for the next load.

They worked well together and Hedy took the opportunity to find out more about Jasmin and Leia. According to Leia, Jasmin's mother had died at her birth and she was raised by an aunt, who may have been her mother's sister, but then all older women were called "aunt" by the children, no matter what their relationship might be.

Leia was told that the Mufti was her uncle as Jasmin was the property of the Mufti's brother. He died shortly after Leia was born and Jasmin joined the Mufti's household. The Mufti believed in educating women, for the purpose of reading the Koran, and sent Leia to school in Damascus. She learned to read and write in Arabic and French, a little arithmetic, enough geography so she could follow the travels of Mohamed and some history of Europe that clearly indicated that all the Christian countries of that area had been Moslem at one time and needed to return to the one true faith.

After six years in Damascus Leia returned to Jerusalem at the age of twelve. She then spent another two years in an English school where she learned the language and that the British considered themselves the only people qualified to rule the world. Later she learned that the Germans had the same idea and so now the two factions were at war.

"After they have all killed each other." she told Hedy, A Moslem Caliphate will emerge. The whole world will be Moslem and there will be peace."

Hedy tried hard to keep a straight face as she asked Leia, "Do you read any books?"

"Oh yes!" was the quick reply "I love to read about Mohamed and his family. His wives and daughters had such interesting lives. Then there are books about the saints and martyrs. Their lives are so inspiring. Learning about the hardships they endured helps us to endure our own lives."

As the three women worked, their black robes and head coverings became soaked. They did not dare to roll up their sleeves, as a guard was posted at the top of the stairs and he might just decide to come down and check on them before they called for him.

It was late evening before all the clothes were hung up on the lines, the vats drained, the basket stowed under the table where the laundry had been sorted, and the cart placed against the wall near the laundry chute.

Tired and very hungry the women climbed up the steep and winding stairs, their damp robes weighing them down at every step. Two guards were waiting to escort them to their room. As they walked the long corridor, Hedy's eyes swept from side to side, hoping to discover a window. To her disappointment they passed only two doorways.

She guessed they might lead to rooms or perhaps broom or storage closets. It would be good to know what lay behind those doors. She guessed that the building might be a square with a courtyard in the middle, but the shadow from the sun had shown an L.

When they entered their room they began to hear the drone of the bombers that were heard each night. The explosions were still at a distance and no sirens were blowing near the villa.

They took off their wet garments and hung them on a line strung up in the bathroom for that purpose. There was a tray of food on the table and the young women ate while Jasmin made tea. Hedy was too tired to eat much and wearily climbed into the bed with her damp undergarment sticking to her clammy skin, and fell asleep.

The next morning they were again up before dawn and escorted to the basement. Jasmin took four coal heated irons from a wall cupboard that Hedy had not noticed the day before. It was Leia's job to keep the irons filled with hot coals while Jasmin ironed the still damp linens and garments that Leia and Hedy brought her from the clothes lines. The finished products were neatly folded into the cart. When it was full they placed it under the chute, which also contained a manually operated dumb waiter. The cart would then be pulled up by the Mufti's personal servants and distributed to the proper rooms, then sent back down to the cellar until the next wash day in two weeks.

The ironing and folding took all day and the women returned to their room, exhausted and hungry. This evening Hedy ate and drank the spicy tea with relish and had the energy to bathe. The women then washed their garments in their bath water. Hedy learned that mixing female with male clothing in the wash was to be avoided.

Hedy was just starting to fall asleep when the nightly bombers started to drone by overhead. The distant wail of air raid sirens were barely audible as the explosions started to reverberate through the city of Berlin. The villa was still far away from the center of the bombing runs that focused on the ammunition storage areas and the fuel bases.

She lay on her back, waiting for the dawn and the retreat of the bombers. For two years Hedy had tried to keep from thinking. The numbing had begun the moment she stepped off that first train and was torn away from her suitcase and from David. He was her last contact with her old life and what she had considered normal human behavior. The events she witnessed as her new life began shocked her at first and then to protect her eventual return to sanity, her mind sank into a state of numbness that allowed her to stay alive. She had seen one act of brutality after another. At first she wanted to scream and protest the beatings and killings of young children for being childish, but when she saw what happened to the young women who could not control their outrage, she quickly mastered the art of keeping a straight and emotionless face, eyes staring into space or at the ground. If these fiends, many of them female guards, were the new rulers of the earth she didn't want to live on it, but she had promised Konstanza to stay alive.

Leia had told Hedy that the next day they would go to a prayer service and see the Grand Mufti. (He had not yet sent for her and she hoped he had forgotten about her.) She had been carefully tutored about what was expected of the women at the service. They were to sit cross-legged in the back of the gathering and be as unobtrusive as possible. Several times during the service they would be expected to bow forward, their faces as close to the floor as possible, as the men lifted their buttocks, the women were to keep theirs on the floor. The instructions were simple enough and she would just try to be invisible.

To forestall further worry about the prayer service and the Mufti, Hedy tried to find a subject that would engross her mind and crowd out the nagging fears. A vision of David floated into her consciousness and how he had taught her to play chess and in the process had imbued her with his love for the game. During the long train ride in the cattle car they had talked about some of the games they had played. David's chess board was in his suitcase, but it was too dark in the cattle car and much too unstable to set up a board. David had told Hedy to close her eyes and imagine a play on the board. At first she had trouble concentrating but with David's help the board had appeared in her head and they were soon taking turns describing the location of the pieces on the board and what move they planned next.

Now the chess board appeared in her mind as it had then. The moves kept Hedy busy all that night and many other nights to follow. In fact she made up some plays of her own that would have made David proud or even envious.

In the morning the women dressed carefully, not a single hair was to show under the headscarves. They put on the heavy cloaks that were still a little damp and waited at the door for the men to escort them to the prayer service.

Chapter 8

Omar began to work on his plans for Jamal. Although he had been made aware of Jamal's sadistic nature by his contacts in Jerusalem, until now he had not had personal proof. In a casual conversation Abdul had mentioned that Jamal beat Leia. After all it was one of his responsibilities to protect and discipline the women. Leia was young, probably 16, and young women were often careless with their manners, disrespectful, and sometimes even rebellious. Omar knew that Jamal had asked to marry Leia and that the Mufti had given permission, however Jamal's father had not as yet agreed. Jamal was from a different tribe from Leia's and the union which would entail an alliance, needed to be negotiated.

In the meantime Leia was under the "protection" of Jamal and he intended to "protect" her from any inadvertent misstep described in the Koran, where it was written that to keep a women pure it was her master's duty to discipline her at his discretion. Omar thought that the loss of Jamal might not be disagreeable to Leia.

Each morning Omar met with the Mufti to go over the correspondence and news reports. Since the Mufti could not read German or speak it with any fluency, everything needed to be translated into Arabic. Omar had become indispensable to the Mufti in this area and often managed to save lives in the process.

This morning a letter arrived from the German High Command, informing the Mufti that a prisoner exchange could be negotiated whereby a thousand men from the Arab

Brigade, who had been captured by the British in North Africa would be exchanged for 200 Jewish children in one of the ghettos. The children, age 9-11, would be sent to England and the Moslem men were to be sent back to Bosnia.

Over the years there had been several of these offers from the Allied forces for prisoner exchanges, but the Mufti had vehemently opposed them. "Those children will grow up and go to Palestine, become Zionists and destroy the Arab culture. All Jews, regardless of age must die." He had ranted upon receiving these letters.

(Changing two words in the response that the Mufti had dictated, would allow the exchange to succeed. A month later, to his immense gratification, Omar received news that the children had arrived in England.)

Other business that morning was reading the news reports. The news from the eastern front was mixed, and Field Marshall Rommel was stalled in North Africa. There was a letter from the Arab Brigade about the Mufti's impending visit to Bosnia, and another letter with an urgent invitation for him to come to North Africa to rally Moslem support for a German offensive. The Italian troops had surrendered in mass by now.

This meant that the Mufti would be traveling to various locations to meet with both German and Arab leaders. Leaving the villa was always dangerous for the Mufti. Many factions in the Middle East, both Moslem and Zionist, had plans to assassinate him.

Omar decided that this was the opportunity to eliminate Jamal.

"Sir," he addressed the Mufti with a deferential tone. "when you travel, especially to Africa, you need strong, aggressive, people with you for your protection. Amir and I have discussed our concern for your safety and we agree that Jamal is a good choice to accompany you on this upcoming trip."

The revelation that Amir and Omar had talked about him was somewhat disturbing but the Mufti saw the wisdom of keeping a muscular, militarily trained man like Jamal near him when traveling out of Germany. He was very aware of his enemies and took precautions for himself and for Amir at all times. He trusted Jamal but did not love him and he was loath to leave Amir behind.

Omar continued speaking, a trace of anxiety in his voice, "Actually it was Amir who pointed out how useless he would be during any attack on your person. He was the one that suggested you talk to Jamal about your travel plans and how best to protect your revered person."

"How thoughtful of Amir," was the Mufti's curt reply. "I will discuss the matter with Jamal today."

"Sir." Omar cleared his throat and continued almost in a whisper, "It is advisable to not reveal your exact movements and plans to anyone. The fewer persons know where you will be at a given time the safer you will be."

The Mufti nodded in agreement and went to his private quarters to consult with his valet/secretary, Amir, about what to pack for his travels.

Later during that week Omar invited Abdul to have lunch with him and since the Mufti had planned a private meeting with Jamal, he also invited Amir.

The conversation was about the war at first then turned to the Mufti's travel plans to the Balkans and North Africa.

"I heard that the Mufti has plans to meet with Field Marshal Rommel himself." Omar said importantly. "I would think he would take a German speaking bodyguard along instead of Jamal, who speaks only Arabic."

Amir looked up from his food, that was being served by Yusef, in Omar's spacious dining area. Yusef moved around the three men on padded feet with a blank expression. No one had ever heard him talk. Thus he was thought to be deaf as well as mute.

"The Mufti has not mentioned to me that he is taking Jamal with him, but of course, he is the obvious choice for the best protection." Amir's voice was flat as he struggled not to show his agitation. "They will be traveling in one of the Luftwaffe's newest fighters."

Abdul interjected, "Yes, a fast, very streamlined aircraft, but so small. There is only space for the pilot, co-pilot and two passengers. There is hardly room for any luggage. The Mufti will have to rough it." he chuckled.

Later that night, just as the drone of the bombers began to shatter the air and shake the windowpanes, Amir was helping the Mufti with his bath when the Mufti mentioned that he had decided to take Jamal along on his intended travels.

"Jamal is better suited for the rigors of the desert in North Africa." The Mufti explained to Amir. "He is stronger, bigger, and his military training will make him a more competent companion than you my sweetheart."

Amir was not eager to leave the luxury of the villa in Berlin for a tent in the desert of North Africa, but he didn't like the idea of Jamal taking his place beside the Mufti possibly taking his place in the Mufti's bed and in his heart. They had not spent a night apart since they had first met four years ago. The Mufti had been Amir's first lover and he couldn't bear the thought of anyone else being in his arms.

On this particular Thursday after the clean and ironed laundry had been distributed to the members of the household, plans were being finalized for the Mufti's departure on Saturday. Everyone, without exception, would gather on Friday morning for their usual prayer service, the lengthy sermon by the Mufti, followed by a festive meal for the men.

On Friday morning the skies above Berlin were quiet. Jasmin, Leia and Hedy had been escorted to the ornate room that had served as a ballroom for the former owners of the Villa. Chandeliers glittered from the ceiling as the sunlight reflected from the crystal. Prayer rugs lined the parquet floor and the women sat down cross legged on the rugs they had brought along. Jasmin and Leia had removed their slippers at the door of the room. Hedy had not been given slippers and she tucked her red, sore, and, scarred feet under the black cloak.

The prayer session seemed endless. The men on their knees kept bending over into what Hedy had learned was the "punishment position" for women (buttocks in the air, foreheads on the floor). The women remained seated, bending at the waist.

The Mufti's sermon went on for several hours. Sometimes Leia translated a few words into French for Hedy, who was fighting to stay awake and not fall over and call attention to herself. Finally the last prayer ended and Omar came toward the women to escort them back to their room. He stood over them and offered Jasmin his hand to help her up. As Hedy noticed this gesture she inadvertently raised her eyes to look at him although she immediately lowered them back to the floor. In the instant that their eyes met they each felt a spark of humanity in the other.

To Omar there seemed something familiar in those deep blue eyes and the pale face. Hedy thought she saw empathy and kindness in Omar's soft, brown eyes.

Their eyes met again for a longer moment as he stood at the door, letting the women into their room. Hedy hesitated, and looked back before she turned and followed Jasmin inside. Then he turned and was gone, locking the door behind him.

Jasmin and Leia sat on their cushions, patiently waiting for one of the men to bring them food from the ongoing banquet. They began to count the prayer beads. It was nearly dusk, but a few minutes before the blackout curtains would need to be drawn. Hedy stood by the window watching a half moon come up over the ruins of Berlin. For the first time in what seemed like a lifetime, Hedy allowed her mind to wander. What would it be like to walk in the garden below the window when the trees were beginning to bud again? Possibly, to walk to the small arbor near the bench, accompanied by the handsome young man with the kind eyes?

After several hours had passed and no one came to their room with food, the women got undressed and went to sleep.

Hedy's last thoughts were of those warm brown eyes and she hardly felt the hunger pangs.

Early Saturday morning the Mufti was waiting in the foyer of the villa, with his small valise. Jamal was to bring the car for their drive to the secret airfield at the outskirts of Berlin. Omar and Amir were to accompany them and drive the car back to the villa. Abdul said his good-by to the Mufti and left to bring food to the women.

Suddenly Jamal's valet came bounding down the curving staircase. "My master is very ill!" He proclaimed in Arabic. "He was all right last night. Now I can't get him up." He was almost sobbing and with outstretched hands he implored the Mufti to come and see. When they entered Jamal's room it was evident that he was dead. He lay prone on his bed, fists clenched, a grimace on his bloodless face.

Omar's valet and Amir had heard the loud voices and came to see what was going on. None of them approached the bed. They were afraid of catching the disease that must have killed Jamal. Amir went to the telephone and called the doctor. Yusef escorted the Mufti back down the stairs where Omar and Abdul were waiting.

"There is no time to change your plans." Omar quietly told the Mufti. "I will go with you, unless you prefer Amir?"

For a few moments the Mufti didn't answer and then he spoke in a slow and thoughtful manner. "Omar, I need to go as you say. Someone in authority needs to bury Jamal, within the 24 hours as required, to notify his father, and to ascertain the cause of his death."

Omar thought that the Mufti was asking his advice about whom to leave in charge, but instead the Mufti went on. "I will take Amir with me." The Mufti put his hand on Omar's shoulder and continued. "You are in charge of my household until my return. Abdul is to help you and obey you."

As Abdul and Amir came down the stairs the Mufti repeated the last sentence for their benefit.

Amir ran back up the stairs to the rooms he shared with

the Mufti to pack a few things and re-appeared within a few minutes. Omar suspected that he had already prepared for the trip the night before.

Abdul drove off with the Mufti and Amir while Omar went back up the stairs to attend to the necessary arrangements for the burial of Jamal. The cause of death was ascribed to a heart failure due to overeating.

When Omar finally had the time to go to the women and tell them of Jamal's demise, their reaction was what he expected. Jasmin sighed and began to pray from her place on the floor. Leia forgot herself and raised her eyes. A glimmer of relief seemed to cross her face before she dropped her eyes to the floor again. Omar thought he caught a quick smile on her full lips. Hedy, who didn't understand the Arabic, had heard Jamal's name mentioned and Jasmin's deep sigh. Something bad had happened to Jamal and she felt a twinge of joy at the thought.

The Mufti was away for many weeks. First he went to Bosnia, where he got the news that the Arab Brigade was about to be disbanded. The British had retaken North Africa and Field Marshal Rommel had been sent to Greece to fortify the troops in case of an invasion in that area. While the Mufti was trying to decide if he wanted to continue to Greece, as some of the Arab Brigade had been sent there, the news arrived that Field Marshal Rommel had been sent on to the North coast of France, where it was believed an Allied invasion was imminent.

The small plane refueled in Belgrade, where the German army was being harassed by Yugoslavian partisans. There was only enough fuel available to fly to an airport near Vienna (which was now the capital of the German State of Ostmark). It was there that the Messerschmidt was requisitioned by the governor of the state who needed transportation to a meeting with leaders of the German High Command.

The Mufti tried to telephone Berlin to advise Omar of the situation, but the lines were not available. Amir tried to make the Mufti as comfortable as possible in one of the abandoned apartments along the Schottenring, where the affluent professional and merchant class of Vienna used to live. Since many of the doctors, lawyers, store owners, university professors, and talented musicians who had lived there were Jewish the lucky and smart ones had fled Europe. Most had been relocated to concentration camps.

Eventually the two men made their way back to Berlin with an army convoy that took two weeks along back roads. In the past this would have been an overnight train ride but the trains were all tied up with shipping Jews to their deaths.

Chapter 9

Nearly a month passed before Omar had a chance to see Hedy again. It was an eventful time for Omar. While Hedy was fighting off boredom. Jasmin and Leia seemed to be satisfied with the routine of eating, sleeping, doing laundry, and praying for long hours every day.

Omar postponed the elimination of Abdul, who, without Jamal to give him orders, could be a pliable pawn in the dangerous game that Omar was playing.

Abdul had a predilection to the unquestioning obedience that was so necessary for the evil manipulators of the world to stay in power. His loyalty was easily shifted to whomever was in charge and had the power to "protect" (actually "murder") his family in Jerusalem. At the moment Omar was certain he could make use of Abdul and perhaps arrange for him to even bring back information without rousing his suspicion.

The lines of communication were erratic in the villa because of the nightly bombings, so Omar sent Abdul into Berlin (a lengthy trip by motorcycle) every other day, to find out if there were news of the Mufti and Amir. By now the electricity and the water supply were also frequently interrupted, although life and death went on in Berlin pretty much as usual.

During the Mufti's absence, correspondence had arrived from the German general who had been left in command of the fleeing Africa Corps. Both German and Italian soldiers had surrendered to American and Australian forces. A prisoner exchange was again offered for the lives of Jewish children. Abdul suggested that this matter needed to await the Mufti's return and Omar didn't dare to contradict him. To show any sympathy towards such a plan could undermine his usefulness at best and cost him his life and that of many others at, worst.

~

One evening, just before dusk and a few minutes before the continuing air raids, the Mufti and Amir came back to the villa in a black Mercedes that had seen better days. They climbed wearily out of the battered car. There was no luggage and the man driving didn't even get out of the car to open the doors for them. Omar came down the portico steps to greet them with appropriate words of relief regarding their safe return.

The Mufti introduced a young man who climbed out of the back seat with him, as his cousin, Hassan, who would be joining the household to replace Jamal. After asking if all the arrangements had been made properly for Jamal's burial, he announced that Hassan was to marry Leia in the near future. "When the war is won, and we all return to Jerusalem," the Mufti added.

Hassan nodded politely to Omar and followed the Mufti and Amir into the villa. Later that evening Abdul returned from the inner city and expressed delight to see his master back safely and deep regret about the news from North Africa.

When the Mufti saw the correspondence from the War Department about the prisoner exchange, he immediately wrote a letter in response declaring the idea preposterous. The Allied forces were offering to exchange 500 Jewish children between the ages of 6-12 for 2000 Italian and German prisoners of war. The Red Cross had been in contact with two orphanages where the children were housed. The ghetto, in Poland, was running out of food and the exchange would be a humanitarian gesture. When the letter went on to say that the children were to be sent to an orphanage in Palestine the Mufti flew into a rage.

He ordered Omar to write letters to the German High Command, addressing the same subject to the Feuhrer himself and to several of his top henchmen. He expressed his disappointment that they would even consider such an exchange. When the war was won, as it soon would be, the cowardly prisoners would be sent home, in the meantime such men were not needed. Then he poured out his outrage at allowing 500 Jewish children, who would grow up to be Zionists, to be sent to his precious Palestine. They must be destroyed as soon as possible, he insisted in his letter. Doing so would further the goals of the German Reich, as well as his own.

Omar as the scribe had full knowledge of all the proposed aspects of the exchange plan.

The 500 children were to be sent on a train of cattle cars to a transport camp near the French border. Then they would continue by a regular passenger train to a port where the German and Italian prisoners would arrive on a neutral ship. The same ship would then take the children to Palestine. A Zionist organization guaranteed the funds.

According to the plan laid out by the Mufti and agreed upon by the German High Command, only the first part of the plan was to be enacted. After the children were loaded into the cattle cars, the train would head directly to an extermination camp. The children, with a few handpicked exceptions, would be murdered immediately,

A few days before this diabolical plan was to be set into motion, Omar went to the sex trade part of Berlin. It was not unusual for him to be seen in that area. After all he was a healthy, 24 year old man, living in an almost all male household. It was to be expected that he needed to have an occasional outing. He visited several brothels and was careful not to show favoritism to any one girl. Many years later, one of the ladies revealed how she was privileged to help pass on information about the orphan transport and how enraged and frustrated her contacts had been at their inability to save the majority of those children.

~

On the designated night the children were rounded up from 3 different orphanages and sorted by age. The older girls were put in charge of the younger children, and the 10-12 year old boys were herded into a separate cattle car which had been designated to be the last car of the train. Then the train departed for what would be a two-day trip through a wooded area of Poland and over a wide river. During the first day there was excited anticipation about their new life, but by evening there was the same hunger and thirst.

As the train passed over a high trestle it slowed considerably. No one noticed the two men who had come out of the forest and worked to unhook the last car. They quickly disappeared into the surrounding forest as the train began to leave the trestle. The train began to pick up speed as it traveled through the dense forest and the last car came to a stop. Several men ran out of the woods, unbolted the door and urged the boys to run into the forest. Some of the boys were afraid it was a German trick, but the men assured them in a familiar language that they were being rescued.

The boys soon disappeared into the thickets while some of the men pushed and pulled the cattle car along the half a mile of track back to the trestle. There was an explosion, not very loud, since only a small piece of the rail needed to break, to assure that the rail car would fall into the river.

When the train arrived at its destination and there was a cattle car missing with 45 Jews unaccounted for, the Germans, who kept meticulous records were puzzled. An inquiry was sent to the departure point. When it was ascertained that the missing Jews were the special boys picked out for possible use by certain members of the German High Command and some of their associates, it was thought best not to probe into the loss.

When Omar again visited the brothel he came back to the villa with mixed feeling. The rage he felt was difficult to conceal and barely assuaged by the small victory of saving forty-five lives.

During the four years that Omar spent in Berlin he had been a link in the chain that had on occasion, pulled Jewish children out of the grip of death. Sometimes he had an inkling of the results of his work, but more often he could only hope that the information he had passed along would be useful in some way and save lives.

Once and only once, he had taken an enormous risk with his own life. And lives of others in that vital chain. On that occasion a letter had arrived at the villa with news of a large ransom that would be paid for the lives of 400 Jewish children.

Once again the Mufti dictated an emphatic denial for giving Jewish children entry to Palestine. Omar found that changing just two words would change the original results desired by the Mufti. He managed to rewrite the letter, over the Mufti's signature and send it off to Heinirich Himmler with copies to the British officer in charge of the proposed exchange. The 400 children from Terezin concentration camp wound up at a train station near the port of Trieste while nearly a thousand German prisoners of war landed in neutral Sweden and were sent directly to the east to fight the Russian army that was nearing the German border. Meanwhile the children, aged nine to twelve, were warmly received in a kibbutz near Haifa.

The Mufti gritted his teeth in a monstrous fit of anger, but as his Arab League fighters were scattered in various parts of North Africa, he didn't dare protest to the Germans.

～

Omar's contacts were furious with him for taking such a blatant risk with the whole operation in which he was involved. A coded message was relayed to him that left no doubt that he was never to interfere like this again. There were threats to his life if he disobeyed or jeopardized his mission again. He was, in the future, to relay information and nothing more.

But unbeknownst to Omar his daring ploy of changing words was used again, with similarly rewarding results.*

A few weeks after the return of the Mufti the Friday prayer sessions resumed and Omar took the opportunity to whisper a request to Leia. He told her that as the weather improved there would be walks in the garden again and it would please the Mufti if she asked Hedy questions about herself and her former life. Omar would pass the answers on to the Mufti. Leia nodded her consent and determined to begin the questioning her as soon as they returned to their room.

*During some of the worst bombing raids on Germany the cattle cars kept rolling to the east, bringing mostly women with small children to be murdered immediately upon their arrival at their destination. Many of the infants had been brought to the train station in recently purchased baby carriages. Hundreds of these prams were left at the railroad stations and as each train pulled away local women were hired to wheel them to a wholesaler of children's furnishings.

On several occasions these, practically new, prams were sent by the carloads to a Swiss wholesaler who supplied the retail stores of several countries.

A letter of transport, a properly stamped bill of lading and other documents were required for these items to be shipped across borders. These documents came to the attention of a clerk who took it upon himself to change one word in the description of the shipment. (The letter of transport described a shipment of 100 prams (kinder wagen). The clerk changed the letter to read 100 orphans (weisen kinder). As the train progressed through Germany the merchandise in the freight cars was exchanged at several unscheduled stops. By the time the train arrived at the Swiss border it contained over 100 orphans. The inspector at the border read the letter of transit and waved the train on to St. Moritz, where the cargo melted into the Swiss and Italian countryside. Many of the orphans were expected at convents, while others found homes with peasant families who welcomed another pair of hands to help with the harvest.

After the war many of these "orphan train" survivors went to Israel, some stayed with their adopted families, and converted to Catholicism. Several of these converts became nuns, and three became priests. It was one of these priests that traced the original letter of transit to its source in the office of the German wholesaler, from there to the daughter of the man who had been part of the rescue plan.

Chapter 10

After seeing the Mufti again at the prayer service, Hedy wondered if he would send for her or, as she hoped, he had forgotten all about her. The nightly air raids on the inner city and surrounding suburbs seemed to be getting closer but according to the Mufti's speech, parts of which Leia had translated for her, Hedy gathered that the German army had been victorious on every front and the Luftwaffe was bombing London into a pile of rubble.

When Omar and the new secretary/bodyguard, Hassan, escorted the women back to their room Omar spoke some Arabic words to Leia as she stopped in front of him as he ushered her into the room. She acknowledged his quiet words with a slight nod of the head in his direction and stepped inside. Hedy followed and turned her head deliberately looking up at Omar. Again their eyes met, and again the warm feeling spread inside Omar's chest. Her eyes had been dark and questioning. She had heard a reference to the Mufti and a twinge of fear coiled in her stomach.

Hassan slid into the room and stood before Jasmin, as she began to lower herself on her pillow reaching for her prayer beads. He said some words to Jasmin, pointed at Leia who stood beside Hedy just inside the door. Then he turned and went out to join Omar.

Hedy was bursting with curiosity about what had been said about the Mufti and what Hassan had wanted from Jasmin.

"What did the men say?" she asked in French.

"It has been decided that I am to marry Hassan when

the war is won." Leia said in an even tone. "He was asked to inform Jasmin of the plan so she can prepare me for that event. We are formally engaged and can exchange words during properly chaperoned periods." Leia sighed with resignation. "He is handsome and closer to my age than Jamal."

Hedy congratulated her and wished her happiness, as was appropriate according to what she had been told of such occasions. Leia shrugged and said nothing.

The winter was finally over and one morning Hedy looked out to see the lilac bush in the garden starting to bloom. She longed to open the window to smell the fragrance of spring. Hedy was determined to keep from worrying about the future. At the moment she was getting food, very good food, twice a day, she was warm and dry for the time being and that should be enough for the present. It was very likely that there was no future to worry about. The routine of eating, sleeping, doing the laundry and reading the Koran seemed to be enough for Leia, but Hedy was getting bored. So one day when a French translation of the Koran appeared on the food tray, Hedy began to read it.

The Koran covered all facets of human life. There were references to hospitality and family loyalty that showed some human feelings were considered to be good, but it should never overshadow family honor. The text dealt with punishment and justifying the murder of a female family member, if need be, to save the family honor. There were whole Chapters that dealt mostly with the sins of women, who were considered lesser beings, who were not wise and rational like men, and must be disciplined by them. The book was repetitious but Hedy was sincere in looking for beliefs and things she might have in common with Leia and Jasmin, in the hope that they might be friends, but each day it became more clear that, although, they might not be her enemies, they were her jailers.

They had not mistreated her since she came to the villa but neither made any friendly overtures, except to read the Koran to her. Jasmin had helped her with her wounds, and made sure she got her share of the food, but Hedy could not remember her ever looking at her directly. Leia answered Hedy's questions about her life but showed no curiosity about Hedy's life or her interests.

On this lovely spring morning, after a night of teeth rattling bombers flying towards their not- so-distant targets, Hedy asked the question that had been foremost in her mind for weeks.

"Do you ever go outside into the beautiful garden?" She tried to keep her tone casual.

"Not since you came!" Leia answered, with resentment in her voice.

"I would like, very much to stroll in that lovely park under this window." Hedy sighed.

Leia translated her words to Jasmin who looked up briefly at her daughter with a blank expression.

However a few days later Leia told Hedy to hurry with her morning tea, as they were going out. She explained that it was the birthday of a saint (Hedy was too excited to catch his name) and there was a small shrine in his honor in the garden. Once a year, just before Ramadan, (a festival that is celebrated for 30 days, with no food during daylight hours) the women were allowed to visit this shrine and spend a considerable amount of time praying there. One of the few times of the year when women could leave their homes and be outdoors.

Hedy walked carefully on the graveled path as she still had no shoes, and whenever possible she walked on the grass, which was cool and smooth under her bare feet. She had not dared to ask, but only hoped she would get shoes before the next winter.

Surreptitiously she looked around at the gray stoned villa hovering over them and raised her eyes to the sky above, quickly lowering her head again, to look at her bare feet.

Omar followed the black clad women, with Abdul slightly behind him. He wanted desperately to talk to Hedy alone and was plotting on how to do so in the near future. It was imperative that he keep the trust of the Mufti. Even the slightest suspicion could put his mission in jeopardy which in turn could cost many lives. Omar was very aware of his responsibilities and how important is was to control his emotions at all times. He was a tightly wound spring that dared not let himself unwind. If he had any hope of helping this girl to escape he had to be extra careful.

The pleasant feel of the grass had triggered a memory for Hedy. Her mind flashed back to a Sunday afternoon during one of her summer visits to Vienna. Hedy, about five years old at the time, had been chasing a butterfly on an expanse of green lawn. Her grandmother, clad in her Sabbath black was dozing on a bench nearby. With a quick glance in the dozing woman's direction, Hedy had sat down on the damp grass and removed her shoes and stockings. The pleasure she had felt while wiggling her toes in the cool grass was cut short when her grandmother had discovered her barefoot state. Now she remembered that feeling of freedom and closed her eyes to prolong the moment.

It was then she stumbled, losing her balance. Omar automatically put out his hand to steady her. He briefly touched her elbow. The warm flesh made his fingers tingle and sent a wave of pleasure through his body. If she noticed his touch she gave no sign.

After the women had prayed at the small shrine, just a square stone with Arabic writing on the front, they started walking back to the villa. The scent of lilacs was in the air and Hedy breathed it in gratefully.

When the group entered the dark hallway and started up the narrow stairway, Hedy stumbled on the first step. This time the hand on her elbow remained in position for several seconds. Hedy turned her head to see which of the men was holding her. Neither Omar or Hedy spoke, but as their eyes met they understood each other as if they had.

During the summer months that followed the women

were allowed to walk in the garden, among the flower beds nearly once a week. They were always followed by Omar and after that first walk, Hassan joined him.

It seemed strange to Hedy that during these walks Leia began to ask her questions about her past. Why this sudden interest in her life after almost a year of living together, Hedy wondered. As she began to tell Leia about herself she became aware that Omar drew nearer to her while Hassan fell back a few steps.

On Leia's part, she was following orders, relayed to her by Omar, that the Mufti wanted information about this girl in preparation of sending for her in the near future. The questions brought out that Hedy spoke German, albeit with a Viennese accent, that she played the piano and also like to play chess. There were never any questions about what kind of future she might envision for herself. After all, if she were allowed to live, she would be a wife and mother. The Mufti would find her a suitable husband.

During these walks Hedy was careful not to look up at the men following them, but at least once during each walk, she found occasion to catch a glimpse from his warm brown eyes. It was enough to lift her spirits until the next walk.

One time after returning from a walk, Hedy asked Leia why the men had to be there. Leia had told her that they were there to protect. She explained to Hedy that "women were not allowed outdoors alone."

"Even in a walled garden like this?" Hedy had asked curiously.

"The men protect us from the evil eye." Leia had whispered as if someone were listening. "No telling what can happen to a woman, especially a young woman, if she wanders around outdoors alone. Have you not heard of Djinni?"

Hedy had not heard of the Djinni and Leia went on to explain. "They are evil spirits in human form, but so ugly they make your hair fall out. They are sent by Allah to punish wicked women by taking them away to Jahannam. The presence of a pious man can save them."

She had read some version of this story in the French translation of the Koran and thought she might have misunderstood it. Her astonishment that Leia, a girl with some education, actually believed these stories was no less than Leia's when she heard that Hedy actually knew how to play chess. In Leia's world it was a man's game. Women did not play games, they only worked and prayed. Recreation was for men only.

One day Hedy asked Leia "Do you ever have the desire to go outside into the city? To see what is beyond this wall? To see other places and other people?"

The answer was one word spoken with finality. "No!"

That summer of 1944 Hedy began to be aware of time again. Her body and mind were recovering from starvation. She would soon turn 16 and could feel herself turning into a woman. Sometime during each day she remembered the last words of Konstanza. "Stay alive! Do whatever you have to do to stay alive."

With that in mind, Hedy asked for the third time about getting shoes but this time she asked about it in the garden, loud enough for the men to hear. Leia had not answered her, but the next Wednesday morning Abdul dropped a pair of slippers in front of her as she started out the door. Hedy suppressed the natural urge to say "Thank you," slipped her bare feet into the cloth straps and followed Leia down the hall. Just in time she had remembered that women did not speak to men in public. She was finally learning the rules and had avoided being beaten for almost a year now. Hassan, Jamal's replacement, was reluctant to be around the women and although he would have been allowed to talk to Leia, he seldom even looked her way and Leia never looked at him.

Chapter 11

The winter of 1944-45 arrived with a snowstorm in early November along with a hail of bombs from the Allied forces. Berlin was being systematically destroyed, as were many other cities in Germany, while rockets kept falling on London. The trains of cattle cars kept rolling north eastward toward Poland and as many as 10,000 people per day, mostly women and many children were murdered daily in the German built gas chambers, erected solely for the purpose of murdering as many humans at a time as possible.

Hedy had been in the Berlin Villa for more than a year. The Mufti had not sent for her but it had been he who had sent the French translation of the Koran with orders for Hedy to read it and memorize certain marked passages that pertained to the deportment of women. Occasionally Hedy would ask Leia for clarification of a phrase, or try to question the validity of a statement. Leia would listen as if she were trying to understand Hedy, but her answer was always the same. "Allah has decreed."

It was during that winter that Leia kept questioning Hedy about her former life in minute details. Leia asked about her leisure time. With whom did she play chess? The fact that she played with her father, unrelated male friends and an older cousin was shocking to Leia. She was particularly interested that Hedy had been allowed to go to the cinema. Movies were forbidden. Leia had heard of them during her school years, but she had never had the courage to accompany her friends who went to see them.

When Hedy mentioned that she had been to concerts, plays, and even knew how to play the piano, Leia gasped in astonishment. "Yes," she told Hedy. "I know that European men played in orchestras and that females were allowed to listen to music, but I am surprised that they can openly go to concerts."

It was quite by accident that Hedy discovered the real reason behind the interrogations.

One Friday morning, while the thirty or so men and the three women gathered in the spacious ballroom of the villa for prayer, Hedy, bent double over her knees with her head scarf over her face, felt an itch in her nose that she couldn't ignore. As she tilted her head sideways and pushed back her scarf to reach her nose, she glimpsed Leia and Omar obviously having a conversation. Leia's head was bent but she was listening to Omar and Hedy could see her lips move as she was replying to him. Omar was on his knees in front and slightly to the right of Leia so when he turned his head to whisper to her, he was looking directly at Hedy. The startled look in his eyes as he saw her look at him, confirmed her suspicion that they were talking about her. He smiled and nodded his head and quickly turned away. A small spark of elation warmed Hedy's insides as she demurely dropped her eyes, allowing a smile to cross her face. Her palms itched to push the black curls back from his forehead. She wondered if his hair felt as soft as it looked.

On the way back to their room the women were escorted by an animated Hassan and a subdued Omar. Obviously for Hedy's benefit Omar spoke French, which Hassan understood but had trouble pronouncing, so he carried on his part of the conversation in Arabic.

Hedy understood that an Allied invasion on Anzio in Italy had been defeated by Germany in spite of the Italian surrender months ago. The war was over for Italy.

It seemed that the Mufti's prayers were being answered. The cowardly Italians were out of the way and the great leaders of the new order could get on with making the mongrel countries of the Christian world into Fascist prisons and the Mufti would realize his dream of making the Middle East a Moslem Caliphate.

"Of course," Hassan boasted, "eventually the whole world will be Moslem."

Omar wondered which of the many versions of Islam would be expected to rule.

He prudently kept his thoughts to himself and concentrated on how to get another glimpse of Hedy's deep blue eyes. Their color reminded him of the sky one saw over the Egyptian desert. Suddenly he was filled with an all consuming desire to see that sky again, to bring Hedy there to share it with him, to compare the depth of that blue with her eyes. He was aware that allowing his mind to be diverted from his mission was very dangerous for himself and all the many lives that depended on him and the work he was doing.

Yet lately there were times when she was all he could think about. He devised plans that would allow him to talk with her, to look into those lovely eyes for more than just a second. He had become obsessed with the idea of helping her to escape to a safe place. Wild schemes came and went in his feverish mind. One time he had thought to fake her death, like in the play "Romeo and Juliet" when Juliet takes a drug that mimics death. Amir was a master chemist who could undoubtedly provide such a potion. He would smuggle Hedy's lifeless body out of the Villa by way of the underground tunnel that led to the river Spree, and take her to the brothel in the center of the city. For a fee the madam would hide Hedy until he could take her to safety.

Eventually he had formulated a more straight forward plan and began to work on its execution that very afternoon. He needed to use every bit of cunning he could muster in order to show how what he was about to suggest, would benefit everyone concerned. Much of his plan depended on his having read in Hedy's eyes not just beauty, but intelligence, understanding of his feelings and trust.

First he had to clear his intentions with his immediate superiors, but only after he had found a way to talk with Hedy. It was a life-changing decision and given his position he could not make it unilaterally. To that end he planned to go to the brothel nearest the zoo and leave a coded message that he had an urgent matter to relate to his contact and asking for instructions on a place to meet. Omar was very aware of the gravity of what he was undertaking. Disapproval meant death for him and possibly for Hedy as well, but he was desperate to have the matter settled. He was convinced, and had to convince his contacts, that without Hedy his capacity and effectiveness would be greatly diminished.

In the process he had to assure his superiors that since he didn't know their identities, he couldn't reveal them to Hedy and under no circumstances would he reveal his true identity to her or betray the mission. Wasn't it normal for a healthy, twenty-six year old to want a girl like Hedy for a mistress, or even a wife?

It had been over two years since the Mufti had ordered the Jewish girl be brought to the Villa. He had asked to see her only once and when that wasn't possible, since Jamal had nearly beaten her to death, he seemed to have forgotten about her. Now Omar needed to decide which way to approach the situation. Should he ask the Mufti if he wanted to see the girl, which would remind him of her existence or just hope that he had actually forgotten about her and stay with the status quo ? Then he remembered that the Mufti had sent her a French translation of the Koran. Omar knew that the Mufti was not interested in acquiring a wife. Amir would never stand for that, even in name only. She would surely die of some poison on the wedding night. Was he was planning to give or sell a converted Hedy to someone else? Should he take a chance and tell the Mufti that he wanted Hedy? Omar was almost certain that the Mufti would not question him about the matter. The women were like livestock to him. The Koran was explicit about the care of livestock. They must be fed, sheltered and domesticated and at times, bought or sold.

Omar barely heard the bombs exploding nearer and nearer to the Villa. His brain was working feverishly on how to get Hedy alone long enough to explain his plans. He would need to know if she were willing to convert to Islam, or at least pretend to do so. He could not tell her of his own circumstances, since that would be very dangerous for both of them. He planned to tell her he was very open minded and only wanted to save her life. Would she understand his motives? Did she like him? Even possibly love him? He reminded himself that she was little more than a child. At sixteen many Moslem girls were married but Hedy was a European girl, a girl with an education. Yet he could see it in her eyes and in the way she moved that she was not a child. He thought about what she had experienced in her short life and how she must have known that she was on her way to die that day when he had pulled her out of that line of naked bodies. Had she known, yet hoped she was wrong?

Someday, after the war, he would ask her about that and about so many other things he wanted to know about her. The war had to end someday. These fiends would be defeated in spite of their boastings of how they would rule the world. Their end was approaching, but at what cost? The Italians had changed sides. They knew they had made a mistake with their fat, bombastic leader. The fighting in Africa was almost over and the Russians were nearing Berlin. The Germans were still talking about victory and how the Third Reich could not possibly be defeated. They continued the diabolical murder of innocent people. The Russians had liberated some of the death camps in Poland, but the Germans had allocated precious resources and fighting men to forcing the survivors of these death camps to march to locations in Germany. How would the leaders of the Reich justify these atrocities? Their cities were being destroyed, there was no food, no fuel, and very little water, the army was fighting a war on two fronts, yet the cattle cars were still rolling, filled with half dead humans toward a certain death.

What demons had possessed the "Christians" of Europe to so ferociously try to destroy the small segment of Jews in their society, who, in actuality, had been the most decent and productive part of that very society? Omar, along with many others, who eventually had to go into exile or be murdered, wondered how the outwardly civilized people of Europe, with few exceptions, had gleefully deported, totally against their self interest, their best doctors, scientists, engineers, teachers and many of the artists and musicians that had made Europe the center of Western Culture.

After reading the history of "Christian" Europe and the attitude of Church leaders about Jews (who would not convert and thus be destroyed or exiled), Omar saw clearly the roots of Jew hatred. It was not reasonable or even sane to hate a whole group of people who had actually been an asset to each country where they had been allowed to live in peace. The mental disease of Anti-Semitism had spread to the Islamic culture as well, although Arabs and other Middle Eastern populations were Semites themselves.

As part of his reading, Omar had encountered Hitler's book explaining his philosophy. He remembered that it was not just the Jews that would be marked for extinction. There would always be another group, because it was hate that drove the Fascist machine. After the gypsies and the Slavic population he supposed the Arabs would be next. Only the Aryan race (blond, blue eyed and well built people) would rule the world. People of color would be kept as ignorant slaves or be killed. But even now no one was safe in the insane asylum that was Fascist Europe. Any person could be arrested and disappear at the whim of an official. It happened often that a Nazi leader wanted something that another person had, like an apartment, or a wife. There was no real legal system and the hoodlums and thugs were in charge. Omar's one consolation was that at some point these criminals would start killing each other as they had no morals and their greed had no bounds.

Omar stopped his pacing and looked around for Yusef. Then he remembered that Yusef had motioned to him earlier that he was going out to get supplies. It was still daylight and the late winter sun was just slipping behind a cloud low in the western sky. The little patch of blue reminded Omar of Hedy's eyes and the urge to see her, to possibly touch her, was like a fierce hunger in his belly. As he stood in front of the window, the air raid siren started to wail and then was drowned out by the roar of airplane engines. The building began to shake and the windows rattled dangerously. It was the beginning of the daylight bombing runs.

At first it was near the inner city of Berlin, but when the anti-aircraft towers were built right inside the zoological gardens the bombs came closer and closer to the villa.

Shortages became common. Even toilet paper ran out and Abdul brought little squares of torn up newspaper for the women to use. Hedy could read German, although it was not a subject she had learned in school. Her understanding of the long words was sketchy and it took concentration to break them down into understandable segments. One morning in early February Hedy decided to try and read what was written on the four-inch pieces. She took a handful and placed them on the bed. Ignoring Leia's and Jasmin's disapproving frowns. Toilet paper was dirty and not to be taken from the lavatory. After about an hour she learned that the "brave soldiers of the Reich were keeping the Russians from crossing the Oder River."

Hedy could hardly believe it. The Russians were near the Oder and must have conquered Poland away from the Germans.

A few days later she again pieced the newspaper squares together on the bed. This time there was a story about how the Allied forces were stalled and how the "brave warriors of the Reich" would never allow them to cross the Rheine. Hedy surmised correctly that the Allies must be in southern Germany already and the Russians were just outside of Berlin. She said nothing of this to Leia or Jasmin, just put the paper back in the bathroom. The other two never asked her what she read in the paper. They showed no curiosity about what was happening in the outside world. Only once did Hedy ask Leia if she knew anything about the war going on around them and Leia gave her a vacant stare.

It was during this same non conversation that Hedy asked Leia if the Mufti might send for her or if he might have forgotten about her presence.

"Our dearly beloved Mufti will let us know his wishes when he is ready." Leia had told her. In a tone that closed that subject.

One morning there was no hot water. The Villa had only a small amount of coal left and it was not be used for unnecessary purposes like women bathing or even for washing clothes. Then there came a morning where there was no water. It was a Friday and as the women were escorted to the ballroom Hedy noticed that there were no electric lights on anywhere, even in the hallways. The men carried kerosene lamps and the ballroom was lit with hundreds of candles which were placed in the sconces that had been the original candle holders when the Villa was built.

The sermon was short as the noise from the exploding bombs made it impossible to hear the Mufti's words, even though he was shouting at the top of his lungs. Hedy thought she heard artillery fire and wanted desperately to ask Omar if the Russians were just outside Berlin, as she hoped. While walking back to their room, Hedy managed to say the word "Ruskis?" and got a glimpse of Omar nodding his head in the dim light of the lamp. Leia and Jasmin were ahead of her, holding hands and visibly frightened. Hedy wished she could hold Omar's hand instead of nervously clutching her own fingers.

Chapter 12

The residents of the Villa had practiced air raid drills only when the officious German air raid wardens had insisted that they go to a sheltered place. The washroom in the basement was considered safest and after a quick inspection the area was designated as the official shelter for the Villa.

So far the Allied bombers had not come directly into this neighborhood. It was thought that they wanted to spare the animals in the Zoo next door to the property. Then the Germans built huge anti-aircraft installations in the zoological gardens and the bombers came by to destroy them. The Villa could take a direct hit at any moment but for many days the Mufti would not give the order to take shelter. "Allah will protect us." he kept saying until one day the wall around the Villa was destroyed in several places.

Returning to his room from a morning working in his office, Omar heard the whistle of the air raid warden coming towards him from the Mufti's quarters. As he approached his own room he had a fleeting thought of Yusef, who had left early this morning to find supplies and bring back any messages from Omar's contacts.

The hallway was suddenly filled with men walking quickly toward the stairs that led to the basement washroom. The Mufti and Amir were already down the steep steps, while the other servants and guards were following, carrying chairs, small tables, food, blankets, and kerosene lamps. The Mufti's favorite chess board was safely in the arms of Abdul while Hassan followed him closely with his hookah pipe.

The way to the basement went by the women's room, but no one stopped to let them out. The women had never been a part of the practice drills thus no one thought to include them now. Since everyone was already heading down the stairs, Omar quickly unlocked the door and stepped into the women's room. Hedy was sitting cross legged on the bed, her black robe tucked around her, Her head bare. The long, golden braid dangled down between her shoulder blades, almost to her waist. She looked up from the book she was reading, forgetting to lower her eyes and stared in surprise at Omar's frightened face. Jasmin and Leia were under the bed. Without a second thought Omar swept Hedy off the bed and went out the door which swung closed behind him.

Hedy clutched the book with one hand and threw the other arm over Omar's shoulder to steady herself. Her long robe flowed behind them, her thick braid looped over his arm. He followed the man in front of him, who was carrying a lit kerosene lamp. Almost everyone going down the steps was carrying a lamp or candles.

Omar had his hands full with Hedy. She was heavier than two years ago when he had snatched her from the line of naked children. When he reached the top of the stairs he stopped and decided to speak to her in German. Leia had told him she was Viennese.

Hearing the soft, lilting twang of Omar's Viennese accent was a shock and a thrill for Hedy. Inadvertently her arm tightened around his neck and his lips brushed her forehead and she began to tremble. He repeated the warning that he was about to put her down on her feet and added "Don't be afraid. I'll protect you." He was fairly certain that no one in the Villa would understand the Viennese dialect. She loosened her grip and he lowered her to the floor. It was almost totally dark at the top of the steps where they now stood. A thin ray of light came from the lamps far below them. There was just enough light to exchange a quick glance, each of them hoping the other understood the affection it was meant to convey.

Hedy followed Omar down the familiar steps. When he reached the bottom he took her arm just above the elbow and gently pushed her into the dark area under the stairs. The servants had set up the tables, lit the lamps and were putting food and bottles of mineral water on a board they had placed over one of the washtubs.

Omar inspected the scene with an air of nonchalance that he was far from feeling. He was certain that he was the only person in the room that knew of the tunnel below the basement and of the secret door hidden under one of the washtubs. During the previous air raid drills these men had spent only a few minutes in the basement and then returned to the upper floors. Now they might be here for hours. Was there a chance that one of them might accidentally find the tunnel entry? He had known about the tunnel which ran all the way to the Spree River, but hoped he would never need it. Like so many Jewish homes in Europe, the Villa had been built with an escape route. Even after a hundred years of tolerance, a volatile situation could arise and a hiding place would be needed. Just knowing of the tunnel's existence had been some comfort to Omar.

The explosions kept thundering into the night. Omar knew that the Allies were "carpet bombing" Berlin and Hamburg. The plan was to flatten the cities, destroy the infrastructure and hopefully demoralize the Germans so they would finally surrender. The bombs had not come this close before and the residents that lived near the zoo had become complacent, thinking they would not be targets.

Hedy huddled beneath the staircase, clutching the French version of the Koran that she had been trying to read when Omar had picked her up off the bed. Eventually Omar brought her a bowl of rice and an apple.

"Eat!" he ordered, seeing her reluctance and the anxiety in her face. He stood in front of her, shielding her from the men who walked by trying to see this uncovered female. Becoming aware of the congestion by the stairs the Mufti, with Amir close behind him came to see what was causing such interest.

"It's the Jewish sow." One of the men told him as they all stood aside to let him pass. Omar stood his ground as long as he could, but when the Mufti demanded to see what was behind him, he had to give way. Even for Omar, who would have gladly killed him, it was unthinkable to confront the Mufti and disobey a direct order in the presence of his followers.

Hedy raised her head just in the moment the Mufti stood in front of her. Even in the dim light she could see the disdain on his face, as if he had just seen a dog turd in his path. The Mufti stepped back quickly and turned to Amir.

"It will be a long night," He sighed, "Set up the chess board and round up some players."

The Mufti liked to play chess with men of his own rank, none of whom were in Germany with him. He had occasionally played with members of the German High Command and once with a Cardinal who was an emissary from the Pope. Here in the basement there were only his underlings and none of them would dare win a game against him. He decided to have some sport and weed out the poor players before he got into a match himself. He ordered Amir and Omar to line up some competitors. The board was set up, chairs were put on each side of a couple of low tables, six men were found who admitted they knew the game. The Mufti said he would play the man who won the most games and eliminated the five other players. The prize, he announced would be the "Jewish Sow." He went on to remind the assembled players that it was incumbent on devout Muslim men to take infidel females into their beds and make them good Muslim wives.

If the Mufti's four personal secretaries/ bodyguards knew how to play chess they had wisely never admitted it. Omar remained at his post in front of Hedy, his face expressionless, his eyes blazing. The roaring overhead abated a little and the explosions seemed to be farther away, but still loud enough to cause alarm in the dim basement.

It was after midnight when the last man of the six original chess players had just conceded to the Mufti. Chuckling softly the Mufti stood up to stretch. "Omar!" he called out, "Bring that Jewish sow over here. I want to see her in the light!"

Omar hesitated for a moment and looked at Hedy. He could not see the expression on her face in the dim light, but he heard her gasp at the Mufti's raised voice, obviously giving a command. She could read in Omar's eyes that it concerned her.

"Maybe I'll just give her to one of you lousy chess players. Is there another player who wants to give it a try?" The Mufti challenged the group standing around him.

Hedy stood beside the chair across the small table from the Mufti. She was still clutching the French translation of the Koran, her eyes cast downward as she had been taught. The lamplight shone on her bare head, reflecting gold sparks from the strands that had escaped from the braid and now curled around her ears and on her forehead.

"You men all played like stupid girls and don't deserve this prize." The Mufti's tone was arrogant, dismissive. He spoke in French for Hedy's benefit.

Hedy had suppressed all emotion for a long time, but suddenly a fierce spark of anger shot through her whole body. She recognized it as a small sign that she was still alive, able to think and feel. She raised her head and met the Mufti's flat, beady black eyes. The hatred was palpable and fueled her own rage which gave her courage.

"I can play chess as well as any man in this room," she said in French. There was no mistaking the defiance in her voice and her words were a challenge. She sat down on the chair, placed the Koran on the table, making a show of smoothing the cover with a steady hand. It was the Mufti's right hand that began to twitch as it lay beside the chess board. He was getting ready to strike this impudent girl, who, against all the rules, was looking into his face with her blazing, blue eyes, her head bare and sitting in a chair in his presence. He planned to hit her so hard that she would land on the floor, where he would kick her to death. He envisioned this scene with relish when he abruptly stopped himself as he remembered that the Koran advised men not to hit a woman while angry.

This admonishment might not apply to an Infidel, a Jewish one at that, he thought. But why take such a chance. He was, after all, a religious leader and must set a good example. He took the opportunity to lecture the young men around him with a short sermon.

"The Muslim religion is merciful. Women must be beaten when necessary, it is a duty not to be shunned by a devout Moslem male, but never should he hit her with a rod thicker than a man's thumb and a man should never beat a female while he is angry."

As he finished speaking he looked down to see Hedy picking up a black and a white pawn from the chess board. Extending her closed fists with a pawn in each one she waited for the Mufti to pick one to see who would make the first move.

Hedy had played chess since she was four years old, when she had received her first chess board for her birthday. Her grandfather had taught her several opening moves. One of them was the Queen's Gambit. It was considered old fashioned but remained a favorite opening among Viennese champions. Her game had outgrown several cousins, her father, and more recently she had been able to give her piano teacher, a master player, a bit of competition. She had played to win, but was a gracious loser, ready with a compliment and congratulations for the winner. Except for the mental games she played with an imaginary David, she had not played a real match for over two years. However, the moves were in her memory and as she looked at the board several opening strategies were forming in her mind.

The Mufti pointed to her left hand and Hedy dropped the white pawn on the board. The Mufti's face had changed from cold hatred to mere dislike and then as he set up his men and looked up, there was a hint of curiosity. His glance fell on the book beside the chess board and he recognized the small volume as the French version of the Koran he had sent Hedy some months ago. Then he slowly lifted his eyes to her gleaming hair.

He knew that his men had snatched her from a line waiting to go into the gas chambers and had witnessed such lines several times. Once with the Feuhrer himself, who had pointed out the efficiency of these structures in eliminating unwanted populations. The women in the camps he had inspected had shaven heads. How did this girl have such long hair? Why wasn't it covered? He fought down the urge to ask her those questions. Instead he said in French, "We play for your life. If I win I will see you are beaten to death for your impudence. If you win you will be allowed to live as the property of one of these handsome, young men around us."

Hedy had read most of the Koran by now. She had come across several passages in which Moslems were held to different standards of honesty when dealing with Infidels.

There was wording to the effect that it was acceptable to lie to, break agreements and treaties and otherwise mislead non-Moslems. She was certain that if she dared to win a match against the Mufti he would have her killed. If she won, but just barely, after a lengthy battle he might be intrigued enough to play her again in order to study her strategy. She dared not take that chance.

The Mufti's thoughts were elsewhere. Besides being distracted by her lovely hair, he hoped for a reward from Allah for converting her. As much as he hated Jews, he had followed the advice of Mohamed on how to defeat Infidels. The Prophet had told his followers to capture as many enemy females as possible, impregnate them and convert them to Islam. The Mufti had urged the Arabs of Palestine to follow this admonition.

Omar stood at the side of the table between the seated players. He tried not to look at Hedy but concentrated his gaze on the Mufti's hand as it moved a white pawn on the board. It was cool in the cellar, but loose ringlets of hair stuck to Hedy's moist forehead and Omar's clenched fists tingled with the desire to brush them back from her eyes. He moved to stand a little to the Mufti's side of the table where he could observe Hedy as well as asses the Mufti's features. He struggled to keep his own face as neutral as possible. Only once did Hedy look up at him. The flash of her blue eyes made his stomach churn and he could feel desire rise in his groin. He did not dare to look at her again.

The Mufti opened with The Queen's Gambit. Hedy decided to accept the challenge. It meant that each player had to sacrifice a pawn and the center of the board would be open to the white pieces. Hedy's black ones would be crowded to each side of the board. But thanks to her grandfather's patient instructions Hedy was able to maneuver her pieces into a favorable position. The Mufti was a strong player, but he was visibly getting tired. Omar noticed his hand shaking a little as he moved a piece and there were damp stains at the edge of his turban. Finally, Hedy saw her advantage and after lengthy deliberation, moved her knight in the wrong direction. Instantly the Mufti's triumphant "checkmate" rang out. He rose from his chair in a quick motion that caused Omar to stagger backwards. Hedy picked up the Koran and began to retreat into the shadows under the stairs to await her fate.

The bombers had retreated but explosions could still be heard coming from broken gas lines and fuel storage areas. When the siren sounded the "all clear" the men began to file out of the basement.

Omar moved to the stairwell to stand in front of Hedy. As the men walked by they tried to get glimpses of the girl and Omar heard some of them speculate about her fate.

"She is a pretty little bitch." One of the younger men said in Arabic.

"I wouldn't want a Jewish sow in my bed," replied another.

One of the older men, that Omar had recently encountered coming out of a brothel, stopped in front of Omar. Put his hand on Omar's shoulder, leaned forward to get a look at Hedy and made a suggestion to send her to the German Army brothel.

"They like blonde girls," He sneered in a tone that indicated he did not. "I saw the place where they keep the Jewish whores. They brand 'Field Whore' on them, use them day and night until they wear out. Lots more where they come from."

Omar had also seen the army brothels when he had accompanied the Mufti on one of his inspection tours of a female section of a concentration camp near the Polish border.

He shuddered inwardly at the memory of the emaciated bodies that were offered to the German soldiers, for two Deutch marks for twenty minutes. These women did not live long under these brutal conditions. (The few who survived often killed themselves.)

Chapter 13

"Omar, you can have the Jewish sow if you want her."
The Mufti called over his shoulder as he started up the stairs
with Amir close behind him. He stopped on his way up and
looked back down at Omar, who was helping to gather up
the chess pieces and directing the dozen men who were busy
with the clean up operation. Everyone stood at attention as
the Mufti continued speaking. "If you don't want her, take
her back to Jasmin. She can use the extra hands, the washing
will be doubled this week when we get the hot water back."
Then he was gone.

While the men filed up the stairs with their loads, Omar
went to Hedy, still huddled under the stairs. He took her
hand and gently pulled her up and she followed him up the
steep stairs, then to his rooms. When they reached his door
he propelled her inside and softly closed and locked the door.
He stood quietly for a moment waiting for his heart to stop
pounding and his breathing to slow down.

Still holding her hand, he looked at Hedy by the light of
the kerosene lantern he held in his other hand. Their eyes
were nearly level and he could see the confusion mixed with
fear in her expression. The hand he held was trembling.

"Don't be afraid." He said in the Viennese accented
German that was to be their private means of communica-
tion. It was best not to speak and Omar tried to convey this to
Hedy with a finger over his lips.

Like all private rooms in the Villa, Omar's quarters were
furnished with listening devices. All conversations were being

recorded on a wire recorder and listened to by persons who reported anything they considered subversive to the Gestapo.

They were startled when the overhead lights came on and they saw Yusef standing near the light switch by the bedroom door. The erratic electricity had been temporarily restored. The valet's questioning look made Omar turn to Hedy and then back to Yusef.

"Yusef, this is Hedy," Omar spoke in French so Hedy would understand what he said.

By way of explanation he continued speaking, holding Yusef's eyes with the fierce look in his own. "She is now my property and I intend to make her my wife." Then added in Arabic "If she is willing to convert and consents to the marriage."

Yusef stared at them with wide, astonished eyes and shook his head in disbelief or was it denial. Something in his eyes frightened Hedy. His mouth was moving and she thought she could make out words, but it looked like he was screaming "No, No, it's not possible, not permissible, it is disastrous!"

Omar smiled back placidly and led Hedy to his bedroom. On the way down the hall he pointed out the bathroom door and the door to Yusef's room on his right.

He turned left at the end of the hall and opened the door to his spacious bedroom. A wide bed stood between two narrow windows. A nightstand was on one side and a chair was on the other side of the bed, behind the chair stood a tall armoire which took up most of the wall next to the door. The bed was covered with a high featherbed. Several books were on the floor. Book shelves took up the remaining wall. Daylight was seeping into the room around the edge of the blackout curtain. Omar stepped over to one of the windows and drew back the curtains. A heavy fog from the river obscured any view and also had sent the bombing mission back to its base in France.

Omar and Hedy stood inside the door. He turned to close it and then took her face between his warm hands. "Hedy" He said her name in a soft, caressing voice. "It has been a long night." His lips brushed her cheek and he whispered into her ear. "I love you."

She stood perfectly still, her hands by her side and raised her eyes to his. He saw her begin to smile. "I need to use the bathroom," she whispered back.

He released her with alacrity and stepped back to open the door. She went to the bathroom door, looked back with a questioning glance and stepped inside. It was an austere, masculine setting. A toilet, (with the lid up) a small bathtub, a mirrored medicine cabinet over the sink revealed a pale, haggard woman with deep blue eyes. The black robe emphasized the dark rings under her eyes.

Hedy used the toilet and noticed that the water service had been restored as well as the electricity. She found blood on the brown paper that she had used for wiping. Her periods had come back recently and Jasmin had given her a two sets of rags to use for padding, which were to be washed out every night and every morning. She would need those rags now. As she stood before the sink to wash her hands she tried to think of how to ask Omar about getting them. It was then that she saw the toothbrushes. There were two, each in its own glass. She had not seen a toothbrush for over two years and suddenly her mind went back to the little bathroom in Poland. The emotions she had fought to suppress into a closed compartment of her mind came rushing out. Like a dam breaking the horrors she had witnessed flooded by in front of her like a newsreel she had seen once at the cinema.

There were the townspeople, their features distorted by hate, screaming insults as the handful of Jews that had been rounded up on that day, walked through the narrow streets towards the train depot. Hedy had tried not to look at them, but then she heard a voice she recognized. A friend from school. As she passed by Marta, the girl screamed at her and then spat at her. Hedy could only wonder what she had done to produce such viral hatred. It was during that walk to the train that she had begun to shut down her emotions and her brain. Over the next two years she had seen such unimaginable brutality that if she allowed her brain to register what she had seen, the rage would have consumed her. She had been ordered by Konstanza to stay alive.

To do so she had to block out all human emotions. But now she was helpless against the tidal wave of horror. She saw again the SS guard snatch the crying baby from the arms of the woman in front of her as they waited in yet another long line. He swung the baby by its ankles and dashed its head against the light post beside them. The brains and blood spattered his shiny black boots and Hedy saw the grin on his face. Then two guards came up and dragged the screaming mother out of the line and kicked her until her inert body was a heap of bloody rags. A wheelbarrow was brought from somewhere and two of the dazed women were ordered to load the bodies onto it. Then a man from the town took it away. Hedy had fought down the vomit in her throat but as the line moved forward the guard with the spattered boots yelled at her and the girl beside her, to clean his boots. The rag he threw at them was the bloody blouse of the dead woman. It only took a few minutes, but the stench of the blood stayed in her nostrils a long time.

By the time Hedy was put in charge of the group of young orphans she had buried all her emotions. She had learned by observation the futility of protesting or even slightly objecting to unjust accusations. Trying to protect another prisoner always resulted in brutal beatings or more mercifully, in instant death. She did her best to get the children some food and water, to find a place for them to sleep, to keep them calm by telling them stories, but she did not allow herself to develop a personal relationship with any of them. This detachment saved her life on several occasions when she had been forced to watch one or the other of her little charges being beaten (sometimes to death) as a punishment for peeing in their pants, scratching their heads or just fidgeting during the long periods when they were told to stand at strict attention for the twice daily head count, or when in line for the latrine or food. Often the children were beaten because the guard thought he heard them make a small sound. A sob could mean a painful death. Evidently all human feelings had been trained out of the guards. There was no sign of kindness, compassion or pity. After only a few days in this environment, the prisoners were also brutalized.

Being able to totally squelch screams of outrage became easier as time went on. Eventually Hedy hardly remembered having any feelings. Pity, sympathy, affection, were dangerous.

The dam had broken and the pressure was overwhelming. Hedy sank to her knees. Her fists began to pound on the white marble floor. She heard loud screaming, but didn't recognize her own voice."Mama! Mama! Why? Why?" was all that came out of her mouth. Even as Omar and Yusef carried her to Omar's bedroom her screams were echoing through the rooms. She became very hoarse and her voice gave out. Totally exhausted, Hedy collapsed onto the bed, barely conscious or able to move.

Yusef went to get a cold cloth to put on her forehead and Omar began to unfasten the black robe. Hedy lay limply on the bed as the men managed to disentangle the ample garment. As she lay on her back in the cotton undergarments Omar saw the blood between her legs. He covered her with the robe and went to the desk in the sitting room, wrote a note in Arabic, gave it to Yusef, with the keys to the women's room and went back to be with Hedy. She was no longer trying to scream, but her whole body was trembling as if in an epileptic seizure. Omar brought the chair closer to the bedside and took her hand into his. He began to stroke her twitching fingers and to talk to her in Viennese about the chess match, about the walks in the garden, and how he loved looking into her eyes. His voice droned on and she began to relax. The trembling became an occasional twitch. Her eyes closed and she seemed to be dozing. Omar didn't move until Yusef came in with the supplies that he had been sent to fetch.

Omar turned to Yusef as he came into the bedroom. "Let's put these things in the bathroom." He said in Arabic. "She needs to sleep for a while." With one last lingering glance in Hedy's direction the men left the room.

Yusef kept watch while Hedy slept. He sat dozing in the chair, the clean sheets he had brought in were on his lap as he waited for Hedy to wake up. Hedy had turned on her right side, her long braid dangled over the edge of the bed.

During the morning hours, the water main had been repaired but there was no coal for the furnace so the Mufti would have cold water for his bath. Although the electricity was on, it was not dependable so the kerosene lamps and matches were kept nearby. The fog had lifted and a shaft of spring sunshine danced on the wall across from the bed and lit up the room. The clear day meant another bombing raid shortly and everyone was tense waiting for the air raid sirens to start.

Omar had gone to the Mufti's quarters where a stack of correspondence awaited him. As he sat at his desk, pen in hand, a German-Arabic dictionary beside him, the words on the pages swam before his eyes like fish in a tank, not holding still long enough for him to get their meaning. After a half hour of useless staring, he got up and went back to his own rooms.

The air raid sirens blared just as he entered the door. The bombings were going on for the third day and night. In the Villa only a few of the men accompanied the Mufti to the cellar. Omar and Yusef decided to stay in their own quarters. They didn't want to wake Hedy, who had slept through the wail of the sirens. It was evening before she turned on her back and opened her eyes. The first thing she saw was the crack in the ceiling and then her eyes fell on Omar standing by the bed, a worried frown on his handsome face. As he saw her eyes open, he smiled and his features relaxed with relief. Yusef still sat in the chair, holding the clean sheets. The three of them looked at each other with unanswered questions on their faces. The bombs began to explode and they were undecided about going to the cellar or remaining in their rooms. Wordlessly they agreed to remain in Omar's quarters.

During a lull in the bombing Omar spoke. "Hedy, do you feel strong enough to get up?" For an answer she began to climb out of the bed. "You can go clean up if you like." Omar added sounding more like a question. He reached out his hand to help her up and taking her arms guided her to the bathroom. She shook off his hand and strode out of the room, head down, reluctant to meet his eyes. He stepped aside to let her pass.

Hedy found the cotton strips and a clean set of undergarments folded next to the water closet. Clean towels were hung on hooks in the back of the door, and a bar of soap lay in a soap dish at the edge of the claw footed bathtub. She noticed there was no lock on the door, but at least there was a door. Stripping off her blood stained chemise she got into the tub and turned on the water. It was cold, but then cold water was best for removing blood stains. She washed herself and used the towels, then rinsed out the stained chemise. Not finding a place to hang it, wrapped it in the towel. Feeling clean, dry and protected by the cotton strips she opened the door. She heard Omar laughing softly as she approached the bedroom door and when she went in she could see Yusef's features pulled into a soundless laugh. The men were standing on either side of the bed engaged in changing the sheets. Omar had just told Yusef that when Jasmin saw the blood stained sheet she would think that he and Hedy had consummated their union. When Hedy came in he thought of sharing the joke with her and then thought better of it. Instead he sent Yusef for some food.

Omar led Hedy into the sitting room and handed her the black robe. She put it on over the chemise, grateful for the warmth it provided. Then he handed her a snifter of brandy. As he held it out to her their eyes met. His were warm, tender, concerned while her eyes were full of suspicion and a hint of fear. Alcohol was forbidden. Was this a trap? She sat down in the arm chair across from the divan and at Omar's urging took a sip of the brandy, grimaced at the strange taste and set the glass down on the small table next to her. She looked confused.

"Hedy" Omar spoke in a pleading voice, "Please trust me.

I will protect you." Seeing her features harden into a skeptical mask, he reached out and took her hands in his and sat down in the chair next to her, holding her gaze. He remembered a poem he had read in an English Literature class. The poet had compared the eyes of his beloved to deep, blue pools in which his soul might drown. Now he had a similar sensation.

How could he gain her trust without revealing his true identity? How far was she willing to go to save her life? He had no one to consult about this complex matter. Over the last six years he had learned that Yusef could be trusted to give wise and sensible advice when he needed it. But getting Hedy to trust him without giving himself away required a discussion that would need more than yes or no answers.

Hedy sat quietly watching Omar. She could see that he was struggling with his thoughts, perplexed about using the right words to assure her of his feelings for her.

Chapter 14

Six years ago his superiors in the Zionist Intelligence Agency had introduced Oskar, who then became Omar, to Yusef. It was during the briefing session meant to prepare him to be the personal secretary and interpreter to the Grand Mufti of Jerusalem. In such an important position he required a completely trustworthy valet. Yusef's inability to speak proved to be an asset.

After his graduation at the top of his class from Dar El Ulum University, one of the most prestigious schools in the Middle East, Oskar, now known as Omar had shown himself to be a devout Muslim, not much interested in females, with overt Anti-Zionist tendencies and a talent for languages. These attributes guaranteed him the position he was about to seek.

According to his references, Yusef had no vocal cords which would actually be beneficial, as gossiping with other servants, thus inadvertently divulging secrets would be out of the question. He was several years older than Omar, a little gray was sprinkled in his dark, reddish hair. The two men were about the same height but Yusef had a well trimmed, pointed beard on his chin, in imitation of the Mufti while Omar sported a thin, black mustache that needed constant grooming. Yusef understood several languages, but Omar was ordered to speak only Arabic to him.

The Zionist contact that was instructing Omar was just finishing the last of the details when he added cryptically, "Yusef is as devout a Muslim as you are." To Omar this meant that drinking brandy would be acceptable. There had been a sizable stock of good brandy in the wine cellar of the Villa and Omar and Yusef had been put in charge of supervising the disposal of all the alcohol in the cellar. Some of the best and oldest disappeared into their quarters, while the rest had been distributed among the German High Command.

Now Hedy took another sip of the brandy and after the third sip it felt smoother and she was becoming calmer. Omar chose his words carefully and fought to keep his voice even. He was aware of the listening devices, there was no privacy in these rooms.

"Hedy, I mean you no harm." He spoke in French, hoping she would understand that this was not a personal conversation. As he spoke he pulled a pad and pencil from the desk drawer. He put his finger to his lips for signaling silence and began to write. All the while talking in French about how good the Mufti had been to him. In German, he wrote that she must learn to trust him and he would help her escape. Hedy wanted to believe him. He looked so sincere. He wrote that there were listening devices in the room and to be careful what she said.

He continued writing. "We must be seen as devout Muslims and devoted to each other. Do you understand?"

Hedy nodded. She had already decided to outwardly show her devotion to Islam. After all it was not that much different from the Orthodox Judaism she had seen practiced in her hometown in Poland. Females were treated in a similar way by the Orthodox in both religions.

Omar continued speaking in French. "Yusef is totally reliable and loyal. He understands several languages, but only admits to understanding Arabic. I noticed you know some words by now." As he spoke he tore the paper in his hand to tiny bits, then went to flush them down the water closet.

Just then Yusef came in with a tray of food. Pita bread, several little pots wafted an appetizing fragrance through the room. The Mufti's chef could make the most mundane vegetables into a tasty spread. A mountain of saffron flavored rice wafted a delicious aroma. Omar wondered where the Mufti's chef had obtained saffron, when there was hardly a potato or a cabbage to be had in all of Germany.

They sat on the floor, Arab style, and devoured the warm food, washing it down with a little more brandy. Then Yusef made tea in the samovar on a sideboard and served it in little, handless cups. When they had finished eating Omar took Hedy's hand, helped her up and motioned her to his bedroom. "Sleep well, my beloved." He said to her in Arabic while he went back out to the sitting room. He then told Yusef that they would be sharing his room that night.

The next day the bombing of Berlin continued but by dawn the Russian artillery was in the process of surrounding the northern outskirts of the city. No bombers came during the night, but just in case of an air raid, the Mufti called his retinue to the cellar for a conference. He told them that the Fuehrer had retreated to a bunker under the center of the city and that he had ordered the whole country to be totally destroyed. "The man is insane and has forbidden anyone to surrender." The Mufti explained. "We have made plans to leave this mad house. Our people will win, in the end, of course, but we must be armed and ready when the time comes. A plane is waiting to fly me and my staff to France, where I am guaranteed protection. Eventually we will make our base in Cairo. From there we will march victoriously into Jerusalem and exterminate all the infidels living in our holy lands." After making this speech the Mufti invoked Allah's blessing on them all and their plans and dismissed everyone.

The next day while the explosions were definitely coming closer, but still some distance away, the Mufti sent Amir to discreetly gather his personal secretaries in his private quarters. When the five men were assembled the Mufti told them the exact details of his plan.

The five of them were to meet at a short air field just beyond the zoo. They needed to make their way to the field

on foot and separately in order not to arouse attention from
the German guards that might still be around the Villa. It
was a small plane with space for five passengers, the pilot,
nothing else. They were each given specific instructions with
the date and time to meet at the plane. They had three days
until their departure. During that time Amir was to pack
a few items for the Mufti to take along and to prepare the
poison for the women.

"We cannot take them along. Death will be more merciful
than leaving them for the Russians." The Mufti's tone was
somber, as if he regretted the murders he was about to order.
"Abdul and Hassan you will take a last meal to the women
and make certain that they drink all of their tea. He added
and then turned to Omar. "Sort the necessary papers into a
small briefcase and use the coal burner in the cellar to destroy
the rest.

When Omar reminded him of the coal shortage, the
Mufti told him there would be a load of coal at his disposal
the next day.

As the men left the room Omar spoke to Amir," Give me
some of the poison for my wife. I don't want to leave her for
the Russians, either." Amir reached into his jacket pocket and
with a knowing smirk, handed Omar a small vial.

On his way back to his rooms Omar finalized a plan for
Hedy's escape. He had worked out several scenarios of how
to get her to safety. For several months, actually for over a
year, going back to the moment he had first seen her after
Jamal's beating, he had begun to devise escape plans for her.
His mind always came back to the tunnel that started under
the washtubs in the cellar. He had been told of the exit by his
contacts and shown how to access it, where it led and studied
the original plans of the whole structure. But getting out of
the Villa was only half the problem. Finding a safe place to go
was the more difficult part. In fact, Omar thought, that had
been the main problem for the condemned Jews of Europe.

In the beginning the idea had been for every Jew to depart

Europe, and of course, leaving all their worldly goods behind. But then almost all the countries in the world closed their borders or opened them just a crack. They demanded that the potential immigrants show that they had a certain amount of funds to sustain themselves. Since all their funds had been confiscated, the Jews of Europe were trapped. There was no homeland for them to which they could flee. The Grand Mufti of Jerusalem with the full co-operation of the British Mandate Government had made certain of that. Omar had to stand by and witness the glee on the Mufti's face as he received news of the mass murders. "Thousands less Jews to overrun our Palestine," The Mufti had gloated when the reports came in about the initial success of the gas chambers.

During these meetings with the Nazi leaders, Omar had to fight the urge to grab an automatic rifle from one of the guards, kill the Mufti and as many of the fiends in the room as possible. His orders, on the contrary, were to keep the Mufti alive as a source of information. He knew he was making a difference, but such a small one. He had been able to help save a few hundred children at a time, when thousands were murdered every day. Now he had a chance to save this one girl, but at what cost?

He realized at that moment that nothing mattered more to him than saving this girl. He had chosen her from a line of naked children. There were many other girls of her size among these teen aged girls who had been assigned to keep the younger children calm as they filed into the "showers." He had felt that there was something special about her.

It was rare for a girl to still have their hair at that stage of the extermination process. This one had a long, gold braid tied back with what must have been a shoestring. To Omar there was something familiar about her. He had the feeling that he had seen her before.

That feeling grew stronger as he got glimpses of her at the Friday prayers and later as they walked in the garden. It wasn't until he heard her speak in the Viennese accented

German that he realized that she reminded him of his step-mother. Although she had died sixteen years ago, and he had lived a totally different life then, he could still hear her soft laughter when he told her of some amusing incident or a joke he had heard on his way home. It was she who had taught him to say the "Shema" (the prayer he thought to himself each time before he went to sleep). The prayer he dared not utter or even mouth with his lips and tongue. Amalia's voice was the last thing he heard each night and he was sure it would be the last voice he would hear before he died, no matter when that might be.

Omar's plan was falling into place and the Mufti's orders were just what he needed. When he got to his room he called out for Yusef who came out of his bedroom. Omar heard the water running in the bathroom, so he motioned Yusef back into the small bedroom that the men now shared. Quickly he explained the Mufti's flight plan. Yusef listened attentively. Then Omar added as an afterthought. "I need to go to my friends in Berlin to say good-bye."

Eventually the two men would need to find a safe place to talk. Omar had to tell Yusef his plan for him and Hedy to escape. But first of all Omar needed to notify his contacts in the resistance. This meant a trip into the bombed out areas of central Berlin. The brothels that he had frequented were mostly gone, and those still in operation were located in the deepest cellars of the rubble filled city. Each night someone came to each of the establishments to pick up any possible messages. The code was simple, but no one knew the identity of anyone involved.

Omar arrived at the "House of Dreams" at the southern end of the Kurfustendam during a short lull in the bombardments. The piano and the beds had been moved to the basement of the demolished building. He spoke to several of the women but only the first one was receptive to his message. He told her "I have seen an owl on a tree with only two branches." Then he spent a half hour with another young girl and left.

Since his message was in French and she would repeat the message verbatim to the contact, that person would know that Omar would be at a certain church at two A.M.

Devising the original code and distributing the information was complicated but it had worked well for almost four years now. Omar and his superior, whose identity was unknown to Omar, had an understanding of every language and several dialects spoken throughout Europe. The word for owl was different in each language and not used often. The code worked in the following manner. The language used designated the place to meet, the numbers mentioned was the time of day, (on a twenty-four hour clock) the word owl was the assurance that the speaker was a trusted contact.

The message that Omar had conveyed to the brothel contact meant that he would be at the Catholic Church near the mostly destroyed art museum at two o'clock that morning.

He would go into a confessional booth which were used to good advantage by many underground organizations throughout Europe at that time. The person waiting in the confessional would repeat the exact words back to Omar after he asked to be blessed.

That morning Omar revealed the Mufti's plan for leaving Berlin, including the murder of the women. He said nothing of his own plan to save Hedy and Yusef. He had worked out a scheme with the woman who ran the brothel whereby he would deliver a blond virgin to her establishment. He also assured her that he would arrange for her to sell the girl to an Arab dignitary for a sizable profit.

When Omar returned to his quarters that morning he went directly to his bedroom to see if Hedy were asleep. The constant rumble of artillery blasts made sleep difficult but after months of this type of noise the human brain adjusts and eventually it is possible to sleep. Omar expected Yusef to be in the chair next to the bed but it was empty and Hedy lay under the covers fully clothed. Omar sat down on the chair and took off his boots. He unbuttoned his jacket and hung it in the armoire. Hedy watched him with mixed feelings. Part of her was afraid of what he might do to her and a deeper feeling hoped he would want to touch her as much as she had begun to want to touch him.

She saw the sliver of light coming into the room from the slightly open door. Had he left it open on purpose? She saw him unbutton the top of his khaki shirt and roll up the sleeves. Then he sat back down into the chair. He met her steady gaze, aware that she had been watching him.

"Where is Yusef?" he inquired in a matter of fact tone.

"He took away the dishes," she answered in French

Omar motioned her to move over and he threw back the thick feather duvet and lay down on the bed next to her, also fully clothed. He pulled the cover back over them. He could not see her face, but he thought he saw a flash of teeth and imagined she was smiling at their rather awkward positions. He placed a finger over his lips to caution silence and pulled the cover up over their heads. This barely muffled the explosions that began to sound closer each time, but were still some distance from the Villa.

Omar began to whisper into Hedy's ear in his Viennese dialect. "Hedy, I have a plan to help you escape. It is complicated and I don't have time to explain. In order for it to work, you must do exactly as I say and trust Yusef and me completely."

Hedy was silent for a long moment as he waited for her reply. She brought up one hand and touched his cheek. A gesture she hoped would be understood as her acquiescence.

Chapter 15

Omar turned on his side, facing Hedy under the feathered quilt. Her hand was still softly touching his cheek as he covered it with his. As he moved a little closer she moved her hand down to his chest. She could feel the warmth of his skin under the rough shirt and pounding of his heart. She breathed in sharply. This was a grown man, alive and breathing lying next to her in bed. It was something she had thought about when her mother or Konstanza talked about her getting married someday. Usually it was a way of consoling her when there was a small scar on her face or on her arm after falling from her bicycle or an ice skating mishap. "It will be gone by the time you get married." were the usual words. As she approached her teens these words got her to thinking about what happens when people get married. She knew they slept together. At least her parents did that. However her grandparents had separate rooms. (They even called each other Mr. and Mrs. Menkes when addressing each other.) Even now she only had vague idea of how children were created. It was a subject she had pushed off into the far future and left for a time when she was forced to address it.

Now she couldn't help but wonder if a girl could become pregnant if she lay in bed with a man. Wasn't that what she had read in the biblical texts and even in the Koran?

Omar gently put Hedy's hand down to his side and pulled her into his arms. He kissed her lips softly and she returned the pressure. They lay like that for several minutes. Just holding each other, feeling the warmth and their quickening heartbeats.

Finally he whispered, "How old are you Hedy?"

She answered with a question, "What year is it?"

"1945," he said, a little surprised.

"I am seventeen, or will be in March," she whispered, then resumed touching her trembling lips to his.

"Don't be afraid of me," he whispered." I want you for my wife, but not yet. Someday when I can tell you everything, when you can meet my mother and we are free to live our own lives. After a proper ceremony we will consummate our union with pride and joy.

"Yes." She breathed into his ear.

With one more soft kiss on her warm and smiling mouth he slowly extricated himself from her embrace. He picked up his boots and went out the door closing it behind him.

Just as Omar entered the sitting room, Yusef came in. Omar motioned him back out into the hallway. The men walked in different directions. Eventually they met outside the walls of the Villa's extensive grounds, having used different routes and methods to arrive at their destination. Omar had gone underground, by way of a trap door near a Greek statue. A short tunnel brought him to an area just outside the wall that surrounded the Villa. Yusef knew of a narrow opening in the wall, far from the house and over-grown by a thicket of ivy.

The sky was beginning to lighten in the east, but it was still dark under the low branches of the fir tree where the two men finally met.

Omar did the talking and Yusef only nodded or raised his hand if he wanted more explanations. The subject was the escape plan for Hedy and Yusef. There were many details that Omar had worked out that needed exact timing and care-fully calculated actions. However just plain luck would play a major part and both men knew that success was anything but guaranteed. Yusef was to carry a vial of poison just in case.

When Omar consulted Yusef about whether to warn

Jasmin and Leia about the plan to poison them, Yusef shook his head vigorously to indicate his disapproval of doing so. Omar said he would think about it. As it turned out his indecision about warning them almost cost him his life.

The men parted, leaving the cluster of fir trees near the zoo at different intervals, and walking in different directions. Yusef returned to the Villa by the same route he had come to the meeting place. A half hour later Omar walked to the road that fronted the Villa. He waited until the morning motorcycle patrol came along. He knew most of the Germans who went by each morning on their rounds to check the damage to bombed buildings and report casualties to the ambulance service. On more than one occasion they had seen Omar stumbling along the wall looking for the gate to the Villa.

This morning there was only one motorcycle with two German Police officers. The driver stopped when he saw Omar weaving unsteadily along the sidewalk that ran beside the wall. Omar put a hand out towards the wall to steady himself and looked at the German sitting there on the motorcycle blocking his way.

"Only one bike?' he slurred.

The policeman recognized him and chuckled. "My cycle ran out of gas." Called the passenger and added "Are you lost again?"

Omar waved an arm in what looked like a greeting and perhaps an answer to the question as he pointed in the direction of the gate. He carefully made his way around the motorcycle and continued, staggering slightly, toward the main entrance of the Villa.

The German policemen started up their cycle and continued on their way without a backward glance while Omar walked into the main gate of the Villa, ignoring the fez-wearing sentries who in turn pretended not to see him. Once inside the Villa he walked briskly to his room where Yusef opened the door when he heard Omar's key in the lock.

Omar went into the larger bedroom where Hedy was sound asleep. His eyes caressed her pink face and rope of honey-colored hair that hung over the edge of the bed behind her.

"I need to start sorting the papers for burning." He told Yusef, upon his return to the sitting room. Omar had donned his military like jacket and put on a tie. He looked a little tired, but not at all like a man had not slept for forty-eight hours. He would not sleep again for at least another day and another night.

Yusef pointed to the coffee urn on the table. The cups were ready to be filled. A plate of rolls and a small jar of jam sat at the ready. Omar nodded and sat down in the chair that Yusef held for him. The hot coffee was refreshing and the rolls and jam refueled Omar's energy.

"Thank you, Yusef," he said as he again headed for the door. "I am coming back to get you when all is ready. I will need your help to carry the load to the cellar."

The visit to Jasmin and Leia was short and decisive. Omar asked them if they wanted to return to Jerusalem or stay in Berlin and die with the Mufti. Leia had told him that she and Jasmin would rather die than forsake the Mufti. Hedy had not been mentioned, nor was the poison.

When Omar entered the Mufti's quarters it was evident that the Mufti and Amir had spent the night sorting paper, and correspondence out of the filing cabinets. Two long tables were piled high with notebooks, account books and file folders. The Mufti looked up and stared at Omar with bloodshot eyes.

"So, you finally got here!" He barked in Arabic. "The honeymoon must be over. When you dispose of these," and he waved his hand over the two tables, "you can go back to your Jewish sow and make your final goodbyes." He smirked at Amir as he said this.

"Are you certain you don't need any of these papers and accounts?" Omar kept his voice neutral. "You had asked me to come this morning to help you sort the files, sir. Would you like me to double check any of the material just to be positive that you really want them destroyed? After all you are one of the most important men of this century, and you and your accomplishments will be a part of world history."

The Mufti gave Omar a searching look to as if to verify his sincerity. Evidently he was satisfied that Omar meant what he said. He pointed to an attaché case that stood by Amir's feet. "We have put everything we need into that case. We might have overlooked some trivial correspondence or accounts that will interest future historians. You have my permission to fill up an attaché case of this size," said the Mufti. Still pointing to the case next to Amir, who had not moved, but looked annoyed. "There may be some material that would explain my life to future generations and enlighten their understanding of why some actions had to be undertaken and the sacrifices that were made in their behalf." The Mufti continued in his pedantic tone as he waved his hand over the tables again and again.

Omar hoped his own features looked sympathetic as he nodded his understanding. "I leave it to you," the Mufti said and added, "however I trust that you only save documents of historic value and destroy anything that might give a negative impression of my heroic efforts to save the world for Islam."

Amir, who seldom spoke in the presence of the Mufti, said, "Yes!" in a loud emphatic voice, as if he had suddenly come to conclusion in his mind. The other two men looked at him and he had their full attention. They waited for him to continue as his tone clearly indicated that he had more to say. Amir cleared his throat and continued speaking in his high pitched, Moroccan accented Arabic.

"The thoughts, deeds and writings of our beloved Mufti will have historic consequences and must be preserved for all times. His guidance will be an inspiration for future generations of Arabs." With these words Amir picked up the satchel at his feet and turned to leave the room.

The Mufti looked sharply at Omar. "My legacy is in your hands!" He exclaimed with a dramatic gesture towards the tables. "I will see you at the designated time tomorrow." He added in a lowered voice.

Just as Amir reached for the door handle, a soft knock was heard on the other side of the door. It was Yusef, who they all knew, had been listening behind that door.

Omar and Yusef exchanged glances and each knew what the other was thinking, as they had heard Amir's words.

Yes, the Mufti's influence would have historic consequences.

No one foresaw the chaos, destruction and bloodshed that the disciples of this monster would unleash on the Middle East and subsequently on the rest of the civilized world.

Now it was time to instigate their plan for Hedy's escape, so Omar and Yusef began collecting the papers piled up on the tables. They each took an armload to the laundry chute in the hallway and sent it down to the bins below. Leaving most of the ledgers and notebooks on the tables for now, they went back to Omar's rooms.

Hedy was awake and drinking coffee as the men came in. She looked up shyly from the low stool where she huddled with the black robes spread out around her. She had covered her hair with the black scarf Yusef had brought with the other garments from the women's room, but the thick braid hung provocatively down her back.

Yusef busied himself with gathering the cups and saucers, taking them and the coffee urn into the bathroom to rinse. He observed that the toothpaste was not in the cabinet but lying near the glasses that held the toothbrushes. He also noticed the female undergarments hanging over the bathtub. He smiled to himself, remembering his sisters. Then quickly pushed the distracting memories from his mind. Saving this girl might bring him some peace.

Omar took Hedy by the hand and led her to the bedroom. Motioned her to get under the covers again as before. When they were under the voluminous feather comforter, facing each other in the total darkness, he began to whisper her plan. Not all of it, only the part that would need her unquestioning cooperation.

"Please listen carefully to what I say to you now, as we do not have much time. When we leave this room we speak French. I will use a disdainful tone when I address you. We will act out a charade for the benefit of the listeners just in case there are still any there. Yusef and I have a plan for your escape. You must trust us and ask no questions after we leave this room. We will hold a French conversation after you come out of the bathroom. When I give the signal with my finger on my lips you will not speak again until you are well away from the Villa. Do you understand, not a sound until you are driving away from the Villa?"

He wished he could see her face, but her soft "Yes!" would have to do. Then she continued in the Viennese dialect. "I have a confession to make. I used a toothbrush that I think is yours."

He had to chuckle, it was such an unexpected diversion from the serious words he had imparted to her. "Hedy," he told her with an amused smile she could not see, "what is mine is yours. When you love someone that is how it is."

She had listened carefully to his plan, not interrupting even when he hesitated, waiting for her to question him. Omar had known she was intelligent and intuitive from listening to her converse with Leia. Her experience had made her mature, she was no longer a child and had full knowledge of how vile and dangerous life was for prisoners of the Third Reich. (Weren't all the people who lived within the grip of that regime prisoners?)

Then Omar told Hedy that if his plan for her escape succeeded they would meet again. He also warned her that if any phase of his scheme went wrong one or both of them would surely die.

"I know." She whispered in the Viennese dialect. There was no hesitation or sign of fear in her soft voice.

Before they got out of the bed he held her gently in his eager arms. They kissed, hesitantly at first and then with the passion of lovers who know it might be their last kiss.

His hand moved up from her waist and brushed across her breast. The touch of his fingers on her hardened nipple sent a shock of pleasure down her belly and into the area between her legs. She gasped as his other hand moved down her back and over her buttocks. She could still feel numb spots even though more than a year had passed since Jamal had beaten her. Totally unexpected the thought of that almost unbearable pain and the terror of being so utterly helpless brought on a wave of pleasure that burst inside of her in an explosion of ecstasy. With what little control she possessed at that moment, she moved her mouth away from Omar's warm lips and pressed it hard against his shoulder to stifle the scream that came into her throat from somewhere deep inside her. His grip tightened as he held her against his firm body and she began to relax. When he again sought her lips with his, he tasted tears on her cheeks.

Hedy's mind was in a whirl. She knew that what she had just experienced was powerful. The feelings and her reaction had been beyond her control but even in her innocence she had the cognizance that this was the feeling that made the world go round.

Omar sensed what had happened and by the way she was trembling, he knew she was frightened.

"Everything that happens between us is very special," he told her, then called her, "My sweet little treasure." in the Viennese dialect that he remembered his father had used when showing fondness for Amalia, Omar's lovely stepmother. He had seen them embracing in the dark corners, heard them whisper, laugh and sometimes hum a waltz as they danced a few steps along the hall. What endearments, if any, did his father whisper to Amah? Why should such thoughts come into his mind just now?

He returned his full attention to Hedy. He could sense that she was very disturbed, but he couldn't know that her sexual feelings had been imprinted by Jamal's brutality, but Omar did surmise that she might have been attacked before.

That was the abhorrence of sexual abuse of a child. Such abuse left permanent imprints and often a deviant mindset that affected all future sexual relationships. It was a crime that destroyed the pleasure that is every human's birthright, to experience ecstasy born of love and real passion, instead of terror and unbearable pain.

Omar could feel his own body responding. It took all his self control to hold himself in check. As Hedy became calmer, her sobs subsided into soft sighs Omar began to relax and feel himself become limp. With a deep sigh he began to move out of the bed.

He reached down and smoothed her hair, letting his hand run down the long, thick braid. It felt like silk and he ran his fingers to the end, pulling out the band that held it together.

"I'm going to wash and change my clothes now" he told her in French. The language they would be using when others could hear.

Chapter 16

When Omar came back to the bedroom he took Hedy by the hand and led her to the bathroom where a bathtub full of hot water was awaiting her. He pulled her black robe over her head and motioned her to wait. For a minute she stood there in her undergarments. She wanted to ask him where he got the coal to heat the water, but before she could form the words he had left the room.

Upon his return to the bathroom, carrying two towels, Omar saw that Hedy had taken off her undergarments and was sitting in the bathtub washing herself with the small bar of soap. She leaned back, spreading her hair into the water. He got down on his knees next to the tub.

"Let me help you with the hair," he commanded. And began to rub soap into the strands and messaging her head. Hedy was surprised at his skilled movements. He had filled a pitcher with water and used it to rinse the soap from her hair. He let the water out of the tub and motioned her to stand up. Then wrapped one of the towels around her head and the second one around her body.

"Stay here and dry off," he ordered. "I am bringing you some clothes."

A few minutes later he came back with four pieces of clothing which he hung on a hook behind the door. Hedy stared at the male garments. There were boxer shorts, the kind her father wore, a knit undershirt, a pair of black trousers, with a rope dangling from the belt loops and a khaki shirt, like the one Omar was wearing. She saw that Omar had changed into freshly ironed clothes, similar to the ones he just hung up on the hook.

"Dry off and get dressed!" He spoke in French. His tone was like a military order as he pointed to the garments on the hook and left the bathroom, closing the door.

Hedy came into the sitting room stumbling over the pants that dragged along the floor behind her, the shirt sleeves hung below her knees. Omar and Yusef couldn't hide their amusement as they knelt on either side of Hedy and set about rolling up the pant legs and the shirt sleeves. Yusef tied the rope around Hedy's waist to hold up the baggy pants then handed Omar a brush and he began the lengthy process of combing out the long, damp tresses while Hedy sat quietly on the low stool.

Omar began to talk in French. "All Arab boys of my station learn to groom horses," he told her. "Braiding tail hair is part of that job." He continued in the disdainful tone that he had warned her about. "I thought all you Jewish sows had your heads shaved when you were *relocated*. How is it that you still have your long hair?"

He motioned Hedy to answer. The daylight faded from the narrow window and the sound of explosions were once again heard in the distance, Yusef closed the blackout curtains, lit the kerosene lamp and busied himself with making tea, she began to tell her story.

After the train arrived at the camp all the women and older girls were lined up single file outside a long building, guards with guns watching every move. As the line moved slowly into the building, Hedy was one of the last ones, with perhaps only two or three more girls behind her. It was the head shaving area. They could see into the room as they neared the entrance. Suddenly there was a commotion in the room ahead of them. One of the girls had objected to having her hair cut off. She had screamed and the three girls still in line outside the door could see how she fought the women trying to hold her down. Some of the other women began to get out of the lined up chairs. Someone called to the guards to come in and help.

*The men pushed past Hedy and the two other girls, there were more
screams, then several shots. Hedy began to back up and she and the
two other girls ran around the corner of the building then hid in a
latrine that was nearby.*

*They stayed there, huddled together, until a woman came in
and saw them. She was a Polish Blockova (a prisoner who was given
charge of a barrack).*

*"Get back to your children!" she had screamed at them in Polish.
"You lazy Jewish sows." Then pulled a whip from her belt. The three
girls went out of the latrine and there were about twenty, very small
children huddled in groups according to their mother tongue. They
seemed to range in age from about three to eight years old.*

*"Get them on the train!" The woman had barked at the girls
who didn't dare say a word.*

*Then the woman started herding the children and the three
teenage girls along towards the waiting cattle cars on the nearby
tracks. Hedy started calling to the children, in Polish, to come with
her. Only eight of them seemed to understand her and they clustered
around her and she herded them towards the train. The youngest
was five years old and the oldest was eight. They became her responsibility as they were shipped from one camp to another. By the time
they were lined up at the last camp, their clothes were nothing but
dirty rags hanging on their bony, little bodies. At the last camp they
were told to undress for a shower and a medical examination. Hedy
had tied her hair up with a shoestring she had found on one of the
train rides and had forgotten all about her hair for months.*

~

Omar gave the signal that Hedy was not to speak again.
Then he gave a disdainful laugh.

"You are one lucky Jewish sow." He had almost finished the
long braid of Hedy's hair and was tying the end with a ribbon.

Yusef brought a tray with tea cups which he set on the
table next to the samovar. An empty vial lay beside the cups.
Omar poured tea and the contents of the vial into a cup,
took it into the bathroom, poured the tea into the toilet and

quickly pulled the chain. Then he brought the cup back to the tray. Hedy was still sitting on the low stool as Omar took scissors from the desk drawer and clumsily tried to cut the braid at its base. Yusef's hand moved into the folds of his caftan and came out holding a curved knife. With one swift motion of his arm the braid was detached and lay in Omar's left hand

Before Omar or Hedy had seen it, the knife with the razor sharp edge had disappeared into the voluminous folds of Yusef's robe.

Omar used his right hand to stifle Hedy's gasp as she felt for her hair. When she stood up to face the men she looked like a twelve, year old boy wearing his father's old clothes. Yusef took a cap from a hook by the door and put it on Hedy's head. Then both men smiled at her, holding their fingers up to their lips, reminding her to be quiet. Then the three of them went into the bedroom. While Hedy watched with wide eyes, the men arranged the bed to look like Hedy was sleeping in it with her braid hanging over the edge of the pillow, and her face towards the wall away from the door.

When they returned to the sitting room Omar took a scrap of paper and a pencil from the desk drawer and quickly wrote. "We will be back" then motioned Hedy into the bathroom. After she had seen the words he tore the paper into small bits and flushed it down the water closet. With a stern face and forceful hand motions he let her know that she was to stay in the bathroom until he and Yusef came back to get her.

The men left carrying a blanket from Yussef's bed. When they returned the blanket held a load of the Mufti's papers and notebooks. They spread the blanket on the floor, removed its contents and motioned Hedy to lie down on it. Then they piled the notebooks, folders and some lose papers on top of her and rolled up the blanket around her. Yusef opened the door, took a look around, seeing no one, as was expected, since most of the guards had fled to avoid the Russians, he and Omar each took an end of the blanket and started towards the basement.

As they proceeded down the hallway, Abdul came out of Jasmin's and Leia's room. Omar kept his head down, giving the impression that he was too busy with his end of the blanket to see him. Omar had not told Yusef of his visit to Jasmin and Leia. Yusef was hoping that Omar had not warned the women about the Mufti's plan for them. Omar gripped his end of the blanket a bit tighter and kept walking. In a second he would know if Leia had told Abdul about his visit that morning.

Abdul raised his hand in greeting and turned to lock the door. Yusef had shifted his end of the blanket under his left arm, his right hand had disappeared into a fold in his robe as he followed Omar down the hall. Abdul walked away in the other direction. In a moment he called out to the two men who did not stop, only turned their heads,

"I arranged for the grave diggers to pick up the packages. Is yours ready to go?"

Omar kept walking, as he called over his shoulder. "I'll bring the package down myself, after I get Yusef started burning this stuff."

If Abdul made a reply, Omar didn't hear it over the roaring in his ears. When they reached the basement, the men put the blanket down gently. Hedy lay still, waiting. Omar and Yusef used a gripping tool to loosen three of the bolts holding down the rinsing tub. Then they swiveled the base to reveal a large hole in the cement floor. A moldy rope ladder hung down one side, fastened with rusty bolts just below the opening.

Yusef got Hedy from the blanket and showed her the hole. He then climbed down the rope ladder, carrying one of the kerosene lanterns that had stood at the edge of the wash basin. Omar lifted Hedy into his arms and held her over the hole in the base of the rinsing tub. For a moment he held her tightly. Letting her go would be one of the hardest things he had done in his short life. His lips brushed hers and then she was climbing down the rope ladder into Yusef's arms.

Omar looked at his watch. By this time tomorrow Hedy should be out of Germany and he would be in France.

Yusef led Hedy into the mile-long tunnel that led to a road along the Spree River. Hedy could almost walk upright, but Yusef, carrying the lantern, had to bend at the waist It took the best part of an hour for them to reach the opening, which was hidden from the road by a thicket of bramble bushes.

They hid behind the bushes until a car with no lights came along. Yusef uncovered the lamp for a second and then put out the flame. The car stopped a few yards past the bushes where they were hiding. Yusef approached the car which the Madam had sent to pick up the promised virgin. The driver was a boy of about fourteen. Yusef opened the car door and the boy spoke the two words that cost him his life. "Heil Hitler!" he barked.

Before the youngster could make another sound he was lying beside the car, his throat slit from ear to ear. Hedy started to come out of the bushes, Yusef motioned her back. Quickly he undressed the dead boy, flung his shirt, pants, coat and hat into the car and pushed the body into the ditch between the river and the road. Then he went to get Hedy from behind the bushes, motioned her into the back seat, put the car into gear and drove to an area near the river.

Hidden from the road he turned off the motor and turned towards Hedy, who sat frozen in the back seat, clutching the front back rest with white knuckles.

Yusef put his index finger to his lips and cleared his throat. To Hedy's astonishment he began to speak in very bad, American accented German.

"Please, not speak," he said. "I answer questions later."

All Hedy could do was nod in disbelief at what she was hearing.

He continued speaking, but in French this time, which was even worse than his German. He told her to put on the boy's clothes, which were a much better fit than the men's clothes she had been wearing. Then Yusef exchanged the robe and fez for the shirt, trousers and hat that were his in the first place.

Hedy didn't dare say anything until he gave her permission. It was evident that his native language was a type of American English, which she had heard spoken in Vienna on one of her visits. Her cousin had explained that it was a very different language from proper British English and that no one in Europe bothered to learn it because no one, who was anyone, would ever go there.

When Americans, usually those from the southern areas, tried to talk German, especially the Austrian version, it was torture to the ears of the natives and also a source of amusement. Hedy had to smile a little as she thought of how terrible it must sound to the French natives to hear their language distorted by an American. They were so particular.

She had learned a few words of English and Arabic and knew that Yussef understood Arabic quite well. She debated with herself which language she should use when he finally allowed her to speak. She had so many questions.

The artillery blasts from the east of the destroyed city were coming closer. Yusef bundled up the dark caftan and tied it to his back. Then they walked west towards the river bank. The clouds parted and a half moon provided sufficient light for finding the trail that followed the river. Eventually, hidden under the low branches of a willow tree they found a rowboat with two sets of oar locks.

Yusef threw the bundled caftan into the rowboat, helped Hedy get into the farthest seat, untied the rope from the tree and got in himself. He found the two sets of oars in the bottom of the boat, placed them into the locks. Hedy grabbed one set of oars, grateful that she had learned to row during her summer vacations on the Austrian lakes. Yusef smiled to show he was pleased with her expertise. She followed his lead and they traversed the river before the half moon had set. Even with the distant shelling in their ears, Hedy felt a quiet pleasure at being outdoors under the moon and the starlit night.

On the western shore of the river they found another willow tree where Yusef tied up the boat, carefully stored the oars and helped Hedy onto the slippery bank. Using the moon to follow the narrow path that led south west away from the river, they walked through a forest of budding birch trees. By the time they reached a wide meadow it was dawning in the East.

The Russian army was marching into what was left of Berlin while the Allied armies were waiting on the western periphery of the destroyed city.

Yusef and Hedy skirted the dew covered meadow, trudging along an almost invisible trail. Yusef, bending over with the caftan tied to his back looked like a hunchback.

Just as the full sun came into view behind them, they heard a shout in English, "Who goes there?"

Yusef dropped to the ground, pulling Hedy down beside him, while shouting back,

"Americans from Texas. Don't' shoot, ya'all!"

Yusef and Hedy were both kneeling in the grass, with their hands up, when the two American sentries strode up. The men exchanged words and ordered the two potential prisoners to walk in front of them.

The captain behind the makeshift table in the tent, listened to Yusef's story with a degree of suspicion. Asked questions about Texas, which Yusef seemed to answer to his satisfaction. After emptying all the various pockets in the caftan and examining the papers he had found, he handed the bread and cheese from one of the pockets to Hedy.

"You must be hungry," he drawled in an accent similar to Yusef's.

The Allied troops were preparing to head east to cross the river and meet the Russians. They were almost ready to move out. A detachment of British soldiers had been assigned to take German soldiers prisoner and help civilians, who could prove they were not German, to make their way behind the lines. A canvas covered truck was waiting. Yussef carrying his caftan, and Hedy joined a group of ragged and hungry looking boys. They looked at the two new passengers with haunted eyes. Hedy broke the bread into smaller pieces and passed it around. She and Yusef had already stuffed the few pieces of hard cheese into their own mouths.

As the truck moved past a column of German soldiers, hands on their heads, Hedy had the sudden urge to push aside the American manning the machine gun at the rear of the truck and to mow down the whole column of men wearing the hated Nazi insignia. She clutched the side of the truck until her fingers were numb. In her mind she could see the heaps of bodies. She was shocked by her overpowering rage and forcefully averted her eyes from the defeated men trudging along the road behind them.

The truck was taking them to a British held area where a camp was set up for the thousands of people who had survived, (against all odds) concentration camps, or had been used as slave labor throughout Germany and had lost all hope of returning to their homes. At the displaced persons camp, Hedy had to part from Yusef. There were so many questions she wanted to ask, her mind was screaming with frustration.

Yusef put his arms around her. "Omar will find you," he whispered in his bad German. Then he drawled in English and she understood him, "Wait for him. He loves you." She could only nod in reply. The lump in her throat made speech impossible. Then he was gone, walking toward a waiting jeep, clutching the caftan under one arm, his gray sprinkled, red hair gleaming in the spring sunshine. Hedy felt something hard against her left breast. There was a toothbrush in the breast pocket.

Chapter 17

After Yusef and Hedy disappeared into the tunnel, Omar rifled through the pile of papers before burning most of them in the coal fire under the washtub. He put together a small stack of papers to add to the ones already in his attaché case. He wrapped another stack of notebooks and folders in the blanket and pushed it into the niche under the stairs. Making sure that the rinsing basin was firmly back in place and secured, he headed for the stairs. In the hallway leading to his rooms he passed one of the gardeners carrying a blanket wrapped body over his shoulder.

"I'll be up to get your package next, sir," he said respectfully in Arabic.

"Thank you, Yasir," Omar replied in a casual tone. "I will bring it down myself shortly."

"Very well," answered the gardener and continued on his way.

When Omar arrived in his rooms he stuffed the papers he had brought into the attaché case. Then he went to the closet to get his jacket. During a quick look in the mirror that hung above the sideboard, he noticed coal smudges on his face so he went into the bathroom to wash. While there he noticed the toothbrushes were gone. A knowing smile flitted across his face. He shrugged into his jacket, took a picture out of the inside pocket. He stopped for a moment to look at the girl in the studio portrait then started to slip the picture into the inside lining of the attaché. It was of his step-mother at the age of seventeen. He had used the photograph (given to him by his father before he left for that last trip to Vienna) to show the "Madam" of the brothel as a sample of the merchandise for which she then paid a few English pounds and arranged to send her car for transport.

Omar hesitated and took one more look at the fading photograph. The resemblance between Amalia Menkes and Hedy Mandel was unmistakable. He was acutely aware that if the picture were found in his possession it could seriously compromise his mission and possibly cost him his life. As he carefully refastened the lining he rehearsed his explanation in case the picture were found. "The attaché case was confiscated from a Jew entering Dachau, and could understandably contain a hidden photograph taken in a Jewish photographer's studio in Vienna. He, Omar, knew nothing of its existence.

Buttoning his jacket, he went into the bedroom, flung the pillow-stuffed blanket over his shoulder, picked up the attaché case with his free hand, and strode out of the room and down the hall towards the garden entry, the long, blond braid bouncing against his back.

The gardener and Abdul were shoveling the last few shovels of earth over the second grave. A third grave was ready for Omar's load. He set down the attaché case and lowered the body-like bundle down with both hands. The braid was lying on the outside of the blanket. Omar needed every ounce of his self control to keep his hand from stroking it. At the last moment he had an overwhelming desire to snatch the silky object from the grave. Could he get it into his pocket before Abdul saw him? Wisely he decided not to take that risk. Instead he took the shovel from the gardener and started the burial process. Then he handed the shovel back to the gardener, who had lit a cigarette from the kerosene lamp near his feet.

With a quick "See you later." to Abdul, Omar picked up the attaché case and headed for the front gate with a deliberate stride, not looking back.

The clouds had parted and a half moon gave a dim light from the western sky. He had about three hours to get to the airfield. Explosions sounded every few minutes. The Russians were advancing. Fortunately the small airfield was in the opposite direction but across the river. All the bridges had been destroyed by the German army in order to delay the Russian advance. Omar walked several miles along the river until he came to a wooded area where he remembered finding a foot bridge during a summer outing. He could only hope that it was still intact. Lines of red were showing on the eastern horizon when Omar spotted the narrow bridge. He could see, even from a distance, that it had deteriorated over the last four years. The winter ice flow and the spring floods had washed away most of the pilings. He would have to try it in any case. Walking quickly and treading lightly, Omar felt the bridge swaying and vibrating dangerously as he looked down at the rushing water, churning with the spring runoff.

Grateful to be on solid ground, Omar surmised that the Mufti and Amir would have a motor boat at their disposal, while Abdul and Hassan probably had to row across. The orders had been to not share any information in order to avoid leaks and possible assassination attempts.

As Omar approached the airfield, the sun slid up from the edge of the trees around the field, and it was suddenly daylight, and departure time. Hanna Reitch, the Third Reich's foremost fighter plane test pilot, was pacing back and forth beside the plane, nervously blowing smoke from her pink lips. The five men came running from four different directions. The pilot climbed into her plane, started the engine, adjusted her headgear and as Hassan scrambled up into the plane after turning the propeller, she yanked the door closed, and the plane began to move.

They flew very low, barely clearing a high tree left standing in a bombed out field. Most of the territory on the way to Paris was made up of open fields or destroyed towns that looked like a giant had flattened them with his boots. Looking down, Omar saw a world of rubble, burned out fields and many corpses. He stifled a scream of rage that rose from the pit of his stomach, consuming his whole body, culminating like a rock in his throat. It burst like an explosion in his brain. "Why? Why? For what?"

They landed in a meadow near a narrow, dusty road. A black Mercedes was waiting for them. The Mufti had wealthy friends and protectors. The five men spent a few months in a villa outside of Paris. One day a "friend" came to warn them that there was a warrant out for the Mufti's arrest with charges of war crimes. This was a surprise because the Mufti had been assured that the French government would protect him until he could get back to Jerusalem and resume his duties as the religious head of all Moslems in the Middle East. In fact he had sent Omar to the nearest town to buy a car and to acquire a driver's license so he could drive the Mufti to Paris and other areas to visit his friends and supporters. Now it seemed that the vitriolic propaganda, hate filled speeches and the moral support he gave the Third Reich were considered war crimes.

For another week the Mufti paced the Villa, loudly berating the Allied Powers who were run by Jews. Beseeching Allah to curse the French for their betrayal. Finally the Mercedes came and took the five of them along twisting back roads to Marseilles where a small but fast boat deposited them in Alexandria, Egypt. King Farouk sent his personal limousine to the dock and the Mufti with his retinue were ensconced in one of his many lavish palaces near Cairo.

Omar was put to work organizing the Mufti's papers, in order to assure his place in world history. Omar's Zionist contacts were very interested in this process which helped to make certain that posterity would learn about the Mufti and his plans for the Jews.

When he finally found some time for himself, Omar tried to find Amah. After several months he located a friend who told him that she had moved to Alexandria, where her father's family had lived for centuries.

It was also during this busy time in Cairo that Omar found out that Hedy was safe. He had tried, without success, not to think about her or to speculate about her survival. One Friday after prayers, as he sat hunched over on the steps of the Grand Mosque, struggling to put his shoes back on his swollen feet, a hand touched his arm. "The package has arrived undamaged." said a barely audible voice. He dropped the shoe and looked up but there was no one near him. Yet these few words sent a warmth into his heart and he began to hope again.

Soon after this incident Omar traveled to Alexandria and located Amah's apartment in the Ahmadi district, located near the port. (The Ahmadi sect, considered heretics by other Moslem sects, lived near seaports in case they needed to flee for their lives.)

Like the Jews of the world, their safety depended on the whims of the ruling population of the country. At any time they could be attacked for no reason except that their rituals for worshipping Allah deviated slightly from the main two sects. There were some other differences with which the mainstream Moslems disagreed. Such as having respect for women and giving them equal rights with men.

The reunion of mother and son was emotional. They wept in each other's arms for a long time. When they were finally able to speak Omar spent many hours answering Ahma's questions. When he had first told her of his being in the Mufti's service she had advised him to break off all contact with her. Even now being with her was dangerous.

Amah tried to reconcile herself to Omar's work with the Mufti. She knew he had been chosen because of his expertise in languages. He had grown up in a German speaking household, although with a Viennese accent. Almost everyone in Cairo spoke French and English during those years. When Omar had entered the Madras school he had to recite the Koran, say the prayers and converse in Arabic. He had a good ear for the different nuances in each language and spoke them like a native. Secretly he was adding Hebrew as his fifth language. He already had a smattering of it from his Bar Mitzvah lessons.

After Omar had left Cairo for Jerusalem with the Mufti, Amah had followed his career and whereabouts by reading everything that was printed about the Mufti in the various newspapers and listening to his vile speeches on the radio. She was deeply grieved that Omar could be a part of such brutality and unmitigated evil as the Third Reich.

Even now Omar could not tell her of his real mission, as she chastised him for working for such a fiend. He would have liked to ease her pain and sorrow with the truth, all he could say now was, "Trust me. I am still your son, as well as my father's son." It was a cryptic phrase, but looking into the sincerity in his eyes, Amah took comfort from these words with the hope that they meant what she hoped they meant.

He had planned to spend a day and a night with Amah, but decided to stay another day with her. It was doubtful, he thought, that the Mufti would even notice his absence.

Amah had never asked Omar about women in his life. She hoped he would find a wife on his own, since he didn't have official parents to arrange a match. Now she decided to enquire about his plans for a family. During breakfast the next morning she began.

"You are twenty-nine years old," she reminded him. "This is the time in your life to start building a legacy."

The look of pain in his eyes at this remark told her that he had a love in his life and that he wanted to talk about her. Amah spent the day cooking and reminiscing about their years in Cairo, when Omar was still Oskar and there was a warm, family life.

That night, over their last evening meal before Omar was to return to Cairo, he told Ahma about Hedy. He described her looks, her Austrian accent and that she reminded him of Amalia. Of how she endured whatever life dealt her with a determination not to just survive, but to overcome and learn from it. He told of how this young girl, hardly more than a child, had spent much of her time studying the Koran in French, in order to learn more about the Moslem faith. When Amah asked about the details of how Omar had helped Hedy to escape Berlin he flatly told her that he could not talk about this and not to ask any more questions. "Eventually I hope to find her," he said, adding "She is nineteen by now. Not a great beauty, but I will never be happy without her. I pray every minute of every day that I find her before she finds happiness with someone else. "

Just before he was about to leave the apartment for the night train back to Cairo, Amah took Omar by his broad shoulders and sought to look into his eyes. 'He resembles his father,' she thought to herself as she started to tell him about her plans. He was surprised and worried, but he heard her out and swallowed his doubts and objections and told himself she was still young and deserved a life of her own. It turned out she was married, had been for two years. Her husband, a widower, was a carpet weaver and had met Omar's father through the cotton trade. He and Amah had known each other for many years. Salim had been born into the Ahmidayya community but was not inclined to be religious. He had emigrated to Palestine and Amah was planning to join him shortly now that she knew Omar was safe and the war was over.

"We are planning to live in Haifa, a port like Alexandria. Look for Salim's Carpet Emporium." Amah smiled encouragingly and continued. "The Ahmadi live in their own area with a beautiful mosque that has been there for hundreds of years. We feel safer there among the Jews. I have always felt safe among the Jews."

They embraced once more and he promised to come and visit someday. Then Omar ran down the narrow steps and walked briskly towards the train station, the salty air in his nostrils, reminding him of fun-filled days at the beach with his step-mother and sisters.

The main train station in Cairo was crowded, every language in the world could be heard. Just as Omar made his way out the revolving door to the street someone bumped into him. It could have been a tall Muslim woman, her face, completely hidden by a black veil and her body shrouded in a black robe, but the voice was male.

"The owl has devoured eighteen chicks," was all that was said. The word for owl was in Hebrew, the rest of the words were in Arabic.

Omar looked at his watch. In about eleven hours, at 18:00 hours, (6 P.M.) he was to meet a contact at the main Synagogue in Cairo. He took a taxi to the villa. It was a lengthy ride and he had time to think about Amah's plans, the impeding war over Palestine and to speculate about his meeting that evening.

There would be war in Palestine and the outcome would change the Middle East as well as the whole world, and certainly the fate of the Jewish people. Would they really get a country of their own again? Would he finally get orders to go back to Palestine and resume his true identity? How much longer could he keep from murdering the Mufti?

When Omar entered the villa his valet, appointed by Amir, was waiting at the door.

"The Mufti wants to see you immediately." He was stuttering in his excitement.

Handing the young boy his outer garments, Omar hurried down the marble hallway to the ornate room that served as a reception hall, meeting room, and for entertaining visitors.

The Mufti, Amir, Abdul and Hassan were seated around a small round conference table and all eyes looked up eagerly as Omar came in, bowed to the Mufti and took the empty chair next to Amir. His valet had followed him and now stood by his chair, asking if he needed anything. When Omar indicated that he was dismissed, he walked out of the room, quietly closing the door.

The Mufti, as well as the other three men were tempted to ask Omar where he had been, but had learned years ago that Omar gave only one answer to that question, and they didn't want to hear the details of his adventures as it made them very uncomfortable. The first time he had disappeared overnight was while they were still in Jerusalem and the Mufti had asked Omar where he had been. His answer had been direct and explicit.

"A man has needs that must be satisfied in order to do his job with a clear head." Then he went on to describe in detail the services available at a certain brothel that he frequented and enthusiastically offered to take them along next time he went. While he had talked all four pairs of eyes of his listeners inspected the floor and it was the last time he was questioned as to his whereabouts. However, since then Omar had not missed a meeting and had reported for duty each morning, even in Berlin during the worst bombings.

This morning Omar was almost an hour late, no one asked why.

"I can hardly believe the treachery," sputtered the Mufti as his opening remark. Then he continued in an outraged voice. "The United Nations committee on Palestine is proposing a declaration of partition, to give half of Palestine to the Jewish Zionist Swine. It is going to a vote of the General Assembly."

They had all known of the possibility of such a move, but there had been rumors that their British "friends" would not allow their Mandate to be removed from their capable rule. They had successfully kept Jewish immigration to a trickle by diverting ship loads of concentration camp survivors to internment camps on the Greek Island of Cyprus. The British High Command in Palestine had promised the Arab League Nations that they would do everything in their power to prevent the Jews from outnumbering the Arabs in the Mandate.

Now it was clear that if the partition were to come to a vote in the general assembly, the British government would vote for the partition over the strong objections of the High Commissioner of the Palestine Mandate. The Mufti began to gather all his allies and persuade or threaten his opponents into voting against the partition and failing that, he needed to make certain that they would go to war against the new state of the Jews.

Chapter 18

Not all Arab leaders agreed with the Mufti and his policies for the Middle East. But the sensible, forward looking and intelligent visionaries were assassinated over the next few years or threatened into silence. The likes of Emir Faisal and King Hussein of Jordan for example, who thought that allowing Jews to live in their ancestral land, side by side with Arabs, who were, after all, also the offspring of Abraham, would bring the area into the modern world. These moderates understood that some of the best minds of Europe were among these tortured souls who had survived the most efficient killing machine ever devised. The Europeans had persecuted and murdered their most patriotic and productive citizens and the Anti Semitic members of the Arab League wanted to murder the remnants of Jews to keep them from entering Palestine. The moderates saw this immigration as a way to enhance the standard of living for all the people in their country.

It was clear that the Jews were not a proselytizing people who would push their faith on the majority Moslems. They did not try to convert others to their beliefs like the Christians were doing. For a thousand years there had been respect between the adherents of these two faiths. In fact only a few hundred years ago the Pashas of Turkey had given refuge to the thousands of Jews fleeing the Spanish expulsion of 1492. The leaders of the Ottoman Empire had welcomed the Jews of Europe, persecuted by the Spanish Inquisition. These immigrants and their descendants were an asset to that Empire, both economically and intellectually. With the decline of the Ottoman Empire and then the total destruction after World War I, the Jews of the Middle East were once again at the mercy of a variety of dictators and kings. In Palestine, which was now a British Mandate, the Jewish population and the subsequent immigrants that trickled in, were barely tolerated in what had once been their own country.

The Grand Mufti of Jerusalem and his Arab League allies bitterly opposed a partition of Palestine and the creation of a Zionist State. The Mufti's speeches echoed the speeches of Hitler and his minions, advocating the annihilation of all Jews everywhere. His followers included his nephew Yasir Arafat, soon to be leader of a militant, terrorist group that instigated suicide bombings and kidnappings in the fledgling "Israel."

On this morning in his conference room, the Mufti gave orders for Omar to travel to New York and see what he could do to persuade the representatives of the undecided counties to vote against the resolution to partition Palestine.

"I can't go myself, " sighed the Mufti. "In fact I will need to go into hiding as I have been accused of War Crimes. It is an outrage but luckily I have powerful friends that will protect me." He stood up with these words and the other men rose with him. The Mufti went up to Omar and placed a hand on his shoulder. Amir observed this gesture with blazing eyes. "Your skill with languages has been invaluable and now is the time when it is most needed along with your diplomatic talent." He waved his hand to indicate the other three men. "I have observed you, Omar." He smiled amiably at the other men. "I have seen how you were instrumental in keeping my three other secretaries on friendly terms with each other, helping them understand their area of responsibility and their unique importance to our mission."

Omar waited under the Mufti's hand as it tightened briefly on his shoulder, and their eyes met. Omar dropped his eyes down quickly, ostensibly as a sign of respect, but actually to hide the murderous intent that he was having more and more trouble concealing.

The Mufti continued. "Abdul will have your papers ready by next week. You should be in New York in time to talk to the Arab League delegation before the partition vote comes up in the United Nations General Assembly." Handing Omar a piece of paper he added. "Here is a list of people to contact when you get there. Keep careful notes on those who continue to advocate for partition. We have ways to persuade them to change their minds. Those who vote for the partition will incur the eternal enmity of Muslims everywhere. Eventually we will rid the earth of all infidels, as is the will of Allah." With these words the Mufti patted Omar's shoulder, turned and left the room, followed closely by Amir. Abdul walked off in another direction.

Omar trailed behind him deep in thought. He hoped that the 'Yanshoof' (Hebrew for owl) he was to meet that evening had orders for him to assassinate the Mufti, even if it cost him his own life. He spent the rest of the day practicing speeches in English and in French. He hoped never to need German again, but in spite of himself the lilt of Viennese danced in his head when he thought of Hedy.

He could hardly wait to get to New York. There, he knew, were several newspapers published by refugees that printed lists of names of Jewish survivors. The Red Cross had collected names from the various Displaced Persons Camps. The synagogue where he was to be at 6 pm this evening also had posted lists on the entry wall. The war had been over for almost two years and Hedy's name or any other Mandel had not appeared in the Cairo English newspaper. He hoped the synagogue had a different list.

Omar, disguised as an Egyptian camel driver, with a dirty scarf wound around his head that also covered his mouth and nose, (to protect him from the foul smell of camel dung) walked along the ancient cobblestones of Fustat Street that led to the Ben Ezra synagogue. For a few moments he let his mind wander to the days when Moses Maimonides had walked this same street about seven hundred years ago. Even the Imams in the Madras that Omar attended, mentioned his name and allowed the boys to read some of his wise comments on how to live an ethical life.

The world had also been in turmoil during the life of the great philosopher. The persecution of Jews went back to the Romans and was taken up with a vengeance by the Christians. Since so many countries did not want Jews living there, giving the Jews a land of their own, Omar was thinking, would solve the dilemma of where they could go to live. The Ben Ezra Synagogue dated back to the 12th century. Its Gothic façade had been rebuilt many times and its interior restored after countless pogroms. It was still a landmark in the old inner city of Cairo. It was surrounded by a high and formidable wall, but Omar remembered a narrow, almost invisible crack, just wide enough for a slim man to sidle through. He had found it one day when he and a friend decided to skip a Torah lesson. Now he was relieved and a little surprised that he still fit into the space.

Omar slipped into the building through a rusty side door and shone his flashlight around the dusty storage room. A door led to a narrow hall which in turn opened to the main sanctuary. At the other end of the hall was the steep stairway that went to the women's section. Omar started to walk towards the marble archway that framed the entry to the majestic sanctuary, when he heard a click. It sounded like a metal heel on the stairs to his left. He turned towards the stairway. A flickering light preceded him as he walked to the dark stairwell. He hesitated for a moment, men were not allowed upstairs. Was his contact female? Slowly he climbed the steep steps, holding his flashlight down towards his feet.

At the top he saw the light retreat behind a curtained area in one corner of the balcony. It looked very much like a confessional. Omar reminded himself that this was not a church. As he stood still, the flashlight shining on the curtain, he heard a man's voice. "Come in, Omar." He said in strangely accented English.

Omar pushed the heavy velvet drape aside and stepped into a small room. Just as he entered, letting the drape fall closed behind him, a dim electric bulb, dangling from a cord in the ceiling flickered on. Sitting on a cushioned bench against one wall was Yusef. It had been only two years since they had parted, but Yusef looked like he had aged ten years. His once reddish hair was mostly white and so was his neatly trimmed mustache. His eyes were faded like those of a very old man.

Omar stood frozen, staring at Yusef with amazement, his eyes gliding around the small room for the person who had spoken. There were padded benches on the other two walls but Yusef and Omar were alone

"Sit down, Omar." Yusef drawled in his strange sounding English. Omar noticed that each word had two syllables

The small bulb left the room in deep shadows, but Omar saw that Yusef was dressed in a western suit, with a white shirt and a patterned tie. Yusef continued to speak while Omar still stood in front of him, his mind racing with questions, his mouth open in astonishment. Finally Omar sat on a bench, his feet kicking a foot stool he hadn't seen. Yusef's words were beginning to sink into Omar's whirling brain. He was explaining that this curtained area was a part of the women's section reserved for mothers with very young children who might need care and feeding. It had not been used very often, as few women came to services with nursing infants. However if a woman needed to say a memorial prayer (Kaddish) for a close relative, she must come to a service if at all possible. Rumor had it that some babies had been born in this private enclosure. 'And probably conceived here' thought Omar, looking around at the soft, wide benches.

Yusef seemed to read his mind as he spoke the same words in English, that Omar had been thinking in Arabic. Both men smiled knowingly. "There is always some truth in rumors." They agreed.

Yusef continued speaking in his strange English. Omar had to concentrate, but it became easier to understand the words as his mind began to absorb the cadence and unfamiliar pronunciation. It was a little like learning a new language.

Before Omar could ask, Yusef said, "It seemed best that I just didn't talk at all. I couldn't get rid of my Texas drawl. It is a serious defect for a spy." Omar only nodded, as his lips curled into a lopsided smile. He was not really listening, just waiting to ask the question burning in his mind.

"Where is Hedy?" he finally blurted out. His voice low, but urgent. He had meant to express his surprise and plea-sure on seeing Yusef again and to comment on how pleased he was to hear his voice. But even before Yusef could answer Omar asked again "Where is Hedy? Is she alright?"

Yusef, who had been holding the candlestick with the stub of a candle that he had used to guide his way up the stairs, now set it down on a little table between them and blew out the candle. "I'll need it later." He drawled and cleared his throat while Omar waited anxiously for his next words.

"I brought her to the Allied lines. Vouched for her with the commander, who put her on a truck with eight other survivors to be taken to a DP camp (Displaced Persons Camp). She is safe."

Trying to keep his voice level, Omar asked. "To which camp was she taken?"

Yusef shook his head, indicating ignorance. "I had strict orders to report to my superiors the moment I was able" Yusef explained. "The names of all survivors and their whereabouts are being posted and printed every day. Have your looked at the lists in the local and foreign newspapers? The Red Cross has a list of almost 250,000 displaced persons, and even now two years after the war more names come up every day."

Omar was sitting with his elbows on his knees, his head in his hands, fighting back the sobs of frustration that were chocking his windpipe. Yusef got up and sat beside Omar, put an arm across his shoulder. "She is alive and probably looking for you. Your job with this unit is almost over. Then you can look for her full time. The whole service will be at your disposal."

Omar sighed, "She most likely has a new life. She was just a child when we parted."

"Folks like you and Hedy were never really children. From your earliest memories you knew that there were people who hated you, wanted to kill you for no rational reason, except for who you happened to be." Yusef cleared his throat a couple of times, waiting for Omar to control his emotions. "There's a whole generation of Jewish kids who lost their childhood," Yusef continued. "I was one of the lucky ones. I grew up playing baseball, dancing to the jukebox, going on family trips, not a care in the world. Now there are thousands of Jewish kids who may never have a family memory to pass onto their kids. They won't tell their kids about the concentration camps and the brutality they witnessed. They are ashamed of the humans that were once their countrymen. But their children will feel that something is missing and terribly wrong with their parents. I think it will be several generations before the descendants of these survivors will live normal lives. I have already seen this working with the survivors, especially the young ones. They just want to forget."

"I wish the best for Hedy." Omar, had listened to Yusef's long speech, made lengthier by his double syllables for every word. Even the letter "A" came out as "a-ya." Now he gave a deep sigh and finally spoke. "I love her enough to want her to be happy, even if it isn't with me." Then he added with a rueful grin. "Her kisses were not those of a child."

"Omar!" Yusef said in a sharp tone, unlike the tone he had used heretofore. "We have business to do. We will talk in English since you are going to New York you need the practice.

By the way, how is your Hebrew?" At these words Omar looked up in surprise. His thoughts had been far away from this dark little room. Wide eyed he looked at Yusef.

"I haven't used Hebrew since my Bar Mitzvah. I can read, but I am somewhat rusty in conversational Hebrew. I have been trying to practice a little, but it is dangerous for me."

Yusef continued. "When you have any spare time study the Sephardic version of Hebrew. In spite of, or because of, what the Mufti says, we will get a Jewish State." Yusef's confidence was catching. You will be sorely needed after the United Nations passes resolution 181 for partition of Palestine, and eventually there will be a Jewish State. The official language will be Hebrew." Yusef saw the disbelief in Omar's face. "Yes, I know it is an ancient language, but why do you suppose the Rabbi's have kept it alive for thousands of years?" If it was possible for a man to smile and look serious at the same time, Yusef succeeded in showing Omar such a face.

Omar had orders to travel to New York in about a week. The Mufti wanted him to deliver personal messages to the Arab leaders who were attending the General Assembly of the fledgling U.N. His message was for them to vote against a resolution to partition Palestine into two states. He was to tell them that this would be a terrible disaster for the Moslems in the Middle East. They were not ready for a modern world. Tel Aviv and Jerusalem were already westernized beyond recognition and a Jewish State would further dilute the purity of the Moslem faith, that was best lived in the 10th Century or even further back to the time when Mohamed walked the earth.

During the evening Omar told Yussef of his orders and Yussef explained that he must do the exact opposite. It must be done in such a way that the Mufti will not suspect that Omar was working against him, at least not yet.

"Be ready to stay in New York through the winter. Take money, as you may need to buy warm clothes." Yusef said and went on "The U.N. Security Council is meeting to draw up the resolution and it is almost ready. Probably the result will be announced near the end of November. There will be debates and arguments about the borders. The Mufti has a lot of influence, but he is also under indictment for war crimes, as you know, so he will depend on you to represent him."

Omar interrupted, "Why not assassinate him? I could do it easily."

"There are at least four Arab factions that want him dead. Let one of them take care of it. Your life is much too valuable to waste on such scum." Yusef replied.

Omar tended to agree. Killing the Mufti would require a suicide mission.

"See what you can do to persuade the leaders of the Arab League that a Jewish State would actually benefit their people, but even more so their leaders." Yusef warmed to the subject.

"There would be state of the art medical care and irrigation systems that would enhance agriculture for the whole region. Also the reluctant Allies need to be convinced that in a Jewish State all religions would be respected and holy places would be protected: Mosques, Churches, Synagogues and all holy shrines alike.

Omar only nodded his head in agreement, but it was in that moment that he began to develop his strategy on how to approach the Arab Leaders. He would start by planting a seed of doubt about the Mufti's message of chaos and bloodshed. He must find a way to make the men who had the power to create policy to believe that allowing a Jewish State in the region would be a benefit for them and their families. They needed to be convinced this policy was their own idea as part of their vision for a modern Middle East in which they had economic and political power.

"The resolution is a done deal, but the U.N. has to declare a legitimate state. The Jews have a government lined up, a national anthem, money ready to coin, a defense force ready to protect the state, a million people ready to immigrate and start working to resurrect the ancient language of Hebrew and the new/ancient State of Israel."

Yusef stood up. "My mission is over in this part of the world. I need to go home. I am very tired. For the first time in eight years I am going to be home for Thanksgiving. There are no words to tell you how much that means to me."

Omar was turning to leave. He hated good-byes scenes and preferred to just walk away. Yusef put a hand on his shoulder and turned him around. "You need to stay in New York until the vote for the resolution is in place. Do not come back to Egypt. Tell the Mufti, just before you leave for what will be, Israel, that you have decided not to return to Egypt, but to go fight for your country. It will be the truth and he will think that you mean Palestine, and even praise your patriotism." The two men exchanged rueful smiles before Yusef continued. "Good–bye, Oskar Menkes, the next time we meet you can call me Joseph Marcus Langdon, AKA yanshoof - the owl."

∽

When Omar, soon to be Oskar again, walked into the mansion where the Mufti and his entourage were housed he had changed his clothes for a western suit and made his way to the smaller of the five formal dining rooms where the Mufti and King Farouk had planned a farewell dinner for him.

The guests had assembled in the ante-room where small plates of appetizers were passed around by attractive young women dressed in traditional robes and sheer silk veils. A trio of female musicians played softly on string instruments from one end of the room. Omar was greeted with smiles, bows and handshakes. The ten men then filed into the dining room The meal was served by men waiters in black costumes and white gloves, who disappeared between courses. The women from the ante-room had retreated to their quarters, where they waited to be summoned for the after dinner entertainment on an individual basis.

At the dinner table, the conversation concerned the U.N. resolution and the importance of Omar's mission.

The Mufti's eighteen-year-old nephew Abdel Al Husseini, soon to be known to the world as Yassir Arafat, was outspoken in his opposition to a partition of Palestine and especially the creation of a Jewish State. "We," and he gestured around the table, "can't let the Zionists take over. Jews mean trouble. Look what they did to Germany."

The Mufti agreed with his nephew and added. "Germany is a pile of rubble. The poor, dear Feuhrer, he had such wonderful plans for the world."

Abdel then continued in his high pitched Arabic, "We learned at school how bad those Jews are. That night in November 1938, I believe it was the 9th, they destroyed all the store fronts in Germany. From the smallest village to the largest cities not a window was spared. It was called 'Kristalnacht' because of all the broken glass."

King Farouk, at the head of the table nodded in agreement and added, "The Gestapo arrested every Jewish man they could find. Thousands were sent to Dachau concentration camp. Fortunately the guards there were ready for those louts. The German government confiscated all their bank accounts and insurance policies to pay for the damage. Those who were not beaten to death by the irate guards could be ransomed by their families."

Hassan, sitting next to Omar broke in excitedly, "I remember reading about a similar situation in my Russian History book. The Russian Tsar, instead of raising taxes on the over burdened peasants accused the Jews in one of the towns where they were allowed to live, of a ritual killing and threatened to hang every man in that town unless a certain amount of gold was paid in restitution. The Jews were given a week to come up with the ransom and of course they did. Then the Tsar sent the Kazaks to collect whatever gold they could find. The Kazaks burned down the village and killed everyone in sight. They were angry because they didn't find anything valuable. The Tsar had neglected to tell them that he had already collected the gold."

"Smart Tsar!" Farouk laughed.

Abdul who had been quiet until now, said tentatively, "That version of 'Kristalnacht' is not how it really happened."

Everyone at the table looked at him. Some with astonishment some with anger and some with worried looks because they feared he might tell the truth. Omar felt sincere anxiety for Abdul who was an honest and literal person. He was an accountant who dealt with absolutes. He hoped he wouldn't say anything more as truth could mean death in this milieu.

Abdel interrupted him, "Jews are liars. They do not tell the truth. The Imams made that clear. I grew up in the Sakakini district of Cairo where Jews and Christians lived. I was curious about them so I attended services at both church and synagogue Their version of the divine laws are so different from what Mohamed taught. All the truth we need is in the Koran."

The Mufti nodded in agreement, adding, "If the Zionists rule Palestine they will destroy our world. They are an evil influence."

Amir, who seldom spoke in public now sounded a small note of doubt. "They do have very good medical facilities. My mother had an appendectomy at Mt. Scopus hospital last year and she had only good things to say about the place." Seeing the disapproving looks around the table he quickly added, "Of course her nurses were Muslim."

Omar had been sitting quietly during this conversation, his white knuckles hidden under the table, seething with rage as he heard the distorted version of the pogrom that destroyed his family (his sisters had disappeared that fateful night) and heralded the destruction of the Jews in Europe. He also feared that Abdel might have some recollection of his father, Faisal Al Husseini, a textile merchant, having had dealings with the Jew, Rudy Menkes, who was in the wholesale end of the same business.

At that moment King Farouk and the Mufti rose from the table and Omar could excuse himself with the explanation that he had to help his valet pack for his trip to New York.

Chapter 19

On the long flight to New York from Cairo, by way of London, Omar spent the time reading and rereading the agreement for a Jewish Homeland. This document was signed in 1919 by Emir Feisal Husseini (representing the Arab kingdom of Hedjaz) and Dr. Chaim Weizman (acting on behalf of the World Zionist Organization) after lengthy discussions between the two men while they were in Aman, Jordan in 1918 and in Paris during the peace conference in 1919. The Emir was at that time the leader of the Arab League and purported to speak for all Arabs, including those living in the British Mandate of Palestine.

This agreement provided that parts of Palestine would be designated as a Jewish Homeland. The Zionist Organizations promised to use their best efforts to develop the natural resources of the region to benefit all the residents. Several paragraphs mentioned religious freedom for everyone living in, what was then still, the Mandate area. Any dispute should be arbitrated by the British High Commissioner's office.

The Nine articles of the agreement and the wording of the Balfour Declaration left no doubt that it was the intention of all concerned to establish a National Home for the Jews.

After living in luxury with the Mufti for the last seven years, post war New York was a surprise for Omar. The area around the fledgling United Nations was in various stages of construction and the hotels in the neighborhood were still struggling to recover their pre-war splendor. He checked into the nondescript hotel closest to the mansion that was rented by the Arab League delegates. The Mufti had given strict orders to deliver his message to these delegated about defeating any resolution that would create a Zionist State. His actual mission was to make contact with these representatives and persuade them that it would be to their benefit to have a modern country in the region which would improve the lives of the people they ruled.

As Omar began to talk to the men (there were only men in all the delegations) their eyes began to glaze over and they lost all interest in his words. They were not disrespectful, after all he was an emissary of their dear, beloved Grand Mufti, but Omar could see he was boring them. He laid out the facts that Tel Aviv had a sanitary sewage system while in Cairo and Alexandria barefoot children in rags played in open sewers. That these sewers crossed the city and dumped raw sewage into the Nile River and on into the Mediterranean sea was of no interest to these men. That there were modern medical facilities in Jerusalem when only the most primitive clinics were available to their people didn't concern these leaders since they and their families went to Europe or to Jerusalem if they needed anything beyond basic first aid. Reminders of how the best minds of Europe were teaching at the Haifa Teknion and how the advances in science and technology being developed there would help their own countries advance into the twentieth century, fell on deaf ears and totally closed minds. Time was running out, the vote for the partition of Palestine would come up very soon.

Since talking was having no effect, Omar began to listen to the conversations among the Arab League delegation. Quickly it became clear to him how naïve and shortsighted he and Yusef had been about the real motivations of the men who ruled the countries of the Middle East. The only interest these men had was to be absolute rulers of their respective countries and making certain that most, if not all, financial gain be funneled into their personal coffers for their personal use. Their subjects were allowed just enough personal freedom and income to keep them loyal to the ruler's particular tribe. They suppressed any opposition or outside influence with brutal force. Most of them had no interest in providing a better life for anyone but their own families. The huge profits from the oil industry were used to enhance their opulent palaces, provide Mosques for the Imams that helped keep them in power and to increase their funds in Swiss Banks.

It was not their concern that in many Middle East Moslem counties streets were not paved, sewage ignored, clean water and indoor plumbing were only for the elite, electricity was a luxury as was medical care. Unlike the elected officials in the United States of America and other democratic countries with parliaments, these men were not at the mercy of the voters. If their people lived in unsanitary squalor, their children died of hunger and disease, while the rulers lived in luxurious splendor, it was the will of Allah. Muslims must submit to their designated fate. Modernization was for infidels and the Koran was very clear about what should be done to them.

There were speeches for and against Resolution 181, which concerned the partition of Palestine. Omar listened to the intelligent, reasonable and eloquent arguments put forth by the likes of Abba Eban, leader of the Zionist delegation. Eban was only a few years older than Omar, but his stage presence was formidable and he was the essence of the visionary focus of Zionism. His calm, cultured voice was a sharp contrast to the bombastic, hysterical shouting of the delegates that opposed the partition. Omar had seen Eban on several occasions, walking in the hallway between sessions, once in the makeshift cafeteria drinking tea with members of the British delegation. Squelching the strong desire to shake the hand of this man that he admired and hoped one day to emulate, Omar had to feign indifference, even hostility when their eyes met during these encounters. He looked forward to the day when he no longer had to hide his admiration of this great man and the pride he felt in his accomplishments.

Omar decided the best he could do was to keep the Arab League members from voting. One at a time he talked to the delegates, reminding them that they needed the good will, if not exactly the friendship, of the Western countries. After all it was these infidels who bought the oil and paid with hard currency, which could then be used to buy the armaments they would need to fight the war against the Jews. In less than a year, he reminded them, the British Mandate would end and even if there were a "Partition" it could be eradicated by the Arab League. So why antagonize the Western Powers by voting against a partition? Of course they could not vote for a partition since that would provoke hostility in their own countries. So the best thing, Omar convincingly argued, was to save face by not voting at all and to simply walk out.

He couldn't be certain what effect he was having until November 19th, 1947 when the resolution for the partition of Palestine came to a vote and the representatives of the Arab League walked out of the great hall at Flushing Meadow without voting.

Omar was now free to leave the cold, damp streets of New York. He sent the telegram, as agreed, to the Mufti in Cairo, informing him that he planned to travel to Jerusalem, where he could be of more valuable service. Leaving the hotel that evening he strode through the lobby wearing the caftan and fez that emulated the style of the Grand Mufti. His attaché case was stuffed full of lists, from various newspapers, of survivors of the catastrophe that would soon be called "The Holocaust."

The doorman of the hotel called up a taxi and asked Omar "Where to?"

"International Airport," Omar shouted over the city noise, and got into the taxi.

At the airport he paid the driver and walked into the lobby by one door and out again through a door that opened to another street around the corner. A gray sedan pulled up to the curb as Omar walked along as if looking for a taxi. The driver put his hands up in front of his face, made circles with his thumb and forefinger, placing them over his eyes resembling binoculars. (In the game of Charades, this formation might represent an owl.) Omar stepped into the car. A few minutes later the car stopped at the outer edge of New York Harbor. The man who got out of the car had a winter coat over one arm and carried an attaché case with his free hand. He was dressed in a three-piece business suit, his white shirt, open at the collar, gleamed in the dim harbor lights. A wide brimmed hat hid his face. Without looking back, he walked briskly towards a pier at the far end of the wharf and onto the lowered gangplank of a French freighter and disappeared. In that moment Omar Samir also vanished and was not seen or heard from again. Oskar Menkes was on his way to a place he longed to call his homeland.

Chapter 20

On the deck of the "Vent Amide" a slim, balding man with very thick glasses motioned Oskar to follow him. The men wound their way down an iron staircase and then along a narrow passage until they stopped in front of a door marked "infirmary." Once inside with the door locked, the balding man said in French, "The owl flies out of the ten foot tree." Oskar visibly relaxed, held out his hand to Dr. Mortenson, whose diplomas were displayed on the pale green wall. The framed documents showed that, Jacque Mortenson, MD (artistically altered from Jacob Morgenstein) had graduated with honors from Montpellier Medical School in 1928, the oldest and most prestigious medical school in France (and possibly in the whole world) and from two other universities in Europe.

"Dr. Mortenson, I am Oskar Menkes," the younger man said as they shook hands.

"Oskar, please call me Jacque." The older man replied, "I will show you where to sleep. Is that all your luggage?" he asked, pointing at the attaché case at Oskar's feet.

Oskar nodded and followed the doctor into an adjoining room, obviously used for storage. A closet with a sliding door took up one wall of the room and inside was a pillow and a blanket. The door took up one wall and bare shelves lined the other two.

"This is the best I can do" Jacque said, waving his arm in the direction of the closet. "Of course this space is only for when someone comes into the infirmary. Otherwise you can be in the main room and use one of the hammocks. I will give you some comfortable clothes for the crossing. You can put the clothes you are wearing on the shelf in the closet."

The two men went back into the main room of the infirmary. It was a small space but well organized, with a table, two chairs, a two drawer filing cabinet and two hammocks, strung from the ceiling against opposite walls. The six foot table had multiple uses as an examining table, operating table and several times a day as a dining table. A sideboard held medical supplies and several bottles of various sizes and colors. They contained lotions, potions and a variety of French wines and liqueurs. The top drawer held a few pieces of cutlery, the lower one contained a tablecloth, a blanket, and rolls of bandages. A large black medical bag sat on the floor under the table.

Oskar began to undress as Jacque handed him a rumpled shirt and trousers. They were obviously not Jacque's as he was several inches shorter than Oskar and these clothes just fit.

"We sail at 10 pm?' Oskar inquired and Jacque nodded. Now both men were more relaxed. The code had been understood. Jacque told Oskar that the captain and first mate were not aware of Oskar's presence but there were two other crewmen aboard who were. One of these trusted men would bring food from the galley and there was a "head' right by the infirmary. Oskar was to be very careful before going out into the "gangway" to use it.

"If you get seasick use this bucket." Jacque said as he pointed to a metal pail next to the medical bag. "Better take it back into the other room with you in case you can't come out for a while." As it turned out, Oskar made much use of the pail during the ten day journey.

He spent most of each day looking through the lists of survivors among the stacks of newspapers he had brought. It was frustrating and unbelievable that the names he sought were not on any of the lists he had seen so far. Hedy and his sisters had disappeared. He read and reread the names, but the ones he was looking for just were not there.

Jacque spent his days wandering around the ship to forestall any visits to the infirmary.

The man who brought the meals waited for Jacque and Oskar to eat and then took away the dishes. He never spoke just watched. The rumor on the ship was that the eccentric doctor liked a silent partner to join him at mealtime. Oskar thought of Yusef. Where had he found the willpower to be silent for five years? Oskar would always miss him.

Chapter 21

The ship rocked gently as it left New York harbor and headed south by south east, following the route that Columbus had taken four hundred years ago. After the third day at sea, Oskar finally put away the newspaper lists he had brought with him. Since his presence on the ship was not to be revealed to anyone except the three men involved with his transport, he had to remain in the cabin. He and the doctor began to have long conversations after dinner. The brandy from the sideboard undoubtedly helped to loosen their tongues and allowed their minds to expand. Oskar had not partaken of much alcohol for several years. Not so much because of the Moslem prohibition but because he had to keep a clear head and besides he didn't really like the taste or the feeling of losing control.

Now he was "under the care of a doctor" as Jacque was fond of reminding him and the doctor prescribed sipping brandy after dinner as was the custom in France. It was during these late night conversations that Oskar learned about the organization for which he had been working for so many years. The two other men on ship who knew of his mission were also part of the Mossad, the Jewish secret service. The exact number of agents was only known to the top commanders, but they were bringing arms and Jewish immigrants into British Mandated Palestine.

Oskar learned just how difficult and complicated this smuggling process was for the small number of brave and dedicated men and women who worked tirelessly to fulfill the Zionist dream. The British Mandate government had implemented a diabolical plan to keep the Jews of Europe out of Palestine. The number of Jews allowed into Palestine was very limited since that entry required a passport issued by the traveler's country of origin as well as a validated visa allowing travel across borders. Since the Jews who had survived the hell of the concentration camps had no identity papers or any other proof of who they were (just the numbers tattooed on their forearm) they were not legally eligible to enter Palestine. The British set up a naval blockade to keep out the shiploads of refugees that headed for the port of Haifa. When the ships were caught trying to evade the blockade the passengers were sent, by the thousands, to internment camps on the Greek island of Cyprus, surrounded once again by barbed wire fencing and guard towers, or sent back to D.P. Camps in Germany and Austria.

The explanation the British gave for this criminal action was that Palestine was not equipped to absorb so many people. At the same time there was no limit to how many immigrants could enter Palestine from Arab countries (as long as they were not Jewish) and these people were actually encouraged to come with no worry about an absorption problem. These Arab immigrants were allowed to bring or later import armaments, at the same time if a Jew were found with a weapon it meant prison. For reasons that are difficult to understand, the British and, by cooperating with their policies, the rest of the so-called civilized world, wanted to keep Jews out of the Middle East, where they actually had originated.

The Atlantic Ocean could be rough, especially after leaving the coast of Cuba behind. The cargo of medical supplies was well packed. The crates of glass vials, test tubes and microscope slides from the Corning Company were checked and rechecked to make certain that they did come loose in the cargo area. Keeping the cargo safe was a high priority for the one man aboard who knew the true contents of the cargo and the identity of the stowaway and he had orders to abandon ship at the slightest chance of discovery.

Oskar gave in to seasickness for the next four days until they finally anchored off the coast of the Azores Islands. While some of the sailors rowed ashore for supplies, Oskar glimpsed a few palm trees waving in the wind. He longed to be on dry land.

Eventually the small freighter entered the Mediterranean Sea through the Straights of Gibraltar. The massive cliffs were an awesome sight, but Oskar could hardly see the top from the small porthole in the infirmary.

There would be another five or six days at sea, however the Mediterranean was not as wild as the Atlantic and the rest of the trip would be more comfortable.

The long nights were filled with conversation. Jacque and Oskar spent many hours discussing the dire situation of the hundreds of thousands of displaced persons. These people, who had lost everything and now existed in the world like new born babies. They had no homes, no family members, no identity papers. Their lives had to be recreated from scratch. For many it was like landing on another planet since they did not know the language of the people who were giving them orders and trying to help them.

The adults, they agreed, those that had an education or a skill would eventually make a living for themselves, hopefully in the new Jewish State. The children, many born in captivity (rape was a favorite indoor and outdoor sport for Nazis) had by and large no one to care for them. They had no education, were undernourished to the extent of not being able to learn even if there had been a school. Many of the orphans were mentally and emotionally disturbed, as anyone would be who had lived in fear and terror all their life.

The two men gave much thought to what should be done when the Jews finally had their land. Dr. Jacque already had an offer from the Teknion in Haifa to join the medical research department. As soon as the British blockade was lifted he would thank the French captain for giving him refuge, saving him from the Gestapo round up in Marseilles, then abandon ship and head for that research laboratory.

When Jacque talked about this future, his blue eyes shone with pleasure. He envisioned a classroom of eager, youngsters, listening intently as he taught a lesson in chemistry and how one or the other of them would find a cure for a devastating disease.

Now that Oskar's seasickness had subsided he was able to keep the food down that was being brought to the infirmary and only one time during the voyage did he need to hide in the storage room closet. That was when the Captain came to the infirmary with a cut in his hand sustained during the rough crossing of the Atlantic. At that time Oskar took the bucket with him with the fierce hope that he would not need to use it. Retching can be noisy. After more than an hour in the closet, Oskar decided that he was satisfied with his height after all. Being a little under six feet meant that he had space to stretch out his legs.

That night, as he sat in the closet, he overheard the Captain and the Doctor talking. The captain was looking forward to seeing his wife and young sons living in Marseilles. Then he conversationally asked Jacque if he had plans to see his family there.

Jacque's voice was low as he answered, but Oskar could hear him clearly as he told the captain what had happened when he went back to his apartment in Marseilles after the war.

"The neighborhood looked just as I left it in the summer of 1943. Before I reached the apartment building where we had lived, a woman who had known us came up to me. She started to cry and then blurted out 'They are dead! I am so sorry Dr. Morgenstein, so very sorry.' Then she ran away. I did not go up to the apartment. I went to the police station to make enquiries. I was told that the French police officers who had come to arrest my beautiful wife for the crime of being Jewish, tried to rape her. My wife started to fight them off and in the struggle her neck was broken. There were several witnesses who saw the policemen throw her body into the river. My four year old daughter ran after them and they threw her into the river after her mother." The doctor's voice began to shake with barely controlled rage. The captain cleared his throat, not able to speak. "The bodies were never recovered. The officer at the station told me the men responsible had been killed by a mob after the war. I wonder?"

Jacque's voice stopped abruptly as he choked back a sob. Then in an even, controlled voice he said. "Keep the bandage dry. I will come to your cabin tomorrow to change it." Oskar heard the cabin door close as the captain went out. Then Jacque called to Oskar, "All clear. Come have a brandy with me."

Those were the last words Jacque spoke to Oskar until they reached Haifa three days later.

During that night Jacque became delirious. Oskar was awakened by shouts that filled the small room. Over and over the same words came hurtling out of Jacque's distorted mouth. "You bitches! You fiends! You monsters! You could have hidden them, saved them."

For a few minutes he would be quiet and Oskar thought he was asleep. Then the screaming would start over again. During the day the doctor thumbed through his medical journals, stopped to eat, sip brandy and stared into space.

When the freighter docked in Haifa Harbor the British officials came aboard to search the cargo. The boxes that were stamped, LABORATORY EQUIPMENT – FRAGILE, were, according to the manifest, designated for the Teknion University's research department and were loaded on trucks without delay and sent on their way up the steep road to their destination. The other cargo was meticulously searched box by box. While the search proceeded through the night another ship anchored about a mile off shore, out of sight of the port but within rowing distance from a beach. The residence of a nearby fishing village slept while row boats were being readied to approach the anchored freighter, which was flying a Dutch flag. All through that night the small boats were rowed back and forth. The moon intermittently provided some light as dark forms scurried ashore. Some carried armloads of precious guns, while some of the others carried precious children to their homeland.

In the infirmary of the "Vent Amide" Oskar shaved off the bushy mustache he had grown during the voyage and donned the three piece suit he had brought aboard in New York. The doctor took the newspapers out of his attaché case, replacing them with expired insurance claim forms and a current copy of the insurance contract that he had brought from the captain's cabin the night before. The men knew that eventually the customs inspectors would come to search all the cabins and they must act swiftly. It was daylight when Oskar, attaché case in hand and winter coat over his other arm, climbed quickly up the stairs to the main deck and walked confidently down the gangplank to the dock. The British guard stopped him and asked for his passport, inspected it briefly while Oskar waved to the light blue sedan parked near the end of the gangplank. The driver wore a fez and a loose shirt, his mustache drooped almost to his shoulders. Without looking at Oskar he made circles with his thumbs and forefingers, holding them up to his eyes for a split second. Yanshoof Insurance Company was painted on the door of the sedan in black letters on a white square. After the guard returned the passport, Oskar walked quickly along the few feet of the dock and stepped into the car.

The sun was coming up over the mountain behind the Baha'i Temple when the car pulled into the garage under the four story building that housed the local Mossad headquarters, disguised as a marine insurance company, owned by a sheik in Beirut.

Chapter 22

After a change of clothing to a white cotton shirt, loose black trousers and leather sandals, Oskar sat through five hours of debriefing, which was concerned mostly with the United Nations Conference and descriptions of the men he met while he was there.

Finally, towards late afternoon he was free to make his way to Cabbabir, the Ahmadi enclave on the outskirts of Haifa. The small village was situated on a bluff near the oldest part of Haifa. A dusty road ran down the middle of the business section. This area was made up of open stalls selling fruits, vegetables, and fish. Towards the end of the street were several brick buildings with real storefronts and apartments on the second floor. These buildings, where the proprietors lived above their businesses, were called "shop houses." A sign on one of these storefronts read "Salim's Carpet Emporium." A wide arched doorway, flanked by tall showcase windows, gave the establishment an air of grandeur. Inside the high ceilings were interrupted by a skylight that let in the bright daylight that brought out the vivid colors of the carpets that were draped over counters and sofas scattered around the room. Groups of chairs were arranged around two small tables where customers were offered sweet apple tea or Turkish coffee.

Oskar stood in the doorway, enjoying the colorful scene. After eight days in the cramped infirmary he had a new appreciation for the sense of sight and the pleasure it could provide. The expression: "a feast for the eyes," had meaning for him now. Also being on firm ground again was a great relief, although he sometimes still felt the ship rocking under him.

A slim, gray haired man came towards Oskar at a leisurely pace, stopping to straighten the corner of a carpet here, flick a piece of lint off another there. He was slightly taller than Oskar and dressed in a long, pale green caftan with a rounded hat that resembled a turban. He took a quick look into a mirror that covered one wall, twirled the ends of his graying mustache before he turned to smile at Oskar, who was waiting for the older man to speak.

By the manner in which the young man stood in the doorway, Salim, the proprietor of the Carpet Emporium doubted he was a customer so he reached out his hand in a gesture that suggested they shake hands, and said, "My name is Salim, I am the owner of this shop. Do you wish to see anything special?"

Oskar took a moment to evaluate the man in front of him. His voice was soft, clear with an honest, forthright tone. Then Oskar extended his hand, saying, "I am Oskar Menkes and I am looking for Amah, she called me Omar."

Salim's smile widened with pleasure. "She will be overwhelmed with joy to see you, as I am also." He said with unmistakable sincerity. "You will find her in the clothing shop next door. She designs the garments that are appreciated all over the world. Go, go to her." He urged Oskar. "I will come along after I put my assistant in charge."

Oskar had passed a women's clothing store on his way to the entrance of the carpet shop. Now he stopped to admire the tasteful display in the window. As he walked inside he saw a woman near his own age, with jet black hair pulled back into a neat bun, arranging a rack of blouses. Her smile reminded him of Salim and he guessed she must be his daughter. She greeted him in English, looking a little puzzled to see a man in the ladies' store. "What can I show you?" she asked in a soft, low tone. Oskar hesitated before answering because he wanted a little time to just look at this lovely woman, whom he was fairly certain, was his stepsister. She waited while he looked around the shop, hoping to see Amah.

"Is Amah here?" he asked at last. At the sound of her name Amah came in from a back room. It took her a moment to recognize Oskar as it had been over two years since she had seen him. In the next moment they were in a tearful embrace, quietly standing in the center of the store. Then Amah stood back and gazed up at her son. "Omar, this is Salim's daughter, Yadira." She said gesturing toward the slim young woman who was almost as tall as Oskar. Yadira came forward, holding out her hand just as Salim came into the store. He beamed at the three people standing in a circle holding hands. He embraced each of them in turn before herding them into the back room to have afternoon tea.

Amah explained that Omar's legal name was Oskar, but she would always think of him as Omar. Salim and Yadira agreed that would be his name among the family as far as they were concerned. Then Omar /Oskar told them as much as he was allowed about his trip to New York. Everyone knew about the resolution to partition Palestine and the hope was that there would be a peaceful border between the two new states that were envisioned by this process. The Jews had a government ready to take over and were recruiting an army, to be called the Haganah, (Later the Israeli Defense Forces) to protect the new state of Israel. Oskar told his family that he would not be returning to Cairo. "The Mufti was told that I am in Jerusalem, where I will fight for my people. Of course he doesn't know exactly who my people really are." Oskar smiled ruefully. "He is evil incarnate. I still can't believe I didn't assassinate him when I had the chance."

Salim had many questions about the Grand Mufti and the Arab League. "Was it true that they would refuse to recognize the new state even after the United Nations had voted for its establishment?"

Oskar, who knew the plans that were already in place to destroy the fledgling State of Israel on the very day of its inception, decided to be as brutally honest as possible about the situation.

"As you know the Grand Mufti has been telling the Arabs who live in the Jewish designated area of Palestine to leave their homes and go to the borders of the five countries that surround it. As soon as the new state is declared, the five countries bordering it will deploy their armies to annihilate every vestige of the Zionists. Then the Arab refugees are to return to their homes and reclaim their property. Many people have already left for the primitive camps that were set up to house them until after the war."

Salim, shaking his head in disbelief, added "The Grand Mufti is the highest religious leader in the Muslim world. He is telling Muslims to kill all Jews? This is against the teachings of Mohamed and the writings in the Koran."

"The Ahmadis are not leaving their homes. We feel safer under the Zionists than we ever did under a Moslem Government." Amah declared.

Oskar continued, "Many Arabs are blindly obeying the Mufti, just as the German people obeyed Hitler, which was totally against their own self interest, and in the process caused the destruction of Europe. The Middle East will be a wasteland if the Mufti and his minions succeed."

Later that evening the conversation turned to more pleasant subjects as they ate roast lamb, with vegetables from Amah's garden and rice, fragrant with the spices that Oskar had missed. Amah, Salim and Yadira took a long time saying good-by to Oskar. They told him they would pray for his safe return to them. Oskar promised to come back for Christmas, which was not an Ahmadi holiday but which they acknowledged since Mohamed recognized Jesus as an important teacher.

Chapter 23

When Hedy arrived behind the Allied lines that spring of 1945 she had no idea of what to expect next. While she was in the truck with Yusef she had felt safe, but now she was standing next to the truck as it pulled away. Seven boys stood around her watching her silently. From the few words that had been spoken on the long ride to this Displaced Persons Camp she learned that the boys were all Polish and they had been hiding in the forest after escaping a Nazi round up. Hedy assumed they were Jewish from the slang they used. Two of the boys were older, which could be discerned from the fuzz on their faces, but the other five looked to be pre-teen or younger.

She knew by the way the boys talked about her and speculated about her origins that they took her for a boy. That was fine with Hedy and she was not about to enlighten them about her gender. It seemed safer to be a boy for now. What was alarming, and could prove dangerous was that they thought she was a German. She had not thought about how she was dressed until one of the boys referred to her as a "Pifke Pig" (a derogatory term used by non-German Europeans to designate Germans).

Hedy was wearing a Hitler Youth uniform, and even though Yusef had cut off all the swastikas, there was no mistaking the brown shirt and military cap. The collar of the shirt was ringed in dried bloodstains, which scratched her neck. She felt very vulnerable standing in the open area, surrounded by the hostile looking boys, so Hedy began to devise a believable story that would, hopefully, save her life. There were people approaching from a tent covered field below them. As the little group had been ordered to stay there and wait, they did not move away from the spot. Hedy began to speak in Polish, keeping her voice down in her throat with the hope of sounding masculine.

"I've been hiding for two years in the garden of a big villa. My parents were Polish and were rounded up while we were visiting Berlin. I got away and found this garden, stole food from the villa kitchen and also a big knife." At the word "knife" the boys looked more interested. Hedy went on, "One day during a bombing raid a boy about my size came out of the villa and backed up into the hollow tree where I was hiding. He didn't even see me when I grabbed him by the hair and before he could turnaround I slit his throat with the big knife. My clothes were falling apart so I stripped him, put on his clothes and started to walk out of Berlin. I met up with a German deserter and he took me to the British army."

The boys were impressed and when Hedy showed them the bloodstains around the collar they believed her story.

"Where's the knife?" asked Samuel, the tallest and obvious leader of the group.

"The British soldiers took it away from me" Hedy explained. "I had a hell of a time convincing them I wasn't German."

By now the greeting committee had reached the road where the group of boys waiting for them. "What's your name?" Samuel asked Hedy.

She had given that matter some thought so she replied without hesitation, "Zev." (Hebrew for "Wolf".)

Then the three Red Cross ladies were standing among them. "Come along." One of the women said in English and the eight boys straggled along behind the women. As they got nearer to the tents they could see long lines of people snaking around each tent. It was late afternoon by then and they were hoping there would be food at the end of the lines.

Hedy was thirsty and needed to relieve her bowels.

"Save my place." She told Samuel and walked a little way behind a tree, hoping that no one would follow her. When she got back to the group she noticed that the line around the tents had not moved an inch. It was getting dark and beginning to rain. The eight Polish boys huddled together in an effort to stay warm. Two men came walking up to them. They began to talk quietly in Polish. "Do you want to go back to Poland?' one of the men asked no one in particular. They all shook their heads in unison. "It's warm and dry in Palestine" said the other man, casually lighting a cigarette.

Eight pairs of eyes looked up with interest. "Want to go there now?" was the next question.

A unanimous "yes" was murmured and came out as if in one voice.

"Your carriage awaits you," said the taller of the two men. Pointing up the small incline where they could see the outline of a wagon.

"Who are you?" Samuel asked in a suspicion tone.

"Bricha!" was the curt answer.

The boys had evidently heard the name before. It meant "escape" in Hebrew and it was an underground organization that smuggled the survivors of the death camps to Palestine.

With the help of many sympathetic Europeans and worldwide Jewish organizations they had been successful in getting people through the British blockade and into Palestine. Even when ships were intercepted and the half dead passengers were interred in camps on the Greek Island of Cyprus or in Palestine itself, "Bricha" managed to help people escape and find refuge in what would soon be Eretz Israel. (The Land of Israel.)

Discerning a little hesitation among the youngsters, he pointed toward the tent nearest to the road. "This is the longest line. It's for registering. It takes forever to get through that process. Each person tells their story and tries to convince the organizers that they are really Jews. Of course it is easier for the boys. They just show them their pricks."

Everyone within earshot chuckled. Then one of the boys asked the question that was on all their minds. "Do they pass out food?"

"Eventually" was the answer from the taller man., "But it could take until morning. "

The other older boy looked at Samuel and then down at the ground. "I'm staying here in the camp." Samuel looked at him sternly. "I need you, Saul." Samuel pleaded

Saul spoke in a low, but firm voice. "I need to go and register. My family will be looking for me. They won't find me if I go with you."

Samuel nodded. "Keep Hans-Peter with you." He said, going over to the smallest boy who was nine years old, but looked to be six, "He is too young to fight just yet." Hans-Peter allowed Samuel to put his little hand into Saul's big paw and like the child he had not been since he was five years old, he allowed himself to be led down the incline toward the long and very slow moving line.

The five remaining boys and Hedy looked at Samuel. "Let's go!" He commanded.

The men led the way back to the road where the hay wagon now stood with two sway backed horses in harness. The driver was slumped on the front seat, barely visible in the dusk and shadow of the piled up hay.

"Get in." They were told. "There are blankets and canteens of water, Get some rest.

As the boys climbed into the hay the rain stopped and the clouds parted to reveal a bright half moon. By the light of the moon they found the canteens and the neatly stacked blankets at the back of the pile of hay. They passed around the canteens and after several of them peed off the back of the wagon they paired up under the four blankets. The two men from Bricha piled hay over them and they were on their way, once again to an unknown destination and an unknown future.

Hedy was having second thoughts. Had she made the

right choice? It was too late now to change her mind. Samuel had bundled her into a blanket with him. "Zev, how old are you?" he asked. Hedy told him she thought she might be 14 by now but had lost track of time. He seemed satisfied with the answer and in a few minutes all six of the youngsters were asleep.

The wagon rolled westward then toward a southerly direction for much more than the two hours that had been mentioned. It was daylight when it pulled into a dense forest. The rutted trail was just wide enough for the wagon. The horses drew the wagon into a small clearing. At the edge, near the forest, stood a thatch roofed cottage with a larger barn looming up behind it. With a loud shout of "whoa" from the driver the wagon came to a stop. The passengers awoke and shook off the hay and the blankets. It had been the longest, uninterrupted sleep they had experienced in several years. One by one they jumped down from the back of the wagon. They had been told to leave the blankets in the hay, so now they stood shivering in the early morning chill. The driver drove the wagon towards the barn, while the taller of the two men addressed the six huddled figures.

"My name is Avi." He said in Polish. "You all know it means 'my father' in Hebrew?" He asked. Six heads nodded. Then he pointed to the shorter man, whose black, curly hair was escaping from under a woolen cap. "This is Moshe, and you all know who he was?" The six heads nodded again. The smell of cooking came into the air and Hedy's stomach began to growl. Soon the hunger pangs drove all fear from her mind and she asked Avi.

"Can we eat soon?" in such a plaintive voice that he could be seen to flinch.

"Line up here." Avi ordered, pointing to a rain barrel next to the cottage door. "We will wash hands, one by one and go inside." The boys did as they were told. Some said the brocha (prayer) for washing hands before a meal. This was something they had not done since they were snatched away from their homes.

Inside the cottage there was a big table, surrounded by nine chairs of different styles and sizes. The bare stone floor was polished to a shine and it glowed in the light of a blazing fire in a fireplace against the back wall and a kerosene lamp on a sideboard. The two windows, one on each side of the door were covered with blackout curtains. The fireplace would be damped to embers now that it was daylight, to avoid any smoke going up the chimney.

A plump, gray haired woman stood by the fireplace, stirring a big pot. It smelled heavenly. She gestured for them all to sit, then spoke to Moshe in a language Hedy didn't understand, although it sounded Polish. One of the boys was Czech and understood what she had said. "I'm Janus." He said in Czech. "I'll get the bowls." And he proceeded to the sideboard to get the bowls and spoons, distributing them around the table with Moshe while the others all took seats. Avi remained standing by the door.

Just then the driver of the hay wagon came in, removed hat and cloak, hanging them on a hook beside the door. To her surprise, Hedy saw that the driver was a young woman. She wondered if she should reveal her identity, but decided against it. She watched the driver put her arms around Avi's waist and turn her face up to be kissed. Hedy felt her heart give a painful squeeze as she thought of Omar.

While the younger woman held the pot, the older woman started ladling the soup into the waiting bowls. Soon the sound of eating filled the room. Moshe passed around a platter filled with slices of freshly baked rye bread, smeared generously with chicken fat. It was a feast. Avi still stood by the door watching them eat, his arm loosely around the young woman. "This is Marta." He said in Polish. Marta raised a hand in greeting "She speaks French, Romanian, Austrian and a little Polish and is learning Hebrew."

"I speak a little English also," Marta added as she pushed her black tangled curls out of her face. Marta was not a pretty girl by any measure. Her nose was long with a slight hook at the end, her narrow face almost disappeared in the mop of black hair that surrounded it. Her big, black eyes were her best feature. They shone with intelligence and an awareness of everything and everyone around her.

Avi released Marta and she went back outside. The faces around the table looked towards Avi expectantly. He brushed both palms over his soft, blond hair. (A gesture they would come to recognize as a preface to an announcement.)

"We will be staying here for another day to wait for more members to join us and for the supplies we will need. The plans for getting to Eretz Israel must be flexible. We will need to adapt to circumstances as they arise on a daily basis. Your sleeping quarters are in the barn in the loft above the horses. Follow Moshe, he will show you the way." Avi gestured for them to leave. The older woman cleared the table while Avi went to a wall cupboard, took out a roll of maps and spread them out on the table.

Moshe led the newcomers into the dimly lit barn. The only light was coming through the gaps between the walls and the roof. A ladder led up to the hay loft and he climbed up, urging the boys to follow him. They saw blankets strews about in the piled up hay.

A shelf along one wall was lined with boots and a stack, of what looked like, clean socks, was piled up at one end. They all stood waiting for Moshe to speak and as the last boy, who happened to be Hedy, reached the loft, he pointed to the boots and spoke in Polish. "We will be doing a lot of hiking and you will need good boots. Among those, compliments of the German Whermacht, you should find a size that fits you, if yours need replacing. Those socks are clean and ready to wear, but wash your feet before you put them on." (Hedy remembered the column of German prisoners and now she knew why they were barefoot.)

Samuel grabbed Hedy's arm and pulled her to a corner, taking a blanket along with them. "Let's get some rest while we can." He said and lay down on the blanket. She noticed that he, like herself, already had on a sturdy pair of boots. Hedy didn't lie down as Samuel had indicated but shook her head and climbed back down the ladder. The wagon and horses were not there. She wandered outside and was greeted by the sight of two boys having a peeing contest to see who could hit the barn from the farthest distance. They called to her to join them and she waved a friendly greeting as she hurried past them towards the wooded slope below the barn.

After a walking a few yards she heard the sound of running water. She crossed a narrow patch of open meadow, brushed by a weeping willow tree and saw the creek. The water ran swiftly over a rocky bottom, but just under the willow branches there was a shallow pool. Hedy remembered what Jasmin had said about very cold water being the best for removing blood. She took off the bloodstained shirt, then sat on the river bank, removing her boots and sock she put her toes into the icy stream. Then she swished the shirt collar through the pool of water. She didn't want to wash the whole shirt as it would take too long to dry. As she expected, most of the blood disappeared immediately and soon all trace of it was gone. She laid the shirt on the grass to dry. The morning clouds had parted and the late spring sun felt warm on her back. On an impulse Hedy took off the trousers and waded into the pool. The water came up to her knees. It was cold, but felt wonderful. She made a decision and took off the cotton underwear. Slowly she lowered herself into the water. Every pore screamed at the shock. Hedy had to clench her teeth hard to keep from screaming out loud. Once she was sitting on the smooth rocks at the bottom it took only a few seconds for the shock to diminish. At once she felt exhilarated, energized and clean.

She let the river flow slowly past her, remembering the orthodox women who went to the "Mikvah" (ritual bath) each month to cleanse their bodies, (and perhaps their souls) in running water. She thought about dunking herself totally, as was customary, but she had not taken off the hat that hid her short hair, since Yusef had set it firmly on her head. It was best to keep it on for now. When her teeth began to chatter, Hedy got out of the stream, used her underwear to dry off and put the damp garments back on. She pulled on the trousers and lay down next to the brown shirt, gazing up at the patches of blue sky playing hide and seek with the clouds. She felt a sense of peace and freedom and began to doze when she felt a shadow over her face. A man was standing over her. She reached for the shirt and sat up, struggling into the sleeves and fumbling for buttons.

Moshe squatted down, supporting himself on the barrel of his rifle with one hand. He was at eye level with Hedy. She saw amusement in his eyes and in his smile.

"So, Zev" he said softly. "You are really a Zev-evah?" (Hebrew for "Wolverine".) It was not really a question. He saw her draw back with a look of alarm on her face. Her eyes were dark blue with fear.

Slowly Moshe put down his gun and sat cross-legged facing her. "Relax little Zev-evah" he soothed. "You are among Jews. We respect and protect females. We are also Zionists which means we consider all humans have equal value." He put out his hand to take one of hers and he saw she was trembling. He touched her hand gently. "I have a teenage daughter. She lives in Haifa and goes to University." His tone was conversational.

Hedy finally looked at him and saw that there was considerable gray in the dark curls that were receding from his forehead. She put on her socks and boots then waited to see if he had anything more to say, then stood up. With a little grunt Moshe untangled his legs and reached for the rifle to help brace him as he got to his feet.

"My name is Hedwig Mandel," Hedy told him, before he had a chance to ask. "I want to get out of Europe as soon as possible, and be among people I can trust." She looked up into Moshe's understanding gaze and without even thinking about what she was doing allowed him to enfold her in his welcoming arms. Briefly she thought of her father and she felt Moshe's arms tighten as she fought back the sudden tears. In a few moments they were walking back to the barn.

Moshe stopped Hedy at the door. "You will be more comfortable sharing quarters with Marta. Come with me !" he ordered. She followed him to the cottage and into a small room.

There was a set of bunk beds with hooks at the foot end. A window faced the door. Two people were obviously sharing this room. Seeing her doubts, Moshe said, "Avi and Marta will not be back until tomorrow. So make yourself at home here until then."

Hedy noticed a Polish-Hebrew dictionary on a little table and several text books on the floor by each bed. Moshe followed her glance. "Hebrew will be our national language. The sooner you start learning it the better," he said.

"I went to Hebrew school." Hedy said.

"So you have a head start." Moshe chuckled. "Dinner will be in two hours. Start studying." He left Hedy in the room, closing the door behind him. Hedy looked around the room and saw a small mirror on the wall by the door. She had not seen herself with short hair. She took off the cap and shook out her hair. She liked what she saw. The girl in the mirror looked modern and older than her seventeen years. Slowly the realization came to her that she was alone in a room for the first time in what she estimated to be three years. It was a strange feeling to know that no one was watching her or would observe whatever she decided to do. Not until that moment had she known the value of privacy. She stood in front of the mirror for a long time, wondering if her family and Konstanza would recognize her. She pushed back the fear and sadness that threatened to overwhelm her and began to seriously peruse the Polish-Hebrew dictionary until a knock on the door summoned her to the kitchen.

Late that night Avi and Marta came back with more

young survivors. Avi went to sleep in the barn while the two girls slept in the beds. In the morning Marta explained to Hedy that she and Avi were going out one more time to collect another group of young people before they would all leave the cottage.

"You must get all the rest and nourishment you can." Marta warned her in French. "The mountain pass to Italy is very high. It will take all your strength to endure the climb. "

After Marta left the next morning, Hedy spent the day in the meadow by the stream, reading the dictionary and listening to the birds. That evening she continued studying by the light of the kerosene lamp. Being alone in the little room was still a new delight.

Marta and Avi made one more trip and then it was time to prepare for the departure to Italy. Marta and the owner of the cottage stayed behind to care for two of the boys who were much too weak to make the journey. "We will be back for you this summer." Avi assured them as the twenty young people set off on foot.

Chapter 24

Much to Hedy's relief there were two girls, near her own age, among the group that had arrived two days after she had. Neither of them spoke Polish. Marlena was French and Vera was Czech but they all knew a little Hebrew and were able to communicate.

The trek across the Italian Alps was arduous. Progress was slow as the fifteen boys and three girls were not experienced mountain climbers, not even occasional hikers. Most of them had spent their days sitting in a classroom even when they were in the Nazi Ghettos. The starvation diet in the various camps before liberation had weakened them further. As the group wound their way up through the "Smuggler's Pass" which the narrow trail was aptly called by the locals, a sheer cliff dropped 300 feet on their right and a solid wall of rock loomed up on their left. A space of a few inches on either side of the trail left a very small area for maneuvering around the many switchbacks. One misstep meant a plunge down the cliff. The group trudged slowly, carefully in single file.

Avi led the way, as he knew the trail. Samuel was in the center of the line and Moshe guarded the rear with the three girls and some of the smaller boys in front of him.

Moshe ordered a rest stop every two hours (he was the only one with a watch) and everyone sat down carefully and drank a small amount of water from the canteens. They proceeded in this manner night and day for three days, eating on the move. In the morning of the third day, they finally started the descent. This proved to be confusing and dangerous in the beginning as now the trail was flanked by a sheer wall on the right and the cliff dropped down on their left, They were getting lower with each step and the drop on their left was not as long. The younger boys were beginning to doze as they moved along when suddenly little Moritz, who was in front of Samuel, quietly fell headlong over the edge of the cliff. The column kept moving a few more feet until Moshe called out "halt!"

"Don't move!" Samuel spoke sternly, but he didn't dare shout. He peered cautiously over the edge and saw Moritz's inert body a hundred feet below the trail. There was nothing else to do but keep moving down until they reached the bottom of the trail. It took another six hours to get to a place where Samuel could make his way to Moritz.

He had been named Moritz by the others because he was small and mischievous like the boys in the children's stories, "Max & Moritz" who played, not so funny, pranks on the people in their village and were always in trouble with their elders.

When the group arrived at a place where they could all lie down, a grassy ledge near the bottom of the trail, Samuel began the slow climb over the rocks and boulders to where he hoped to find Moritz. Moshe offered to go with him but he was firm, he would go alone.

Samuel fought down the lump in his throat and the rage that burned in his chest. When he got near enough to see the crumpled form, the tears began to run down his cheeks and by the time he knelt over Moritz he was sobbing helplessly. He had thought that he had no more tears left in him, but he had been very wrong. Grief was like a bottomless pit and rage was like a whirlpool with no end. It dragged one down and then spun to the top and down again in an endless cycle.

Moritz lay in a heap, his neck clearly broken, his arms folded under him, not outstretched to stop the fall. He had not cried out perhaps because he was asleep. Samuel knelt beside the small form and thought about how they had met three years ago.

~

They had been loaded into the last car of a train of cattle cars, with 50 or so, other boys. Samuel had briefly thought about how he would probably not live to have a Bar Mitzvah after all. His father, who had been shot in front of him that morning, had always said. "All bad things that happen always have some good things come out of them." The only "good" that he could see was that he didn't have to go to Cheder (religious class) that morning, or ever again. He told himself. Samuel was past being afraid and made bets with himself about how long he would live. He had not wondered about where they were going or why. It was as if his mind had frozen and he managed to doze as the train rumbled along its way. The little boy next to him laid his tousled, blond head on Samuel's shoulder while Samuel braced himself against the back of the boy behind him. Eventually all the boys were lying on top of each other. They traveled like this for another day and night.

When they arrived at their destination they were herded off the train and noticed that they were the only group on the platform. The other cattle cars stood empty, the prisoners already dispersed. Then the boys were divided into groups by size. Each group was loaded into a truck and driven to a well guarded compound where they were herded into a large room. Before they knew what was happening they were told to strip, their heads were shaven and they were shoved into icy cold showers, given dry shirts and herded back into the large room, where they were told to stand facing the wall.

One by one the boys were taken away. Some were taken to a science project geared to gage their homosexual tendencies; the smaller ones were distributed to the commanding officers of the local garrison to be used as they pleased. Most of these younger boys were raped repeatedly and many of them bled to death. The older boys like Samuel (the lucky ones) were sent to barracks and became the burial brigade.

It was their job to dig graves for dead, and sometimes half dead, younger boys.

It was during one of these burial events, while Samuel and several others his age, were shoveling dirt into a ditch full of little bodies that the air raid siren began to blare. While the guards and the other boys ran for the barracks behind the fence, Samuel dropped his shovel and flung himself down into the ditch. The planes came roaring by and he lay very still until he felt something stir under him. He looked down to see the little, blond boy from the train. The planes kept coming for what seemed an interminable time. Samuel looked up over the ditch there was no one in sight. Beyond the ditch there was a meadow with tall grass. Very slowly the 13 year old Samuel dragged the nine year old, whom he would call Moritz, out of the ditch and into the tall grass.

"Can you crawl?" Samuel whispered. Moritz gave a slight nod.

Moritz seemed to be in fairly good condition. He had fainted during one of the ordeals which he was forced to endure. Thinking him dead his molester had thrown him on the pile of corpses on their way to burial.

The two boys inched along through the tall grass until they came to a stand of trees. Beyond the group of trees a dense forest awaited them and they began to run. They ran and ran until they couldn't run anymore. Samuel found a hollow log and they slept inside the damp, mushroom lined cavity until daylight. Once or twice during the night they woke to the sound of explosions in the distance, but fell asleep again immediately.

In the morning they ate berries and Moritz showed Samuel which mushrooms were edible. His mother, he told Samuel, had often taken him mushroom hunting. They had no idea of where they were. After two days they met some local Jewish boys who had run into the forest to hide from the Germans (and their Polish neighbors). They had a camp of sorts, and kept moving every couple of days. They stole food wherever they could. Water was not a problem, the forest had many streams. There was a road and they kept away from it, but went near enough to see what was being driven along it. They slept in hollow logs or used piles of leaves to keep warm. Each of the boys gave Moritz a piece of clothing, as he had been naked when they met him. The boys who knew the nearby village stole not only food but warm clothing. Little by little all seven of them had warm things to wear. In this way the boys survived two winters.

The other boys thought that Samuel and mischievous little Moritz were brothers and the two never denied it.

~

Now Samuel was kneeling beside the only brother he had ever known. He reached out to touch him, run gentle fingers over the numbers tattooed on his forearm. He wanted to say something, a prayer, a good-bye, something meaningful. There was nothing to say. This little man, who never did have a childhood, who helped them get through the toughest time of their tragic, young lives, with his jokes and harmless pranks, deserved a decent burial. Samuel, who had once been assigned to bury him, had to leave him for the buzzards. He did have the presence of mind to check if his boots were worth salvaging and decided they were much too worn out already.

Fifty years later Dr. Samuel Horowitz, who had three degrees in the study of psychology, was on an international board that was studying the psychological, emotional, spiritual as well as physical damage to victims of child sexual abuse. He had interviewed hundreds of victims who had been abused, sometimes for many years, by adult men, (many of them Catholic priests) whom they were meant to trust and look to for guidance. It was clear that there had been permanent damage that many of these victims could not overcome in order to live normal lives. There were two revelations that did not surprise Samuel. 1. That many victims of pedophiles

committed suicide near puberty. 2. After WWII a large number
of German officers were ordained into the Jesuit order of the
Catholic Church. It was during this study that Samuel became
certain that Moritz did not go over that cliff by accident.

Chapter 25

Avi and Moshe had studied the maps and listened to shortwave radio reports about the various battles still being fought in some areas of Austria and Italy. Finally the decision was made. The destination would be the port city of Genoa, famed for the place where Christopher Columbus had begun his life. The fervent hope was that they would all find passage on ships, evade the British blockade and arrive safely somewhere in Palestine.

They had made their way into Italy and it was decided they needed to split up and scatter into three different villages in the Italian countryside. The three girls and three of the younger boys stayed together and found a farm where two women were the sole survivors of the brutal war that had killed their husbands, their children and most of their livestock. The refugees offered to help with chores for food and a place to sleep. The women gestured that they had no food to spare, but the six youngsters could sleep in the empty chicken coop.

The girls found a broom and a shovel and began to clean the floor and make a place where they could lie down. The boys split up hoping to buy, beg or steal food. They came back with a grainy loaf of bread and two apples they had found in an abandoned basement. (The house was just a pile of bricks.)

One of the boys, who knew a few words of Italian, reported that the retreating Germans had taken every morsel of food they could find. If they caught someone hiding food from them, they shot them no matter who it was. Mostly women were shot for hiding food for their children, and the children for trying to defend their mothers.

The men had all been killed much earlier. First by the Americans as they advanced into Italy and then when Italy surrendered unilaterally, the Germans shot any Italian man they found.

There were many orphans and the Zionist youngsters were part of a much larger group of wandering and hungry children.

Avi and Moshe managed to keep their group of orphans in touch and moving along toward Genoa where one morning in early May, the twenty of them congregated outside of the city at a designated church. Church bells were ringing in every village in that whole area and the Cathedral bells of Genoa could be heard for miles around. An American army base was nearby and Avi sent Hedy (who spoke a little English) to beg for food. She encountered a jubilant celebration and ran the half mile back to the church to bring the news to the rest of the group.

The war in Europe was over. The Germans had surrendered unconditionally. The slaughter was ended except for the Jewish Poles who tried to return to their homes. Thousands were murdered with shovels, pitchforks, knives, scythes and axes, as the Christian Poles tried to finish what the Germans had left undone.

The original group stayed together for a few more days. It was uncanny to be able to walk the streets and roads without the roar of cannons or bombers filling the air. Each night Avi came back to the church, brought food and then took 3 or four of the youngsters with him to a waiting ship. When it was Hedy's turn to go, she left with two boys who were probably nine and ten years old. They were given papers that showed they were siblings, traveling to an uncle in Jaffa. The British allowed a few select Jewish orphans into Palestine, if they had a relative who would sponsor them. The stated reason for this policy was fear of overwhelming the absorption agencies. There was no limit on Arab or other immigrants.

~

The navy blue dress had white polka dots and a wide skirt that swirled around Hedy's bare legs. She had been handed a box, tied with metallic ribbon just before she was to board the ship by a woman from the Joint Distribution Committee. There was also a jaunty barrette that matched the dress, shoes near her size and a warm looking gray wool coat. The generous donors had included underwear, socks, a toothbrush and soap. Hedy took off the scarf she had worn for months and stuffed it into the coat pocket (one did not throw away anything that might be useful), and put the barrette on her tousled hair. She felt elegant. It was an outfit that her mother might have worn, accompanied by white gloves and a white purse. It had come in a 'Macy's of New York' dress box, which was now tucked under her arm and contained the shirt, pants and jacket from Berlin and Omar's toothbrush, a keepsake she would always cherish.

Hedy stood on the Genoa dock with her 'younger brothers' waiting for Avi to clear up some final details, when Samuel came walking up to her. "I came to say good-bye or rather '*la hit ra ot*', "till we meet again" in Hebrew. Then he added in Polish, "Hedy, I knew you were a girl the moment I saw you." An amused chuckle rumbled in his throat. Hedy was only a little surprised at the confession, but didn't know what else to say, so she put up a hand to his face and kissed him gently on the cheek. Samuel blushed like the shy boy he would always be.

"I'm going back with Avi," he announced. "They can use my help. Moshe is going with you on the ship." Then he was gone.

Moshe came up to the three small figures on the dock and guided them aboard the Greek steamship Ionia, headed for Haifa, Palestine. The voyage would be twice as long as could be expected for that distance.

Even before Hedy got to her cabin she found writing

paper and pencils as well as a chess set in the ship's salon. She would write a letter to Konstanza and mail it as soon as she herself had a return address and she resolved to teach her two 'little brothers' to play chess. She was a better teacher than player and by the time they reached Haifa she rarely won a match. Moshe came to the salon for an hour every day and gave all the children on the ship Hebrew lessons and then disappeared for the rest of the day.

Chess was not the only thing Hedy taught the two boys in her care. The small ship had been used as a ferry between Italy and Greece so had only six cabins, since most passengers slept on deck for the short trips. The cabins had four bunk beds each and there were two toilets, one at each end of the passage, to serve the twenty-four passengers. Getting the boys in her charge to use the water closet meant showing them how it worked, since these children had only used out houses previously and even those rarely. Each cabin did have a wash basin with one faucet which provided a trickle of water. Passengers were expected to bring their own soap and towel.

Fortunately, each of the refugees had been given a toiletry bag with a bar of soap and a wash cloth, (which none of them had ever seen before) which they called "American towel."

It was all Hedy could do to keep the boys and herself clean. Teeth brushing was a new skill that needed to be learned. The eight year old girl who shared their cabin took care of herself, but spent most of the days in her upper bunk sobbing. She spoke a language that no one understood and shook off all attempts to comfort her.

Eating in the dining room at set times with flatware and table manners was difficult for the boys who had lived like wild animals for several years. With patience and kindness Hedy coaxed her boys to be seated by the designated meal-time and showed them how to eat in a civilized manner. "Watch the other people." She admonished and it worked. However Hedy and many other passengers tended to stuff bread and fruit into their pockets before they left the table.

One day Moshe took Hedy aside and explained that this was not an acceptable practice. She was embarrassed because she knew that people did not behave this way in normal times. After months of starvation it seemed only natural to make certain they would have food in their pockets to forestall the agony of hunger pangs.

"We panic when we don't have food within reach," she explained. And Moshe understood and looked the other way. It was one of his most endearing traits.

The Ionia made slow progress along the coast of Italy and through the Straights of Messina, stopping near small fishing villages to buy food, supplies and water, Sometimes there were K-rations available from American soldiers who even had chocolate bars to spare. The Jewish Agency had leased the ship and provided funds for further expenses like bribes. Each of the Displaced Persons would get a five-pound note when leaving the ship.

The twenty-four documented passengers that had walked up the gangplank in Genoa and would disembark in Haifa Harbor were serving as decoys. The majority of people aboard were being smuggled into their own homeland. Port by port the number of young men in the cargo hold increased and as the ship reached the shores of Palestine the numbers dwindled as they were rowed ashore or even swam to reach the nearby kibbutzim or Youth Aliyah villages.

Aside from keeping the boys clean and getting them to the dining room on time, Hedy seldom saw the two 'little brothers', who for the first time in their young lives could romp around freely. No one was going to take them away, lock them up or beat them.

Max, who had been the mischief-making partner of Moritz, was the ringleader and Daniel was a willing accomplice. If Max felt sorrow or pain after the death of his friend, Moritz, he gave no sign of it. When he had been assigned to travel with Hedy and Daniel, who was a year older, he only nodded his agreement and played his part.

Aboard the Ionia there were many areas marked "NO ADMITTANCE' which did not stop the boys from exploring the engine room, the radio room and even the bridge, where the crew was kept busy making certain that handles, knobs and wheels were not disturbed by busy, young hands. The doors marked "HIGH VOLTAGE' were kept locked.

There were the numerous ladders marked, "KEEP OFF", which were invitations to climb them to wherever they led. Even the chimney ladder was not off limits to the intrepid twosome. It was lucky for them that a blast from the ship's horn had not caused them to lose their footing just as they reached the top.

One day Max invented a game with the deck chairs. First they jumped over one chair and after mastering that feat they lined up two chairs for the next jump. Soon some of the crew were getting into the game and bets were being made about how many chairs could be cleared in one jump. In the process several chairs were broken, clothes were torn, and although there were no broken bones there was some bleeding that left permanent stains on the deck. At the captain's orders this game was not repeated.

The two rascals used the life boats for a game they called "HIDING FROM THE BRITISH" which they would soon be playing in earnest. It was while hiding in the lifeboat that they got an idea for a prank that would give them cause for regret. One day while the noon meal was being served, Max ran into the dining room screaming, "Man overboard! Daniel fell overboard! He's gone!"

The deck crew and many of the passengers ran to the spot from where Max told them Daniel had fallen into the sea. The crew threw life preserver rings and the captain gave orders to launch a life boat. As the life boat was being uncovered in preparation for being lowered, Daniel's grinning face appeared over the edge.

Max and Daniel spent an uncomfortable hour standing in front of the captain while he lectured them on the etiquette of the sea, reprimanded them for their thoughtlessness, and ordered them to remain in their cabin except for meals and lessons.

They had not understood the words, but there was no doubt about the captain's meaning. They were impressed by the fact that this important man had taken the time to talk to them like responsible human beings and astonished that they would not be severely beaten. As a result of the brutality they had experienced they had lost all respect for authority, but this captain had earned their respect with his kindness and decency.

Chapter 26

The weeping girl in Hedy's cabin had not left her bunk for three days, except for a trip to the lavatory. She did not respond to questions or attempts to comfort her. Hedy decided to consult Moshe to see if he could find out what language she might understand.

"I'll come to the cabin after breakfast," he told Hedy in Hebrew. Then he went to the purser's desk where all the registered passengers had left their passports and relevant papers. Moshe showed the purser his credentials, then asked to see the papers from the passenger in cabin 4 bunk # 1.

There was an Italian passport, an entry visa to Palestine (easily granted to anyone who was not Jewish) indicating that Yolanda Russo was Catholic and a letter from the priest, Father Geraldo, for the purser of the Ionia, relaying her father's instructions and a receipt for half of the fare.

The purser was Greek and he could read English, but knew only a smattering of Italian. He understood that he was to deliver the little girl to her parents when the ship arrived in Haifa, but little else of the explanation in the letter.

Moshe told the purser that according to the priest's letter, her parents had left her and her little brother in the care of her maternal grandparents while they established a home for them in Jerusalem. The father, a master mason, had been offered a position as a builder of crypts for the local Catholic Dioceses. Before the parents could send for the children the war had started. The grandfather was shot by the Germans. The grandmother and her younger brother were killed in a British bombing raid. The small hill town was totally destroyed and the surviving orphans were sent to a convent near the Austrian border.

The lengthy letter went on to explain that as soon as the war in Italy was over the priest from the destroyed village, who had accompanied the children to the convent, had sent a letter to Pasquale Russo informing him that his daughter, Yolanda, was safe, and asking if he should make arrangements to send her to Palestine. The parents of Yolanda had sent instructions to put her on the first ship coming to Haifa. That they had paid half the fare and the purser could collect the balance upon her safe arrival.

What Father Geraldo had not revealed in his letter to the purser was that the Russo's had sent sufficient funds to pay for a first class cabin on an Italian luxury liner. That Father Geraldo had cashed the generous money order for British pounds and thoughtfully gave the sisters of the Benedictine Convent a small offering for their trouble. He then arranged for the needed paperwork to assure Yolanda's entry into British Mandate Palestine and paid for half the passage on the first coastal ferry to leave Genoa. The little steamship was a far cry from the luxury liner that her parents had envisioned for her travels. Father Geraldo then ordered several cases of vintage wine to be delivered to his quarters at the monastery. This last purchase used up all the funds that had been sent to him by Yolanda's father.

Moshe made his way to Cabin #4 with a light heart. He had good news for little Yolanda. Over the last five years he had told many children that they would soon be reunited with their parents, this time, thankfully, it would be the truth.

Yolanda was lying face down on the top bunk when Moshe came into the cabin. She didn't look up when he lightly touched her shoulder and attempted to talk to her in his broken Italian. She gave him a cursory glance and hid her face again. It was clear that she didn't understand what he said. Moshe decided to return to the purser's desk where he asked if there were any crew members from the hill country around Genoa. The purser knew of two crew members who were from that region. He told Moshe where to find them. (In the galley, of course.)

Guido, the younger of the cooks, was from a town nearest to Yolanda's home and he was happy to get away from the hot stove. The first thing he saw as he entered the tiny cabin was Hedy's bra and panties hanging out to dry over the railing on her bunk. Guido had a moment of homesickness as he thought about his sister's things that were often hanging in the bathroom of his parent's house. He had been eager to get away to sea a year ago. But now he missed his garrulous family. They were known as the Pagliaci di Luca, (The clowns of Luca) as there was always the sound of laughter in their home.

Guido turned his attention to the weeping girl and gently touched her shoulder. When she heard him call her "little sweetheart" in a familiar dialect she turned to face him. He kept talking to her and in a few moments she was sitting up, legs dangling over the edge of the bunk, face to face with the tall and handsome young man, who kept saying things that eventually made her smile. He was explaining that she was not being kidnapped and that her parents would be waiting for her in Haifa. He told her that she was among friends who like her.

Moshe stood in the doorway, breathing in the scent of garlic and marinara sauce that followed Guido wherever he went. Now Yolanda was laughing at something Guido had told her about his family. Moshe felt like he had won a grand prize in a lottery. Just then Hedy came to the door and saw her underwear brazenly displayed at eye level to the handsome young cook, who was at that moment helping Yolanda down from the bunk.

"We are going to lunch!" Guido announced in English, as he took Yolanda's hand and disappeared up the stairs, but not before he gave Hedy an appreciative look, his black eyes twinkling with pleasure.

The next seven days, as they slowly sailed towards Haifa, Yolanda took part in the daily Hebrew lessons. Max and Daniel practiced Hebrew with her each evening before going to sleep. During the warm, sunny days at sea she walked the deck with Guido, relaxed and happy to be speaking her native dialect.

Hedy learned a few words of Italian from Guido and by the time they reached Haifa she could make out a few sentences as he explained how to make the perfect pasta sauce and how he hoped to be the best chef in Genoa someday. "I will call my restaurant *The Garden of Laughter.*" he told her "When you come, dinner will be free."

While the Ionia was pulling into Haifa Harbor Moshe gave Hedy the address where she should go upon arrival. He also gave her the good news that Vera and Marlena would arrive there soon. All three of the girls had been assigned to work as interpreters for the Jewish Agency after their required stay in an "Ulpan" where they would be submerged in the Hebrew language for several weeks.

Approaching Haifa Harbor was a visually enjoyable experience. The green hillsides were covered with a variety of trees, well kept gardens and lovely villas. Crowning the scene was the impressive façade of the Teknion, one of the foremost technological universities in the world ever since it was founded in 1912.

Hedy stood at the ship's railing clutching the Macy's dress box with one hand and the smaller of her charges with the other. Daniel was carrying her gray coat. At Moshe's insistence Hedy wore the blue dress and new hat. The breeze played with the skirt, sending it up and around her slim legs, much higher than she would have allowed if she had her hand free.

When the gangplank came down and the passengers were finally allowed to leave the ship, Hedy experienced a moment of sheer panic. Walking down the ramp and seeing the uniformed guards with rifles, she was suddenly on another ramp looking at a similar sight. She was fighting down the scream of anguish in her throat when she caught sight of Moshe standing at the bottom of the ramp, smiling up at her. She also saw that the other men on the pier were looking at her with appreciation. For a moment she was uncomfortable, then her natural female instinct took over and she began to enjoy the obvious approval directed toward her. She slowed her steps allowing Max and Daniel to go ahead of her. The officials gave them and their papers a cursory glance and resumed watching Hedy's descent. A flicker of satisfaction crossed Moshe's face as he observed her progress towards him. He took her box and guided her toward the two boys already on the pier.

When Guido came down the ramp with Yolanda, her mother rushed toward the girl she had not seen in four years, but would have known anywhere. Senior Russo started to shake hands with Guido, but on a sudden impulse embraced him like a son, while Yolanda and her mother wept tears of joy in each other's arms. Moshe watched the scene and thought of his daughter. Would she recognize him after six years? What would she call him?

At first Yolanda had not been certain if the woman Guido had pointed out to her was actually her mother, but as she got closer the scent of sandalwood and cloves brought back the memory of loving arms and tender words that had filled her life before the terror. "Mama, Mama, she whispered between sobs of happiness. As Moshe guided Hedy and the boys in the direction of a blue bus at the edge of the pier, a high pitched voice yelled out. "La Hit Raot, Chaverim!" and Yolanda waved a hand as everyone on the pier turned in her direction.

Chapter 27: HAIFA

The light blue bus, each of the seats filled, climbed up the narrow street to the top of the hill and turned left along a winding cobblestone road, then continued out of the city. In a few minutes the stones gave way to a dusty trail and stopped at a two-story brick building. The square structure resembled a school house, which it was. The fifteen newcomers had arrived at their first destination in this, soon to be new, yet old, country.

The Hebrew school for the new citizens of Eretz Israel was called an "Ulpan". There each person was inundated in the new version of the Hebrew language and given an extensive course in the history of Zionism, Jewish history (which was mostly a litany of persecution, culminating with the unbelievable horror of the event soon to be known as the Holocaust). The latest episodes of persecution had been experienced in person by the new arrivals. Now they would learn of the extent and enormity of the crimes that had been perpetrated on the Jews of Europe and many other people who were deemed to be subhuman by the Nazis and their sympathizers.

The bus driver pulled the bus alongside of the brick structure and the young people filed out and into the building where the boys went to an area on the ground floor. Hedy was led to a six bed dormitory on the second floor and assigned a cot and a nightstand. Two sets of sheets with pillow cases were neatly folded on the cot beside a feather pillow and two blankets. The woman who had led her up the stairs pointed to a narrow shelf above the bed. "This is for your books," she said in Hebrew. Then she handed Hedy a square white card. She continued in Hebrew, "Print your name in Hebrew on this card." Then she gave Hedy a pencil and a thumb tack, motioning for her to pin the card to the edge of the shelf. "Change your clothes if you have other ones. We are very informal here." Then pointing to the two hooks on the wall next to the bed she said "For your nice dress. Put the box under the bed." She motioned down. "The water closet is behind the door at the end of the room." She continued. Hedy nodded her understanding and felt gratitude to Moshe for the Hebrew lessons on the ship. "Come down to the dining hall at 6:30." The woman spoke in rapid Hebrew pointing to a clock above the entry door, then turned to go back downstairs. At the door she stopped and looked back at Hedy. "The three girls who have the other beds are in class. Two more girls are arriving next week. Moshe tells me you know them, Vera and Lena."

When she smiled, the woman, who told Hedy her name was Sonja, looked much younger, her plump face was almost pretty and Hedy wondered how she would look without the black headscarf that hid most of her curly black hair. "Todah rabah!" Hedy whispered. Sonja nodded in reply and disappeared down the steps.

Hedy investigated the latrine area. There were two stalls, two sinks and a shower. There was soap in the soap dishes and six towel bars, with towels on them, lined the wall near the sinks. High, wide windows let in the daylight and several bare light bulbs hung from the ceiling, as well as in the dormitory room. Such luxury, she thought to herself as she went back to her cot to change into the trousers and shirt and hung up her dress and hat.

For now, she would wear the blue shoes. The heavy boots didn't seem appropriate. She made the bed, put the extra linens on the shelf and lay down on top of the blanket, intending to rest for a few minutes, but she was soon sound asleep.

∾

The driver of the blue bus offered to take Moshe up the hill to the Teknion. He declined the offer and started walking up the steep road that led to the university and research center. His ascent was purposefully slow along the narrow road as he needed time to sort out his feelings. On the one hand there was happy anticipation on the other, trepidation about what kind of a welcome he would get from his daughter.

Moshe's parents had emigrated from a small town in Poland to escape the continual persecution of Jews in their area. His father had studied ophthalmology and soon opened a clinic in a Haifa neighborhood and served the locals as well as members of the Turkish administration. His mother stayed home and kept house for her husband and their two sons.

Moshe was the restless one, while his younger brother Beni, followed his father into the business of providing eye care. After WWI and the British takeover of Palestine the family learned English and French and the words to the British national anthem. They considered themselves British subjects. After finishing high school, Moshe served with the British police force, where he never mentioned being Jewish. He did, however meet a lovely girl one day while in his father's clinic and their friendship blossomed into love.

Her name was Rachel, and she taught third grade in a British school. In 1928 they were married and two years later they had a daughter, Yael. It was at this time that the Zionist movement began to recruit young Jewish men (and women) to start forming a homeland for the Jewish people. As a policeman Moshe had seen the way the British Mandate government favored the Arab population. Moshe could not understand this prejudice against the Jews while catering to the Arab leaders, who did nothing to better the lives of their people, while the Jews who came to live in what they considered the "Holy Land" put great effort into making the land more fertile, building medical facilities and institutions of learning, the Teknion among them.

Rachel was sympathetic, but not as Zionistic as Moshe.

His Zionist activities kept him away from home for long periods. They drifted apart. Rachel and Beni became good friends. When Moshe came back to Haifa after a long absence he heard his four year old daughter call Beni, "Papa." Beni had moved in with Rachel and Yael and become the father figure in Yael's life. Rachel was calm and matter of fact about the situation. "We need a man in the house." She told Moshe when he asked about her plans. "I love you, but I also love Beni and so does Yael. You don't really want a family life. For you it is tedious but Beni wants the routine and the responsibility. We are encouraging her to call Beni her 'aba' (Hebrew for father). It would be best for all of us if she calls you 'dod'" (Hebrew for uncle).

Moshe loved Rachel with all his heart, her happiness was more important to him than his own desires. He agreed to the arrangement and came to visit as often as he could.

During WWII, Moshe fought in North Africa with General Montgomery and soon came to the attention of the Zionist leaders that led the Jewish Brigade. (In Our Own Hands — a film about the Jewish Brigade in the British army 1944.) When the Allied Powers invaded Europe Moshe started to work undercover for the Zionist cause. Towards the end of the war it was his assignment to recruit young Jews to come to Palestine. (Legally, if possible and illegally if not.) Like most of the other young men of the Jewish Brigade he traveled all over war torn Europe looking for survivors who wanted to go to a Jewish Homeland.

∽

While Hedy, for the first time in years, slept a deep, untroubled sleep, Moshe continued up the road to the Teknion. It had been six years since he had seen Yael or Rachel. In his mind he went over his last conversation with Rachel. It had taken place in the kitchen of their neat little bungalow. (Rachel was an immaculate housekeeper. A trait Moshe admired but sometimes found annoying.) He had been home on a short leave before being sent to North Africa with the rank of Master Sergeant in His Majesty's Fusiliers. "I will be away for a long time." He had told Rachel. She had looked into his eyes, waiting for him to continue as they sat across from each other at the kitchen table, holding hands like the lovers they would always be. "I can't tell you where I am going but I know it is very far away." Her eyes held his and they both knew that this might be good-by forever. There was no need for words; they both knew what the other was thinking. They stood up and Moshe had taken Rachel into his arms. There was no mistaking the kiss they shared as anything but a passionate expression of love. Just then twelve year old Yael had walked into the kitchen and stood transfixed while her parents didn't even notice her. When Moshe had finally released Rachel and turned towards the door he saw Yael, a startled look on her lovely face. Moshe and Rachel had exchanged a brief glance, then Moshe bent and gave Yael a peck on the cheek, brushed her hair lightly with one hand and gave a quick wave with the other. Then he was gone. He had been away for six years and there had been exactly six letters from him to his wife but no communication from her to him. To be fair, there had been no return address.

Through his contacts he had heard that his brother, Beni had been killed five years ago in an Arab riot. The very people whom he had helped to see better, broke into the clinic and beat him to death. His father had died the year before and his mother died of a broken heart shortly after the riot. Rachel's parents had moved to South Africa and tried to persuade her and Yael to join them, but Rachel had stayed in Haifa. Was she waiting for Moshe? He sincerely hoped she was. He loved her so much that he could feel the physical pain whenever he thought of her. He longed to embrace Yael and call her 'Yalda'. Tears were beginning to form in his eyes and blur the road in front of him.

The late afternoon sun was warm and Moshe took off his tie and coat. With his open collar he now looked the typical

Zionist leader as depicted on the brochures he had often handed out to potential recruits. He thought about his image now as he began to feel a little out of breath with his exertions. Twenty years ago he could have run up this hill. Now he was twenty years older and twenty pounds heavier. He felt like a very old man. He had seen more grief and destruction in the last six years than most men would ever see in a lifetime. Finding and recruiting potential Zionists had been a grueling task. Most of the youngsters who came out of the concentration camps were broken wrecks, barely resembling human beings, but if their spirit were intact and they retained the will to live, the demolished bodies could be repaired and revived. His mind flitted to his meeting with Hedy, whom he would always think of as his little "Zev-evah." Actually she was not so little. He remembered that day he first looked into her blue eyes. They were almost at a level with his and the spark he saw in their depth lifted his spirits. Now that he thought of it, he found that often the fierce life force that was needed to forge the new Jewish State was often stronger among the surviving women than in the men.

He walked across the open area around the front of the Teknion and towards the glass doors of the entry hall. To his right was the road he had come on and to his left a flower bed. A young woman was crouching among the flowers, trowel in one hand, pulling weeds with the other. She looked up as Moshe approached, then she stood up and ran towards him. When Moshe recognized Yael, (there was no mistaking her, she looked exactly like Rachel at eighteen) he moved towards her. A thought raced through his brain. Would she call him uncle or dad? Had Rachel told her the truth yet?

"Dod Moshe!" she called joyfully, answering his question. "How did you know I was here?" Yael asked him as she threw her arms around his neck. He held her away at arm's length to get a better look at her. Her white shirt was stained with the soil from the flower bed and her dark blue skirt didn't cover the same stains on her knees. As she shook back her long black hair a faint scent of lavender floated into his nostrils.

"I heard that you worked here," he told her. "I didn't think you were a gardener, though." Moshe gave a little chuckle.

"We all help with this flower bed," Yael explained. "It is a memorial site for the men who were killed in the war, in the Jewish Brigade. I graduated this year and have a job in the medical research laboratory."

"Where can I find your mother?" Moshe asked as he put his arm around Yael, breathing in the familiar scent of lavender and her young beauty.

"She should be at home at this time of day," Yael said. With a quick hug and a peck on her cheek he turned from Yael and headed for the place that he always thought of as home.

Chapter 28

A chatter of female voices woke Hedy from her dream in which Omar was walking beside her. She sat up quickly and looked around. Three girls about her age were talking to each other in rapid Hebrew. When they noticed Hedy they started to introduce themselves, speaking more slowly. Hedy began to answer in Polish, then stopped herself and continued in her fumbling Hebrew. The three young women smiled in understanding and repeated their names. Hedy mentioned her name and waited for a reply.

There was Berta, short and chubby with blond hair and blue eyes the color of Hedy's. Minna was tall and thin with long black hair tied back in a pony tail. Fanny, who looked to be older than the other two, had a bit of gray in her short, brown hair.

Fanny sat down on the bed next to Hedy's. "Shalom, Shalom!" she said and in deliberately slow Hebrew, "There are very strict rules here. Only Hebrew is spoken while you are in the Ulpan."

Hedy had many questions and formulating them into Hebrew would be a slow process. She looked up at the clock, hoping that it was near 6:30 and time for dinner. She was getting very hungry and it was difficult to think. The clock had no numbers, only Hebrew letters, but she could tell that it was 5:45.

They all went into the lavatory and Hedy noticed that there were name cards above each towel rack. Three were blank and she asked Fanny which one she should use. Fanny told her she had her choice and she should write her name on the one she wanted. Since it was obvious that last names had been used on these cards, Hedy decided then and there to change her name from the German "Mandel" meaning almond, to the Hebrew "Shaked."

The other women were dressed in a similar fashion as Hedy. She noticed that they had a skirt or a dress on the hooks by their beds. No one was changing for dinner. A quick comb through the hair or a scarf to cover tangled curls, a thorough washing of the hands followed these gestures and the four of them were headed downstairs.

Two long tables, flanked by benches filled the dining hall. The kitchen was behind a wide counter and fifteen students lined up to be handed individual plates of cheese, bread, cucumbers, onions and tomatoes. A large bowl of yogurt was at either end of the table. There were twenty one place settings on the two tables. Five more students had been expected, but their arrival had been delayed until after dark.

Gina, the housemother, her long black skirt covered by a white apron and her hair carefully tucked into a scarf sat at the end of one table. For Hedy's benefit Gina reminded them to speak only "Ivrit" (Hebrew) and wished them a pleasant meal. Pitchers of water and milk were passed around. Like on the Ionia, the hot meal of the day would be served at noon. Later in the evening, after the homework was completed, everyone in the Ulpan gathered around the radio in the open space they called the parlor. They drank hot tea from the samovar on the sideboard, and listened intently to the latest news in English.

Chapter 29

The next few months were busy ones for Hedy. Vera had arrived a week after Hedy and then Lena joined the Ulpan a week after that. Each of the girls had been accompanied by a "little brother." All of the new Ulpan students had to study and practice Hebrew every spare minute to catch up with the ones who had arrived earlier. They were given pencils, paper and textbooks and spent many hours learning the Sephardic version of Hebrew which would be the official language of their new country. Daily quizzes showed their progress, or the lack of it. The teacher, a middle aged Sabra (Palestinian born person) who had been one of the developers of the new Hebrew version he was teaching, was very strict but not unreasonable. He told the class that when they began to dream in Hebrew it was a sign they had internalized the language. "After that first Hebrew dream, I will give you permission to leave the Ulpan for a few hours to explore Haifa." He told them in Hebrew, a quick smile escaping from his lips.

Three months went by before Hedy, Lena and Vera had mastered Hebrew sufficiently to win a few hours leave. They were reluctant to spend the small stipend that they were given by the Jewish Agency. There was enough to go to a movie, buy a snack in a café, but Hedy was saving her money to buy a pair of shoes for everyday wear. So the three of them, elated with the feeling of freedom to roam where they pleased, decided to share a snack in a café overlooking the harbor. Only the sight of the soldiers patrolling with guns at the ready reminded them of where they had been, but also strengthened their resolve to control their own future.

After another month, all three of the girls passed their final examinations and found jobs in Haifa. Most of the other graduates opted to go to a Kibutz and become more adept at farming. Also it was safer to be away from the main harbor and the military presence.

Hedy worked for the Jewish Agency as an interpreter and translator. Vera had enrolled in an English language class and soon she was hired by the British Internment Department where she helped with the interrogations of the Jewish displaced persons who were caught trying to enter Palestine. Lena was hired by a wealthy Muslim Family to tutor their daughters in French.

Now that they had graduated they would need to leave the Ulpan and find a place to live. A nearby boarding house was suggested as a convenient location. It was near a bus stop, the proprietor provided a substantial breakfast and allowed the three young women to share one of the rooms. They even had a private bathroom with a real bathtub. The room was quite small, but it had a view of the harbor. They discussed renting an apartment after they had saved sufficient funds for a deposit and rental payment. The three of them did not come by this decision lightly. After being forced to live with all types of people that they would never have even met in their former lives, each of them wanted to be certain that the roommate they chose would be compatible and have similar standards of cleanliness, consideration for others, a sense of decency, decorum and moral values.

After meeting in the Austrian hideaway the three young women had become good friends in spite of the fact that they were not able to speak to each other directly. Hedy and Marlena (who asked to be called Lena) spoke French to each other. Vera and Hedy communicated in Austrian. Lena knew a few words of German that she had learned from the guards at Bergen-Belsen concentration camp, but she needed Hedy's help when she wished to talk with Vera.

During their first night in Marta's little room they each had, almost unconsciously, observed each other for clues to their respective background. The way they undressed and dressed, folded clothes, held the books they took from the shelf and their table manners were indications of training and education which two years of brutalization had not erased. As they watched each other, each made a conscious decision to become a family.

Like family members they loved and cared about each other, but also had diverse interests that often took them in different directions. They had survived the murderous intent of their enemies and had seen the face of pure evil. In spite of their suffering they had kept their souls intact and hope alive. There was hope of making life worthwhile again, for themselves and for those they loved and would love.

After graduating from the Ulpan the three young women finally had a language in common and on rare evenings when they were at home they began to talk about the experiences that had brought them to this stage of their lives.

VERA
Vera had been born into a wealthy family in Czechoslovakia. They owned a construction company that was responsible for many of the bridges that spanned the Danube River. Her parents had believed that their social prominence and wealth would protect them. They were sadly mistaken. Their "gentile friends" were quick to turn them over to the Nazis shortly after Germany invaded their homeland and looted their palatial home at the first opportunity. Vera, who had just started high school, her mother, father and younger sister were sent to Terezin (Theresienstat) concentration camp, where her sister died of malnutrition. After a few months her father was deported to a "work camp". Vera and her mother spend another year in Terezin and then were loaded on a train of cattle cars, like so much cattle, and spent

several days traveling without food or water to an unknown destination. One morning the train stopped and when the doors were opened, Croatian men surrounded the women and girls and herded them into a field near the tracks. The women who were with small children were separated from the others and marched away into a nearby forest. Vera and her mother, an attractive woman in her thirties, were lined up with another group. The Croatians indicated they were to line up in rows of five and this much smaller group of women, (Vera estimated there were 25 or so) was marched off along a dirt road that led through a dense forest. Most of the men had rifles, some only had clubs, and they left no doubt that they would use these weapons if anyone disobeyed.

When they were at the edge of the forest the men called a halt and ordered the prisoners to sit on the ground. Two men came over to Vera and her mother. They grabbed her mother by the hair and one arm. She held tightly to Vera with her free hand so that Vera was dragged along with her mother into the underbrush. The men separated Vera from her mother, who was struggling to stay on her feet.

"Run! Run!" Her mother had screamed at Vera.

While the men were clawing at her mother's clothing Vera ran into the woods. She ran without looking back, until she couldn't run anymore. She found a hollow log and crawled into the dank darkness, trembling with fear and exhaustion and eventually she slept. When she woke up and slowly began to crawl out of her hiding place she looked up into the astonished faces of five skeletal forms. The men were Slavic prisoners who had escaped from a slave labor camp. They had survived the winter in the German forest. Now they were looking for the Swiss border. They told Vera that she could come with them if she kept up with them. They stayed in the forest, but followed the road that was visible through the trees. Eventually they met a convoy of British soldiers and were taken to a Displaced Persons Camp where Avi recruited Vera.

LENA

Lena's parents were school teachers in a village near Lyon. Her father taught English (He had been educated in England but returned to France after graduating University.) Her mother taught European History and they had met and married late in life. Lena's grandparents on both sides had died before she was born.

The maid who came once a week to clean the small apartment had offered to take Lena to church with her. It was at that time that her parents had told her that they were Jews and what that meant to the rest of the world, but that it did not mean anything to them. (Lena did go to church a few times and enjoyed the experience. It was like learning about a foreign culture for a social studies class.)

When Lyon came under German occupation, it didn't seem possible that the Jews of Lyon, most of whom were able to trace their French ancestry back to before the Roman occupation, would be rounded up and deported by their own French police force. The day before the arrests were implemented a friend of Lena's came to warn the Lobe family. The friend's father who was one of the police officers in charge of the roundup had mentioned that only the Jewish men were to be arrested that day so Lena's father went into hiding.

The gendarmes came and lined up all the unfortunate Jews in the area including Lena and her mother.

"We are loyal French!" One of the women had screamed. The German officer, who was in charge of the "operation", looked at her disdainfully. Then he pulled his pistol out of the holster and shot her in the head. Lena's mother who was standing beside the murdered woman, fainted and was also shot. Lena was dragged away by another woman. Lena went into a state of shock and couldn't remember much of what happened to her after that. She spent about a year in Bergen-Belsen, where she was liberated by British soldiers. Some of these men were Jewish and helped her to connect with the Zionists.

In early winter of 1947 Lena, Hedy and Vera had saved

enough money to rent a furnished apartment with two bedrooms, a kitchen with a double electric hot plate. They used the kitchen sink to wash their clothes and themselves. In the tiny living room they had to move the dining table to one side every night in order to unfold the sleeping couch. The toilet, out in the hall, was shared by the occupants of another apartment.

Storing their things was not a problem. They each had a small suitcase (a dress box in Hedy's case) which fit under the bed or couch. They had drawn straws to see who would sleep on the couch. Hedy had drawn the losing straw which was just as well, because she was the tallest and the beds were rather short.

Vera's room had a full length mirror and she spent a lot of time in front of it trying to shape her frizzy curls into a fashionable hairdo. She would scrunch up her narrow face as the wiry black strands escaped her combs and pins, eventually getting it under control so Hedy or Lena could take a quick turn at the mirror.

One day Lena brought home a henna rinse that was popular among the social set of her employer. She used it in her dark brown hair and Hedy decided to try it in her golden tresses that gave them a reddish sheen, like candle glow in a dark room. All three young women wore their hair rolled up during the daytime, but for evening they often let it hang loose in the back.

They didn't do much cooking. There was tea for breakfast and occasionally a boiled egg for dinner. Work hours often went late into the night at the Jewish Agency, so Hedy ate many meals from the street vendors. Lena ate with the Muslim family and Vera had a date almost every evening. A year passed like the blink of an eye.

The Jewish Agency posted the names of survivors, adding new ones daily. Hedy spent her spare time reading these lists over and over, hoping against hope to see a familiar name. In the meantime she had changed her name from Mandel (German for almond) to the Hebrew word for almond-"Shaked" without even thinking that someone might be looking for her on one of those lists.

It was during that winter of 1948 that Hedy received an answer to the letter she had sent to Konstanza more than a year earlier. The letter was in Polish from the woman who now lived in the Mandel's former apartment. It was just a short note, telling Hedy that Konstanza, who had been a German collaborator, had fled back to Greece and that Poland was much better off without her kind and her Jewish employers. The note was not signed. Hedy was relieved that Konstanza had escaped with her life but couldn't believe that she had collaborated with the Germans, even though she was half German. It just didn't seem possible. Hedy promised herself that she would find her and learn the truth. Konstanza had often mentioned the name of the village where her mother was born. Greece wasn't that far away and someday she would go there.

Chapter 30

A secret organization was being formed to serve as an elite group for intelligence and espionage. Only a handful of men and women knew the name of what was to become a section of the Israeli Mossad. These special agents, who were picked for their loyalty and skills, were at the forefront of furthering the Zionist cause of establishing a Jewish State in the Middle East.

Oskar Menkes, formerly Omar, was in charge of the Haifa office, which was by far the busiest in the whole enterprise. He had been instrumental in developing a method of screening applicants for the secret service that would later be adopted, with similarly successful results, by the El Al airlines for security screening of passengers and personnel. The method was painstaking and almost foolproof. Since most personal records of the applicants had disappeared along with any trace of their former lives, it was the only way to find the suitably intelligent and dedicated people that were needed.

To start the process, each applicant had to fill out a deposition stating who they were and where they came from, their family history, (as complete as possible), their own life story to that point and their reasons for wanting to join the special forces. No names were used on these, often lengthy essays, but each paper and applicant was assigned a number. After reading each story the committee sent for the applicant, still using only a number. At this point names were exchanged and the applicant was asked to give a detailed oral history of what had been written. Questions were asked about dates and occurrences and also about the applicant's plans and ambitions.

The application essays were written in many different languages, but mostly in Polish and usually by boys just out of their teens who had survived the Nazi camps. There were some girls who were usually given office jobs, but a few were sent on dangerous assignments where it was thought a female could be more successful.

Hedy, at the recommendation of Moshe, had been employed by the recruitment department of the future Israeli Defense Force, currently named the Haganah. All potential recruits were also vetted by the fledgling secret service as possible agents. Her skill with several languages made her a valuable member of this small group who, except for the top leaders didn't know about each other.

The offices of the secret service were in the Jewish Agency building which faced a busy street on the first floor. The second floor had no street access, only two windows that faced away from the streets. The third floor faced another street on the hillside above the lower floors. The people who came into the first floor were directed to a small room to one side of the entry and given the paper and pencils to fill out applications and write their depositions. When they were finished writing they were given a number, which was also printed on their paperwork, and told to come back in two days for a personal interview, which would be held on the second floor.

Hedy worked in an office on the third floor and always entered the building through the street entrance that led to that area. She never saw the applicants. Her job was to translate the stories into Hebrew. Each morning individual folders containing essays were on her desk. At the end of the day she placed the translated and original copies back into their folder. These were picked up after she left and replaced by new ones.

The stories Hedy read each day were emotionally wrenching. These young people had experienced horrors and hardships that would traumatize not only their lives, but the lives of their progeny for several generations. She often wondered how they were going to live normal lives again. Miraculously most of them managed to live productive lives and raise fairly well-adjusted children. Yet there was always an undercurrent of sorrow, fear and rage that was felt by the children and even grandchildren of Holocaust survivors.

One morning Hedy started to translate an essay in Polish and a flash of recognition crossed her mind. 'This could be Samuel' she thought to herself and made plans to meet him. On the morning that she expected Samuel to return for his personal interview (more like an interrogation). Hedy went brazenly through the door marked "Authorized Personnel Only" and lingered on the second floor landing hoping she would seem to be lost, in case someone questioned her presence. As she expected Samuel came up the stairs from the floor below and strode down the hall towards her. He didn't recognize her at first, dressed as she was in a short, flared skirt and pale pink blouse with her henna tinted hair rolled up in a fashionable hairdo. When she spoke his name, his eyes widened and sparkled with appreciation. Hedy put her finger up to her lips to caution quiet.

"Meet me at the Café Safadat at 6 o'clock" she whispered in Polish and quickly turned to walk back to the door that led to the stairs. Samuel didn't know the café but he was sure he could find it.

A door opened at the other end of the hallway. Oskar beckoned Samuel to enter, but before he closed the door again he got a brief glimpse of a female figure retreating behind Samuel. He saw trim ankles above high heeled shoes, a slender figure in pink and blue and a flash of reddish gold hair in a smoothly rolled up style. He wondered briefly what she was doing on the second floor, which was off limits to anyone not specifically authorized to be there. But the committee was waiting and his mind went back to the matters at hand. At the end of the lengthy "interrogation" Samuel asked where he could find the Café Safadat. That question showed him to be at ease and he was hired at once.

By 5:30 pm that evening, Samuel was seated in the busy café, impatiently awaiting Hedy, who slipped into a chair across from him promptly at 6 o'clock. Their hands and eyes met and held for a long moment.

"Hedy" he murmured in a voice that had become several octaves lower in the last year. He brought her suntanned wrists up to his lips as they kept looking at each other across the table. His deep blue eyes, so much like hers, darkened and he whispered in Polish. "My little wolverine you have become a beautiful woman," then he blushed and looked away.

Hedy felt a stirring in her belly, a tingling sensation in her groin and instantly thought of Omar. Three years had passed since Yusef had told her that Omar truly loved her and to wait for him. At twenty she was hardly an "old maid" but was it wise to keep waiting for a man she didn't really know ?

Now looking at the blushing Samuel, his thick, blond hair combed stiffly back from his forehead she thought how much they looked like the ideal example of the Aryan race.

They were blond, with blue eyes, tall, slim and could have passed as German siblings. Hedy pulled her wrists out of Samuel's grip and took his big, rough fingers into her hands.

"We need to talk in Hebrew." She admonished him in spite of the fact that every language in the world could be heard in the café as well as on the streets of Haifa. In the two years she had been there Hedy noticed that Hebrew was becoming more prevalent and just hearing it made her feel safer.

Samuel had not finished with the classes at the Ulpan on the Kibbutz where he had been living since he arrived in Palestine, but he had made sufficient progress to get a few hours of leave. Now he relished the freedom of sitting in a café with a pretty girl. He looked around at the young people, mostly in their late teens or early twenties, talking heatedly about their future, laughing, flirting, and he wondered if he would ever be that young again. He was nineteen and felt as if heavy weights were bearing down on his shoulders. He knew that he would live his life on two levels. On the surface he would try to live like a normal person. Eat, sleep, love his wife and children, work to provide for his family materially and culturally. Beneath that façade of normalcy there would be, for Samuel and almost every survivor of the Nazi brutality, a volcano of rage and sorrow that made forgetting or forgiving impossible. For now he longed, desperately, to join this seemingly carefree crowd of young people around them.

Instead he told Hedy about how he had finally arrived in Haifa. He had accompanied Avi and Marta on two more trips to Displaced Persons Camps in Austria to help bring future Zionists to *Eretz Israel*.

Over slices of cucumber, tomatoes, hard boiled egg and pita bread Samuel told Hedy about the last trip from the Austrian forest to Genoa. The group had boarded a small Italian vessel that got them near to Haifa. A British patrol ship approached, took control of the vessel and began to tow them towards Cyprus. After dark Samuel and two other boys wearing life vests, slipped overboard and started swimming east. They were in the water more than twenty four hours when a fishing boat picked them up.

Hedy had read some of these details in his essay but let him tell her again, as he clearly needed to talk. She kept encouraging him to tell his story in Hebrew and he tried his best.

Once ashore the boys were directed to the Jewish Agency where they were given identity papers and sent to the Kibbutz near Haifa where they now attended the Ulpan.

"What has happened to Avi and Marta?" Hedy asked then. Samuel became very quiet for several minutes and concentrated on eating the food and drinking the beer they had ordered. Thinking he had not heard her, Hedy asked again. "Samuel, how are Avi and Marta?"

He looked at her sharply and answered with a question. "You haven't heard?" Her puzzled frown reassured him that she really did not know. "They are in Atlit" (the prison near

Haifa) Hedy gasped, and Samuel continued. "Someone betrayed them and their whole operation. We know it was someone who knew all the details, from the hideout in the Austrian forest to the safe houses in Genoa and Trieste. The British knew about the Greek shipping line that had modified their ferry boats to allow space for secret passengers." He stopped to rest, exhausted from the effort of the long Hebrew speech.

"Do they know who betrayed them?" Hedy asked in the pause. "I can't believe it was a Jew."

"Jewess!" Samuel said emphatically.

Hedy waited for Samuel to explain further but he just sat in front of her looking sad. Finally he did look up at Hedy and gave her a reassuring smile.

"There is a theory of who it was that betrayed the operation to the British, but until we have proof we don't want to name names. Negotiations are going on for the release of Avi, after all he is a British citizen with residency in Palestine. He and Marta were legally married during their last trip in Italy so she has rights as his wife. "

Hedy sat quietly for a few minutes then said in a level voice. "It is best not to discuss this matter further in public." She wondered, if she should ask Vera if she knew anyone important enough to help. After all Avi and Marta had helped her and so many other people, this might be a way to repay them.

The café became noisier as the evening progressed. A radio was playing American dance music and several couples got up to dance. "Come dance with me!" Hedy called to Samuel over the din.

"I've never danced." He called back as the saxophones wailed, drowning out the rest of his words.

"Neither have I!" She shouted across the table and proceeded to the small dance floor. For a few minutes they stood hand in hand, watching the dancers, then they stepped out together. He was a natural. Eventually Samuel would go on to win dance contests with equally skilled partners, but he never forgot his first time on the dance floor with the first woman he loved who would always be the love of his life. There was no more conversation between them that night. The music was much too loud for talking and besides they were busy following the rhythm. Eventually they were out of breath. Someone had taken their table by then, so they left the café and Samuel offered to get a taxi for Hedy. She laughed and told him she still had enough energy to walk home. Haifa is a harbor town built on steep topography. Samuel and Hedy climbed the hill to the apartment together. After giving Hedy a chaste peck on the cheek, Samuel hurried down the hill to catch the bus to the kibbutz.

Chapter 31

The apartment was dark when Hedy stepped into the living room. What she lacked in privacy by sleeping on the couch was rewarded by the panoramic view of Haifa and the harbor below. At night it looked like a diamond necklace displayed on dark blue velvet. She removed her sensible shoes, wiggling her bare feet. (With her next paycheck she planned to buy stockings.) Dancing was great fun. The music had made her feel light and free. She had not felt this happy since her last trip to Vienna ten years ago.

Walking into the apartment, Hedy remembered how she and Samuel had actually laughed out loud, first at each other then together. It was sheer pleasure moving to the music with no thoughts beyond the next step they would make.

The bedroom doors were closed and Hedy assumed Vera and Lena were asleep. She prepared for bed and fell onto the couch exhausted. During that night Hedy dreamt of Omar. When she awoke the next morning she could not remember anything about the dream except that he was in it and that she was happy to see him again. Before she left to go to work Hedy noticed that Lena had left for work as her bedroom door was open. Vera's door was still closed. Hedy decided not to disturb her in case she was still asleep, although she would have liked to inspect herself in front of the full length mirror before going out.

Just before noon Hedy looked up from the transcript she was working on to see Klara, the woman who worked at the reception desk at the Jewish Agency on the ground floor, standing in the doorway to Hedy's private office. Klara had obviously run up the two flights of hidden stairs. She looked agitated and sounded breathless as she called to Hedy. "We are closing the building. You need to go home." Klara's plump little body was shaking as she spoke and her salt and pepper hair was escaping from the usually neat bun at the nape of her neck.

Hedy didn't question Klara. She presumed that there was trouble with the British Mandate police or some other harassment from that bureaucracy. She had heard about a week ago that some of the officers of the Jewish Agency had been detained for questioning in Jerusalem. Perhaps the British would be questioning the Haifa staff next. Without a word Hedy gathered up the deposition she was working on and locked it into the safe, picked up her hat and coat and went out to the street from the door at the top floor of the building.

It was a warm, clear day in early spring and Hedy could smell the lilacs that bloomed around the side of the building. There was another odor in the air like the faint smell of a wood fire. She decided to walk home

When Hedy arrived in the apartment, Vera was sitting on the couch, smoking a cigarette. A package of expensive American cigarettes lay on the table beside her.

After greeting Vera, Hedy took off her hat and coat and went to the open door that led to the small balcony. In a conversational voice she said, "Vera, we all agreed not to smoke inside. Please go outside to have your cigarette."

Vera got up from the couch, came to stand directly in front of Hedy and blew smoke into her face. "I saw you last night with Samuel." Vera said. Her tone was sharp and accusatory.

"Yes, we met accidentally at the café and we had a nice visit." Hedy replied evenly. Then pointing at the package of cigarettes, she asked. "Vera, where did you get these?'

"That is none of your business!" Vera snapped. "Furthermore I'll smoke where I bloody well please."

Hedy was shocked at the hostility in Vera's voice and the anger that showed in her face and in her posture.

"Did you have a bad day?" Hedy asked with concern. "A fight with your Englishman?"

"I spit on the English, and I spit on the Zionists and I spit on you." Vera hissed and suddenly spat into Hedy's face.

Without being aware of it Hedy's hand had shot up and slapped Vera across the face. Hedy only realized what she had done when she saw her finger marks on Vera's cheek. Vera abruptly sat down on the couch, her fingers still clutching the burning cigarette. She lowered her head while rasping sobs shook her whole body.

Taking the cigarette out of Vera's trembling fingers, Hedy put it out in the ash tray and sat down next to Vera. Little by little the story of betrayal came out. When Vera had seen Samuel and Hedy together, she was certain that he would have told Hedy of his suspicions.

A week before, Vera had arrived at work and had seen Samuel being ushered into the dreaded interrogation room at the back of the British immigration office. He had looked surprised to see her. It was obvious that she worked there as she sat down at her desk. Their eyes had met as he turned his head in her direction before disappearing behind the door. In that moment Vera knew that she had, however inadvertently, been responsible for his presence in this terrible place. Soon she learned of the other detentions, and knew that she was right.

Now Vera waited for Hedy's angry denunciation. She assumed that Hedy knew about the latest arrests and her possible involvement. Vera had lost everything but her life and now she felt that she should lose that also. How could she ever face Hedy, Lena and Samuel? Eventually she might have to face Avi, the man who saved her life and Marta, who had helped her get through the mountains. Marta had been seasick every day of the ferry ride from Livorno to Haifa. It was possible because of Vera that she was now in Athlit detention camp separated from Avi by barbed wire, not much different from Auschwitz.

Between loud sobs, Vera alternated from holding her

head in her hands, elbows on her knees, then sitting up and throwing her head back, waving her arms wildly in the air and shouting. "What have I done? Oh what have I done? I want to die! God let me die!"

Hedy had seen women go mad. She had watched, helpless and paralyzed with fear as they were dragged away, screaming hysterically. No one tried to calm them, they were beaten into the silence of death or shot. Now she stood up, her whole being cringing at the memory of those atrocities. She was afraid to touch Vera. Afraid of what she might do as the rage grew inside her.

Now Vera was starting to pull at her disheveled black ringlets and screaming obscenities when the apartment door opened. Lena stepped inside with Samuel with Avi close behind her.

Avi was the only person in the room who knew something about the reason for Vera's distress. He spoke her name in greeting. She opened her eyes and something about his presence had a calming effect. Vera stared up at him, openmouthed, a mixture of fear and surprise froze on her contorted face. Avi ran his fingers through his hair, a familiar gesture, as a prelude to an important announcement.

The apartment living room seemed suddenly crowded. It was not made to hold five people. Avi motioned the three who stood watching him to sit down. Lena sat on the only chair in the room, while Samuel and Hedy sat on the floor, backs against the wall.

Avi sat down next to Vera on the sofa and took both her shaking hands into his and held them firmly against his chest, forcing Vera to face him. "Vera," he said in an even, but firm tone. "Tell me how you have been doing since we last saw each other." He spoke in slow and carefully pronounced Hebrew. Avi's blue eyes were warm and kindly. His tone was conversational.

At first Vera just stared at him, her dark eyes wide, confused. But within seconds her features relaxed. Avi sat back on the sofa, still holding Vera's cold hands in his warm ones he placed them on the sofa between them. She leaned back and closed her eyes.

"How was your stint at the Ulpan?" Avi asked in a voice just above a whisper.

Vera sighed, "Did you know I didn't pass the final exam?" she asked in an equally slow whisper.

"Yes," he answered, and added "Many people don't pass the first time. Hebrew is difficult."

Vera opened her eyes and looked straight into Avi's warm blue ones. They were so beautiful, like the summer sky in the mountains where she had vacationed as a child.

"Avi, I'm not much of a Zionist." Vera said. "I made a mistake. I'm not Kibbutz material. I want a life like I had before the Nazi horror. I want to be rich again, I need it." She added in broken Hebrew.

"Most of us who have lived through the war would like to erase the past nightmare and wake up in our old world. You know we must all go on from where we are now." Avi's voice was sterner now.

"I'm not strong." Vera said in flat voice. "I gave in to my worst instincts." Suddenly she lapsed into Czech. "They, the British, saw my weakness and used me. I was stupid, and evil, because I could see what he was doing. Even if you and the others find a way to forgive me I will never forgive myself or Henry Ferrel for leading me on." Her voice began to rise. "I thought I loved him!" She wailed and tried to pull her hands away from Avi's firm grip.

"Tell me the whole story." Avi coaxed in a soft, concerned voice continuing to use Hebrew. "Who is this Henry Ferrel, and how does he fit into what is troubling you so deeply?"

Vera took a few minutes to gather her thoughts and her courage. Avi could see the resolve coming into her eyes and almost feel the struggle in her mind as she searched for the Hebrew words. Avi was reminded once more that survivors had a special quality and strength which had allowed them, to not merely survive, but in most cases, to flourish in their new lives.

Vera continued the best she could in her very basic Hebrew.

"I met Henry during the time I studied English at the British high school on Ha Meginim Blvd. near the Italian hospital. The Jewish Agency had sent me there after I flunked the final test at the Ulpan. He was guarding the entry to the office building next door. At first we nodded to each other. He is handsome and about my age and I was flattered by the attention. One day he said, "Good Morning." The next day he asked how my English was progressing. After another day we had a coffee date, ostensibly for me to practice my English. He told me I was good enough to apply for a job at his office building. It is the Haifa headquarters of the immigration commission which is in charge of the internment camps.

"I got the job as an interpreter since Czech is very similar to Polish and I also speak a little German. Henry helped me perfect my English and told me that I deserved to be rich again and to have a comfortable life like his family had in England, with servants, cars, a country house and a mansion in London. He never told me he loved me, but I fell in love.

"He asked me about my experiences and I told him everything about me and how I got to Palestine. I even mentioned names of people and described places where I had been. He seemed so caring, so interested in the smallest details, so willing to listen to everything I said. I dreamt of a wonderful life with him."

Vera stopped talking and looked up at Avi. His face was black and he was no longer looking at her. He released her hands, clenching his fists on his knees while Vera continued talking in broken Hebrew, and a little Czech.

"When I got to the office this morning I heard about an explosion at the British barracks last night. I enquired about Henry since I didn't see him at the entry to the building. Someone, I think it was his commander, told me that Henry was hurt in the explosion and taken to the British Hospital down by the harbor. I got on a bus going to the hospital. It took an hour to find him. The British patients have their own area separated by a covered walkway from the main building of the hospital.

"Henry had an injured hand and a bandage around his head. The nurse from the ward told me in her very Scottish brogue that the Irgun, the Jewish terrorists, had exploded a small bomb near the barracks and several men were wounded and a new latrine would need to be built."

To Avi's credit he totally stifled the smirk that threatened to cross his lips as he heard the last remark. "It was not Jews who set off the bomb." He muttered under his breath.

Vera continued her story as if she had not heard him.

"I came into the ward and found Henry's bed. I leaned down to kiss him and he pushed me away with his good hand. His eyes were cold and his words were colder. 'See what your Jewish pigs did to me. 'Get away from me. I don't ever want to see you again.'"

Tears began to roll down Vera's cheeks as she remembered how he looked at her with loathing and abhorrence.

"I wanted to tell him that I had nothing to do with bomb, but his look stopped me. I went out and started to walk home. On the way I bought the most expensive cigarettes in the tobacco store. My father used to smoke these and suddenly I wanted desperately to smell them again."

By now Vera was more calm and ready to ask some questions of Avi. When she started to speak again after a few moments of contemplative silence he interrupted her.

"Vera, I need to share some information with all of you about what is happening and what is to come. Let's go downstairs and get something to eat."

Vera went into the bathroom to wash her tear-stained face and comb her unruly hair. Avi turned to the three young people who sat looking up at him with stern faces. "Let's find a quiet place to eat and talk," he said.

Hedy led the group to a small restaurant on the corner and they chose a table near a window where they could watch the sun set into the Mediterranean sea. Vera made an effort to emulate the calm demeanor of the others.

Over steaming bowls of chicken noodle soup, which reminded each of them of childhood suppers, Avi told about his latest illegal entry into Palestine and his subsequent internment. He and Marta had been in a row boat with about a dozen young boys they were smuggling into the country when a British patrol boat stopped them. There were no questions asked of them, they were given numbers and sent to Athlit internment camp. Marta was very ill so she was taken to the Italian Hospital where she would be treated for the lung infection that had plagued her for months. After a month in Athlit, Avi and about twenty other prisoners managed to escape. They scattered around into various Kibbutzim. Avi went to the one where Samuel lived.

The explosion at the British barracks had happened while Hedy and Samuel were at the café, dancing. Vera had a glimpse of them as she was leaving with Henry. Henry drove Vera home and went back to his barracks, where he found the latrine on fire. He had hurt his hand and singed his eyebrows in an effort to help put out the fire.

Through contacts in the police department Avi had found out that the explosion had been caused by heat on the combustible matter in the latrine. Blaming Zionist radicals played into the British agenda. There had been several arrests during the night.

"In another month the British will be leaving Palestine." Avi said. The Zionists have assembled a cabinet in Jerusalem and will have a government in place when the United Nations declares the existence of the State of Israel." He continued and went on to explain that he had come to Haifa to ask Hedy to visit Marta. "She is very sick and I can't go there until the British leave."

Hedy promised to go the very next day. Then the friends all hugged and went their separate ways.

Chapter 32

The next day Hedy walked to the Italian hospital. The imposing building was only a few blocks from the apartment in the Kiryat Eliyaho district. As she climbed up the steep incline to the Meginim Blvd. Hedy gazed out at the panoramic view visible from almost every place in Haifa. The sight of the ocean and the green hills rising all around had a calming effect on Hedy's disturbing thoughts.

Recent events did not bode well for the hoped for peaceful future. When the war had finally come to an end, Hedy and everyone else in the world, had thought there would be no more fighting. But in Palestine battles raged on. The British, who had tried to keep order during their mandate over the area, were organizing their imminent departure. All their resources were geared to loading ships with weapons and supplies then sending them to their possessions around the Empire.

The Jewish Brigade had been disbanded but not before many members deserted and became part of the clandestine Haganah and the Mossad. (The future army and intelligence service of Israel, respectively.) These forces were unable to keep peace as yet. Armed skirmishes erupted nightly between Jewish and Arab factions. Just last night Hedy had heard gunfire near the apartment.

When Hedy arrived at the Italian Hospital she saw an armed British soldier on guard at the main gate. He did not stop her, but scrutinized her every move as she walked up the drive and past the huge glass doors. The entry hall was small for such a large structure and the wide desk blocked the hall leading back into the building. A nun in a black habit sat behind the desk, a tall filing cabinet on her right and a telephone switchboard on her left.

Hedy spoke to the nun in the barely understandable Italian she had learned during her stay in Italy and from Guido on the ship.

"I am here to visit Marta Morelli," she told the nun, who looked up at her in surprise.

Marta's papers had shown she was an Italian national, arriving in Palestine on an Easter Pilgrimage. She had stayed on the ship until Haifa, while Avi and Samuel had left the ship the night before its arrival in Haifa Harbor. Marta, had been transferred by ambulance to the Hospital.

Although she had been there over a month, no one had come to visit Marta in that time and the nun at the entry desk was curious about this young woman. She was tempted to ask why no one had come to see Marta before this, but her training prevented her from doing so. Small talk and gossip were strictly forbidden in her order, so she curtly gave Hedy directions to the ward for lung patients.

Hedy's footsteps echoed loudly on the marble floors and she resolved to wear low heeled shoes on her next visit. After several right turns, she found the ward. Twenty beds lined opposite walls. Hedy stopped at the door before slowly walking down the aisle. A young woman dressed all in white with a white veil pinned to her blonde hair, approached Hedy, a questioning look in her clear gray eyes. When Hedy mentioned Marta's name, she was led to a curtained area at the back end of the ward.

Marta stared at Hedy from the narrow bed. Her eyes were dark hollows in her pinched and sallow face. The white pillows contrasted sharply with her tousled, black hair. Hedy fought back tears and hoped her tight smile hid the dismay she felt. The last time Hedy had seen Marta was in Avi's arms a few minutes before the group he had gathered was to depart on their trek over the mountains to Italy. The two of them were in a passionate embrace. They were totally unconcerned about who might be watching, as they kissed for a long time, raw emotion evident in their very posture. Hedy's heart had lurched as she remembered Omar's embrace almost a month ago.

In the few moments that Hedy stood over Marta's shrunken form she thought about how parting from a loved one, for what might very well be forever, must be the hardest thing for a human to endure. But not being allowed that parting moment, not having that chance to say, what was certainly, the last good-bye—was that not even more heart breaking? Hedy knew what it was like to have the people you love just disappear. The not knowing what happened to them meant the pain would last a lifetime.

Pushing back the depressing thoughts that often threatened to engulf her, Hedy sat down in a chair by Marta's bed. Both women started to speak at once, but Marta quickly closed her eyes and waited for Hedy to speak. She started out in Italian for the young postulate's benefit, but as the girl retreated back into the main part of the ward, Hedy lapsed into the French they had used in Austria.

After Hedy told Marta about Avi and Samuel and that Avi had sent her, Marta again closed her eyes. In a few moments she asked Hedy to tell her about her life in Haifa and what her plans were for the future. As Hedy gathered her thoughts, Marta spoke softly.

"Hedy, I know I don't have a future, but I did have an exciting past. It gives me such pleasure to recall my childhood and my teen years. I loved my horses. I never thought I would ever love a man."

Hedy was tempted to keep Marta talking. She was curious about her past, but she could see the fatigue in her eyes and on her pale face. Instead she began to talk about herself and her room mates. She described the apartment and told a little about the translating work and watched as Marta began to doze. Hedy resolved to learn more about Marta's life during her next visit.

When Hedy got up to leave Marta opened her eyes and whispered, "Tell Avi I love him and have only one wish. I want to see him again before I die."

That evening Hedy left the hospital with her head full of ideas of how to get Avi in to see Marta. Meanwhile Avi was working on a plan that he had conceived that very day. Its success was part taking advantage of circumstances, recognizing opportunity as it came his way and luck.

~

A supply truck loaded with British uniforms, weapons, and ammunition was ostensibly headed for the harbor to be driven onto a ship headed for North Africa but instead was driven to the kibbutz near Haifa where Avi and Samuel were living. The driver, a former member of the Jewish Brigade had taken a "wrong" turn at a roundabout intersection. With the help of directions from "an unknown party" he found his way to this outpost near the Lebanese border.

When the truck arrived at the kibbutz everything was ready, as the driver had radioed ahead that he was coming. The truck came to a halt beside the Kibbutz warehouse next to the foundry. A dozen men swarmed around the vehicle and began unloading the contents. When all the boxes, bundles and crates had disappeared into the warehouse, the truck itself was dismantled until it also disappeared. Even the license plates was smelted into bullet casings.

The driver, wearing a British corporal's uniform had papers identifying him as Darryl McPherson, formerly of Glasgow, Scotland. Avi was standing near the deserting corporal and noticed that he was similar in size and coloring. It turned out that the corporal was someone else than what his papers indicated. The real Darryl McPherson was on his way home with a sizable amount of English money in his pocket.

An idea was forming in Avi's mind. He approached the driver of the dismantled truck with a proposition that, he explained, would benefit both of them. The driver agreed to lend Avi his uniform and identification papers in exchange for Avi's help in getting a desirable position in the kibbutz.

The next morning Avi was on his way to a nearby Druze village. He was riding one of the Arabian horses that were the pride of the kibbutz and the reason he had chosen to live there with his beloved Marta.

His plan was to borrow a car from his childhood friend who was an auto mechanic in the village. When Avi arrived at Asfar's garage, much to his surprise and delight, he saw a British staff car parked inside. Asfar had bought the car from a sergeant who had ignored orders to drive it off the pier and instead drove it to the Druze village. The sergeant was now on his way home to England with a little bag of gold coins under his shirt and facing a less uncertain future.

~

Although the Jewish Agency office was still open, and Karla was taking applications from job seekers, the intelligence office was closed. All the members of the staff were supposedly in Jerusalem at their head office or in a British prison. So Hedy, who was still being paid each week, had free time to visit Marta and was finally able to hear her story.

MARTA

Marta's father had been the head veterinarian at the breeding farm for the famous Lipizzaner horses of the "Spanish Riding School" in Vienna. He had wanted to go to medical school but the quota for Jews had been filled when he applied for the first time and also the second time. The director had told him that it was highly unlikely that he would get into the Vienna School of Medicine even on a third try. In fact the dean of the medical school had taken Ludwig Krebber aside and suggested he learn to be a veterinarian. As it turned out Ludwig liked animals and specialized in treating horse. He soon had a reputation among the drivers of the carriages, (known as "Fiakers") that competed with taxicabs in the streets of Vienna. One day a no lesser personage than the director of the Spanish Riding School came to Ludwig's office to ask his help with a rare eye infection that was plaguing some of the famous white stallions. He was able to clear up the infection and found the cause (rat droppings), and was made head veterinarian in the process. In 1915 performances of the Lipizzaner horses were cancelled for the duration of World War I and Ludwig was sent to the breeding farm in Hungary to look after the horses during their exile.

In Hungary he met Marta's mother, who became his assistant and a little later, his wife. When Marta was born in the little village near the farm the Krebbers decided to remain in Hungary. Marta grew up with the horses, rode them, learned to train them and couldn't imagine a life without horses. Arrangements had been made for her to go to Vienna when she graduated high school and work at the Spanish Riding School as a trainer.

In 1938, a day before her 18th birthday, Marta's dreams fell apart and the nightmare of a Nazi Europe began. Dr. Krebber was in Vienna on that fateful night of November 9th 1938 when he disappeared without a trace. A few years later, Marta's mother died of a lung disorder just a few days before the Germans, warmly greeted by the Hungarians, marched into the village and rounded up the few Jews who lived there. Marta was at the Lipizzaner farm that day and the stable master hid her during the Nazi search for every last Jew in the area.

After the war Marta left the farm to go in search of her father. She made her way into the Austrian woods and to the house at the edge of the clearing where Avi and Moshe brought the potential Zionists they found in the Displaced Persons Camps throughout Germany and Austria.

The woman and her daughter who provided the shelter and way station welcomed Marta as she stumbled into the warm kitchen one evening. She had warm bowl of soup and a short nap in the barn. Marta woke to the sound of neighing horses. For a moment she thought she was back at home with her father. Avi came into the barn leading two black horses. A half asleep Marta fell into his arms, thinking she had found her father. Avi held her tenderly and spoke soothing words in the same Viennese accent as her father. Marta began to cry with disappointment and then with fear at being in the arms of a strange man. Avi gently wiped away her tears with a huge white handkerchief. He invited her to come see the horses. Marta fell in love with the horses and became the driver of the hay wagon. She also fell in love with Avi and gave up her search for her father. Avi proposed marriage and they had planned to be married as soon as they arrived in Palestine.

Now Marta was dying of the lung disease that had killed her mother. Avi was in hiding and Hedy had brought the news from the Jewish Agency that her father was presumed dead since his name was not found among any of the living survivors of the concentration camps so far.

"Thank you for sharing your story." Hedy whispered. "Now close your eyes and rest."

Marta closed her eyes and Hedy, still holding Marta's hand, settled back in her chair.

Heavy footsteps sounded in the ward beyond the curtains, which suddenly opened and a British soldier strode to the side of Marta's bed. Hedy raised her eyes and saw the uniform jacket, the khaki shirt and tie and then a face that looked like Avi's.

Avi put his finger to his lips, signaling silence. Then he looked down at Marta and softly spoke her name. Her eyes opened and when she recognized Avi they glowed with pleasure. He quickly took off his coat and tie, put them on the chair that Hedy had just vacated. Sitting on the edge of the bed, Avi gently gathered Marta into his arms. She sighed with contentment as she nestled her head against his broad shoulder.

Hedy watched the scene for a moment, stifling the small spark of jealousy as she imagined herself in Omar's arms again. While Avi cradled Marta, murmuring soothing words and stroking her hair, Hedy stepped out into the ward. An obviously irate nun blocked her way.

"There are rules….." the sister began in Italian then started again in French, since she had overheard Hedy and Marta conversing in that language.

Hedy smiled her most ingratiating smile, put her hand on the nun's elbow and guided her gently away from the curtained area.

Sister Maria Antoinetta was a compassionate as well as an educated woman. She spoke fluent French and had a nursing degree. Her area of responsibility was this ward dedicated to lung diseases and she took her duties very seriously. She had observed Hedy's visits to the dying girl and appreciated the kindness. She decided to listen when Hedy said she wanted only a few minutes of her time, to tell her about the couple behind the curtain.

"It is not an unusual story," Hedy began with the fervent hope that what she was about to tell the nun would sound plausible. After all it did contain kernels of truth, she thought to herself.

Hedy continued speaking. "The two young people met in Italy while he was stationed in her town. He had respectfully courted her. After he had mentioned his Italian ancestors and how pleased his mother would be to have a daughter-in-law from this region, they were given permission to marry. Before they could marry he was transferred to Palestine. She became very ill and the doctor told the family that it would benefit her health to be in a warmer and dryer climate. Plans were made to send her to her betrothed and for a priest to marry them upon her arrival. Marta became very sick on the ship and upon docking was sent to the hospital. No one notified her fiancé and now he has finally found her." Hedy sighed deeply and waited.

As she listened to the story, sister Maria Antoinetta remembered a night at the La Scala Opera in Milan. She was sixteen, enthralled by the music, immersed in the drama of the last scene of La Traviata and weeping uncontrollably. Now she lowered her head so Hedy would not see the tears running down her wrinkled cheeks and reached out to pat Hedy's shoulder, turned and walked out of the ward.

Undisturbed, Avi held Marta in his arms all through that night. In the morning he gently laid her lifeless form back on the bed, picked up his coat and tie and walked out into the dawn.

Chapter 33

Hedy walked home quickly after leaving Marta in Avi's arms at the hospital. She was anxious to get to the apartment before nightfall. The streets of Haifa were no longer a safe place after dark. Recently gunfights had broken out almost nightly. It was not always clear who was involved and why.

Vera and Lena were already at home when Hedy let herself into the apartment, slowly closing the door behind her. They could tell from her manner that there was bad news about Marta.

When Hedy told them that Avi was with Marta and that she would most likely die in his arms that night, the three young women exchanged meaningful glances. They each had the same thought, *Lucky Marta.* None of their loved ones had experienced such a privilege.

Lena had brought home an Arabic newspaper from her employers. While tutoring the children in French, they in turn had been teaching her Arabic. Lena was now able to read and even speak a basic Arabic, so she read and translated parts of the newspaper for her friends. Most articles were about the end of the British Mandate. The front page carried a long diatribe by the Grand Mufti of Jerusalem, who was now in exile in Cairo, Egypt. In the article (a reprint of a radio speech), he exhorted the Muslims living in the portioned Palestine to leave their homes and flee to the borders of the five Arab States (Egypt, Syria, Iraq, Jordan, Lebanon) that were set to attack and shortly eradicate the new Jewish State. The Mufti promised his faithful follower that they would be able to come back to their homes and live as they had before, because all the Jews would be murdered or pushed into the sea.

It was alarming and depressing to read these threats. The three young women were very aware that the army of the new State of Israel would be outnumbered at least five hundred to one if all these five nations attacked as predicted in the news article.

Lena mentioned that her employers, the Midoori family, were planning to move to France shortly and await a visa for emigration to America. They wanted Lena to come with them. Mr. Midoori was in the business of distributing medical and laboratory supplies. He had contacts in Lyon, a center of production for these products. Lena was ambivalent about going to France. Recently she had found her father. He was teaching again at the university in Lyon and had remarried. This was difficult for Lena to accept.

Vera also had plans to leave for England where she felt she had a better chance to become wealthy again. "Money will give me control over my own life," she said. "I am going to be rich again if it takes me a lifetime." Her tone allowed no contradiction.

Hedy was certain that she would stay in Haifa. She loved this city where so many people of different cultures and religions had lived in harmony. Not until recently had there been friction or hostility between the different groups. She acknowledged that there were militant factions on both sides, but they were a small minority. "Hopefully" Hedy sighed, "people on all sides would become more reasonable when confronted with reality." All three of the women spent a restless night. Their fitful sleep was often disturbed by gunfire.

The next day was a Sunday. Hedy, Lena and Vera woke to the sound of church bells from the Carmelite Monastery. It was a cool, sunny morning and Hedy expressed a desire to go on an outing.

"Let's rent bicycles from the rental place on the corner," she suggested. We have talked about exploring the Arab villages in the area. So let's do it today."

The others quickly agreed. The bicycles had to be walked up most of the steep hill but an hour later the three young women were cycling through the Ahmadi enclave of Cabbabir. While eating lunch at a corner falafel stand the three friends agreed to lock their bicycles to a post and wander around on foot. They passed several outdoor stalls where fruits and vegetables were for sale then came to an area of more upscale shops along the same street. Since the three of them had different interests, they decided to split up and meet up at the bicycle shop down in Haifa, at five o'clock since that was the time the bicycles needed to be returned.

Lena, who had developed an interest in calligraphy, saw a shop that sold art supplies and books of instructions. Vera stepped into a jewelry store and spent the afternoon trying on a variety of gold ornaments, pretending she already owned them. Hedy wandered further along the street. Next door to the arched entrance to Salim's Carpet Emporium she saw a colorful display that had the look of an abstract painting. It was not obvious what exactly made it pleasing to the eye, but the collection of scarves, hats, pendants, skirts, blouses and sweaters drew her towards the open door of the shop. As Hedy entered, she heard familiar voices and her heart leapt in her chest. It couldn't be, but she distinctly heard the voice of her mother, then her grandmother and her great-aunt (who spoke Viennese with a very slight Russian accent). Hedy felt her whole body tremble as she slowly stepped inside the well-appointed store.

Three women stood around a glass encased counter where a variety of charms and pendants were displayed. There were blue glass eyes to ward off the evil eye, crosses of various designs, -Greek, Coptic, Roman Catholic, Stars of David pendants in gold and silver, and amulets with sayings from the Koran written in Arabic as well as other languages.

When Hedy saw the three strangers she started to back out the door, but the woman behind the counter called to her in English.

"Come in! I am certain you will see something that pleases you." Her smile was irresistible.

Immediately Hedy wanted to know her better and was curious about how this hijab wearing woman had learned Viennese. She was about to address her in that dialect when she became shy about using it after so many years. Instead Hedy began to look at the objects in the glass case.

The Austrian women glanced at Hedy and moved aside. They were plump, red faced and well dressed in tailored suits and real silk stockings. They had obviously survived the war well fed and affluent. In the course of their conversation Hedy learned that after the war they had resumed their annual pilgrimage to the Holy Land and were looking for souvenirs to bring back for their maids.

"Nothing too costly," one of the women snickered. "Those girls have cheap taste." Then she turned to Hedy, and asked in strongly accented English, "My maid is about your age. Would you prefer a scarf or an amulet?"

Before Hedy could answer the other Austrian woman spoke up in Viennese. "You pay her enough salary you don't need to bring her anything."

"You are right," said the first woman. Her double chins waddling as she nodded her head in agreement. "She had the nerve to ask for a raise before we left on this trip. I told her she was lucky not to be living in the Russian zone of Vienna."

Her friend had turned around to look at an array of hand knit sweaters. "Look, Lisle!" she called out. "Those are just like the angora ones that Jewish girl knit for you."

The woman named Lisle walked over to the pastel pink, blue and green garments hung artfully on a hand woven wicker basket.

Hedy, her back to the women couldn't help but overhear their next words. She was relieved that they couldn't see her face.

"We hid that Jewish bitch for years and she paid us hardly

anything." Lisle sounded indignant.

Her friend was quiet for a moment, examining the lovely sweaters. Then she said in a conciliatory tone. "She did do all the housework and she was a good cook."

"As soon as the Americans came she just disappeared," Lisle snapped back. What's more, the day before she snuck off she had the gall to ask me if I would return her mother's wedding ring."

"Well," retorted Lisle's friend, "it's like we always said, Jews are greedy swine."

At these words Hedy and the Muslim woman across the counter exchanged glances. By the stricken look on their faces it was clear to each of them that they both understood what the Austrian had said.

"We need to get back to the bus." The heavier of the two Austrians admonished her friend. They paid for their meager purchases and left the shop without another word.

Hedy had come into the store with no intention of buying anything and besides she had spent her last shekels on lunch. She turned to the woman behind the counter and again she was struck by her beautiful face, her warm smile, and her kind eyes. There was something familiar about her, but Hedy was certain she had never seen her before.

"I don't have any money with me." Hedy told her in a Viennese accent. "I'll be back some other time."

"Of course." The Arab woman said in Viennese and then added "Until we meet again in Hebrew," indicating that she guessed Hedy was Jewish.

Hedy walked to the post at the end of the street where she had left her bicycle. The other two bicycles were not there. Hedy was relieved, as she wanted to be alone. The hateful words of the Austrian women kept spinning around in her head. She called on all her willpower to push them to the back of her mind and to concentrate on the exhilarating ride back down the hill to Haifa.

Chapter 34

After almost a month in Jerusalem, filled with meetings, conferences, late night secret sessions and many early morning rendezvous, Oskar was finally on his way to Haifa. It should have been a two hour drive, but there were numerous check points. Most were put up by the British, searching cars for weapons in order to keep them out of the hands of the Zionists, who would use them in the upcoming war. A few of the roadblocks were set up by the rapidly growing Jewish Defense Forces, the Haganah, who were also in search for weapons, to be confiscated for use in that same war.

Although his driver was getting more and more frustrated by the long delays, Oskar hardly noticed the disruption to his progress in getting home. His mind was filled with the excitement of having a part in the making of history. A new state was being created from almost totally new and raw material. The concept of a Jewish State was over 2000 years old. The Jews, scattered all over the world had mentioned their return each year at the Passover meal. "Next year in Jerusalem" had echoed through the ages. Now the promise was coming to fruition with a modern, democratic government. Could this handful of leaders really carry it off? Was it possible?

The arguments, the differences of opinion, the intransigence of the Orthodox Rabbis about waiting for the Messiah to deliver the Jewish people instead of the Haganah went on into the nights and continued through the long days. The verbal dueling had been excruciating and in spite of his exhilaration, Oskar felt exhausted. He remembered one of his father's sayings. "Where there are two Jews together, there will be three opinions."

Yet in the final days of April 1948, a working government had been formed. That Ben-Gurion would be Prime Minister had been almost a foregone conclusion, as well as the election of Chaim Weitzman for the first president of the new/old state. After that the cabinet appointments fell into place.

Oskar was impressed by the American woman, Golda Myerson. She had the drive and enthusiasm of Ben-Gurion and the eloquence of Aba Ebban, the new state's representative to the United Nations. If she had been a man, Oskar thought, she would be a good prime minister and her diplomatic skills were wasted as Labor secretary. At the very least she should be secretary of state or an ambassador. The other women, mostly Zionist leaders, who had come from European countries, were of the same caliber. Oskar felt confident that the new state had strong and idealistic leaders who were at the same time realists. They placed great emphasis on the importance of the military and the intelligence service for the survival of the new state.

The car was traveling through the evergreen forest near the outskirts of Haifa. The scent of pine drifted in through the open window. It triggered a memory in Oskar. In his mind he was in a car speeding through the pine woods of northern Germany. His boots were resting on the blanket covered form of the Jewish girl he hoped to rescue from certain death. With a great effort he brought his mind back to the present. Then for a few moments, Oskar allowed his mind to marvel at the power of scent. A whiff of perfume could conjure up the memory of a warm and willing girl, while the cooking odors wafting from a nearby kitchen brought on mouth watering thoughts of a delicious meal eaten with loved ones.

Then he made a serious effort to keep his mind focused on his plans for organizing the Mossad headquarters in Haifa. Before the pine scent had distracted him, he had been making mental lists of the steps necessary to insure recruitment of the best agents available.

Suddenly, without the slightest warning, Oskar felt a strong and urgent longing for Hedy. He almost cried out with the emotional pain that constricted his chest and tightened all his muscles. He clutched the briefcase on his lap as if it were a life raft that was keeping him from drowning.

The car was moving slowly through the late afternoon traffic in the business district of Haifa. The harbor was just beyond the buildings on his left and a steep hill rose behind the buildings on the right. When they reached a clearing between two buildings Oskar told the driver. "Stop, I'll get out here." The driver gave him a questioning look then pulled the car to the side of the road.

"I can't sit another second," Oskar explained. "It will take you a half an hour to drive up that serpentine road to the village. I need to walk to clear my head. The climb up that hill will do me good."

The driver got out and opened the door for Oskar, looked him up and down with obvious displeasure. "Sir, you are not dressed for such a climb," he ventured.

Oskar was wearing a dark business suit with a starched, white shirt, open at the collar. His shiny black shoes were meant for city streets not dusty, mountain paths.

"Meet me up at Salim's, Yitzak," he ordered the driver. Leaving his coat and briefcase in the back seat, Oskar stepped away from the black sedan, and started up the path as Yitzak drove off with a deep frown wrinkling his forehead.

The climb was gradual but steady and soon Oskar was sweating in the hot afternoon sun. He estimated that in about an hour he would be sitting down for a meal in Amah's dining room in the spacious apartment above the carpet store. His stomach growled in anticipation. Although Oskar had every intention of continuing to concentrate on the matter of organizing the Haifa branch of the intelligence service he was to head, his thoughts kept wandering to a more personal matter.

After the end of the war it became possible for Oskar to

send agents into Austria to look for his sisters and their families. He knew they had been sent to Therezin concentration camp near the city of Prague in Czechoslovakia. From there they had written several post cards to Amah in Cairo, but during the war in North Africa all communication stopped. His family had disappeared without a trace.

This seemed almost impossible because each person who entered a concentration camp was catalogued like a piece of livestock. The Germans kept meticulous records. Oskar had witnessed the punctilious entries himself when he went on inspection tours with the Grand Mufti. The name, date and location of birth, last known address, gender and maiden name were entered into the huge binders which were subsequently sent on to Berlin with the date of death entered next to each name beside the number that had been tattooed on the prisoner's forearms. Some of these records were found by the Allied liberators but most had come into the possession of the Russians and the subsequent Communist regimes of Eastern Europe where they stayed hidden for another fifty years.

The fact that Hedy had also disappeared was another matter. Yusef had assured Oskar that she was safe. The irony of the situation made Oskar smile in spite of his frustration. Shortly after his arrival in Haifa, Oskar and his staff devised a system for giving new identities to thousands of Jewish survivors who were potential immigrants. These people had been stripped of everything but their lives. Since there was no possibility of verifying who they were or where they actually came from, new papers were printed with names and plausible dates, then these documents were signed by persons with official sounding titles. These identification papers seemed to satisfy the various bureaucrats who provided the stamps of notarization for the visas needed to emigrate from Europe.

Hedy could very well have procured these papers, have a new name and traveled to any number of countries that were easier to get into for a Jewish girl, than was entrance to Palestine. Oskar had told himself often that to continue to search for her was useless, but try as he might he could not forget her.

A little more than halfway up the hill, Oskar stopped to look at the view of Haifa harbor below him. Looking to his left he took a few moments to admire the Bahai' temple and the well tended gardens. Even with an aching heart and a head full of devious plans for defeating an implacable enemy, Oskar appreciated the lovely scenery that surrounded him. He stood there for another moment then turned around and resumed his climb.

As he looked up the dusty path, Oskar saw a woman on a bicycle descending towards him. He stopped to watch her progress. She was approaching at a fairly high speed and he stepped off the path to let her pass. As she came closer, he noticed she was young and slim. Her dark skirt was billowing out behind her and the wind pushed her white blouse against the soft curves of her body. It was her hair that caught his attention. It was the same color he had seen on the woman in his hallway about two months ago. It was not exactly blonde or red, but had the glow of candlelight in a dark room.

The woman on the bicycle had seen him and began to slow down. When she was about ten feet from him she stopped, got off the bicycle and leaned it carefully against a fence post near the path. For a few seconds she stood still, shading her eyes against the sun. Oskar didn't move but looked at the figure slowly advancing towards him. His heart began to pound in his chest and up into his throat. Something about the way she moved reminded him of Hedy. He looked more intently and saw a lovely, shapely woman with the face of the girl he would never forget.

She took a few more steps towards him and now he could clearly see her deep blue eyes. Finally Oskar managed to say her name over the pounding in his throat. He remained perfectly still, arms by his side and waited. Even if she recognized him, what would be her feelings after three years? Oskar speculated that a woman this beautiful would have a man in her life by now. Also she only knew him as Omar, secretary to the evil Grand Mufti, sworn enemy of her people. Oskar held his breath as she moved closer.

"Omar?" Hedy asked softly. She stopped and looked into his eyes. There was no doubt of the unmitigated joy in her voice as she called out "Omar!"

Oskar felt every muscle and sinew in his body begin to relax. Taking a deep, much needed, breath he raised his arms and she stepped into his embrace.

Epilogue

Characters in alphabetical order:
1. Avie: Became an officer in the Haganah and was killed in the battle for Jerusalem. It would be twenty years before the beleaguered city was united once again.
2. Guido: Together with his brother he opened a successful restaurant on a hillside outside of Genoa. He married Yolanda the day she graduated from high school. Their children gradually took over the business and fifty years later it is still in the family.
3. Hedy and Oskar were married in a civil ceremony in Cyprus. They continued to live in Haifa and worked for the Mossad into their old age. With all the expertise of their organization they never found a trace of their families.* However, with Amah's help they found out that Amalia was the sister of Hedy's mother and thus her aunt.
4. Konstanza: Will be the subject of another book. She and Hedy were reunited due to the diligent search of one of the Mossad agents who set out to find the woman who saved his life while he was hiding from the Nazi and Polish murderers in the wintery forests of Poland.
5. Lena: She went back to Lyon, where she found her father. He had resumed teaching after years in hiding. She tried to live in France but after a year she was able to join the Midoori family in San Diego, California. Mr. Midoori became head of the medical supplies purchasing department. Lena worked there also and her language skills were a valuable asset. She never married but enjoyed

being an aunt to the Midoori children and grandchildren.

6. Moshe: Reunited with Rachel and they spent their retirement tending their garden in the hills of Haifa and volunteering at immigration centers in that city. Yael continued to call him uncle and he took his secret to the grave.

7. Samuel: Lived through the War of Independence and in 1952 started on an education program to become a clinical psychiatrist. He saved many lives in the course of his long career and wrote several books about the permanent damage of sexual molestation and abuse of children. He never married but kept a picture of Hedy on his desk.

8. Vera: traveled to London at her first opportunity. She found a secretarial position in a small cosmetic company, worked her way up to top executive. When the company was bought by a larger company based in South Africa she relocated to that country and became fabulously wealthy. She had many love affairs, but never married.

9. Yusef: continued working for the The State of Israel from his home in Texas. He had influential friends who arranged for Israeli pilots to train on Texas airfields and made certain that the Israeli Defense Force had the best weapons and knew how to use them.

*Afterword:

Fifty years after WWII ended and the communist governments collapsed under the weight of their own corruption the Red Cross finally came into possession of over 300,000 names and detailed information about the people who bore those names. It is a mystery why the Communists hid these records.

There is a warehouse in Bad Arolsen, Germany, where sixteen miles of shelves hold ledgers with hand written entries of name, gender, birth date, and former address of each person with the day they entered a concentration camp. On the same line is the date they were shipped out. A notation next to the name (mostly the name of a child) says, "Did not survive transport." (Translated to mean: "Gassed immediately upon arrival.")

In the late 1990s Oskar and Hedy were sent the information of what had happened to their loved ones: Oskar's sisters and their four young children were sent to Terezin concentration camp for a few months and then sent on different dates, to Auschwitz and murdered in the gas chambers. Hedy's mother and grandmother experienced the same fate. Their husbands were sent to work camps in northern Germany where they died a few months later. No trace was ever found of Hedy's father.

CPSIA information can be obtained
at www.ICGtesting.com
Printed in the USA
FSOW03n1235100816
23447FS

9 780990 582755